GRIST

GRIST

Linda Little

*To Sarah Miller
From one miller to another.
Linda Little*

ROSEWAY PUBLISHING
AN IMPRINT OF FERNWOOD PUBLISHING
HALIFAX & WINNIPEG

Copyright © 2014 Linda Little

All rights reserved. No part of this book may be reproduced or transmitted in any form by any means without permission in writing from the publisher, except by a reviewer, who may quote brief passages in a review.

Excerpts from "The Young Mill-Wright & Miller's Guide" reprinted with permission from Algrove Publishing Limited.

Editing: Kate Kennedy
Design: John van der Woude
Printed and bound in Canada

Published by Roseway Publishing
an imprint of Fernwood Publishing
32 Oceanvista Lane, Black Point, Nova Scotia, B0J 1B0
and 748 Broadway Avenue, Winnipeg, Manitoba, R3G 0X3
www.fernwoodpublishing.ca/roseway

Fernwood Publishing Company Limited gratefully acknowledges the financial support of the Government of Canada through the Canada Book Fund, the Canada Council for the Arts, the Nova Scotia Department of Tourism and Culture and the Province of Manitoba, through the Book Publishing Tax Credit, for our publishing program.

Library and Archives Canada Cataloguing in Publication

Little, Linda, 1959-, author
Grist / Linda Little.

ISBN 978-1-55266-599-2 (pbk.)

I. Title.

PS8573.I852G75 2014   C813'.6   C2013-908695-1

My temptation is quiet.
Here at life's end
Neither loose imagination,
Nor the mill of the mind
Consuming its rag and bone,
Can make the truth known.

—*Wm. Butler Yeats*

*To the women who worked
and the women who work.*

CHAPTER ONE

PENELOPE

My parents were hard-working people. Labour was a virtue. I say this only to paint the backdrop. They worked hard and died young. They were humble, happy people and I took our happiness for granted. I thought happiness grew naturally like ivy along the walls, or dandelions in low grass, or hedgerows ringing the fields and pastures. My father was a kind man, awkward and quiet. Before he got ill I remember him behind the plough, sweat off man and horse alike winking in the sunlight. I remember a day in spring my brother and I followed him to the field to pick stones before seeding. He left us by the stone boat to pick and toss while he wandered farther off searching for larger rocks beyond our strength. He could pry up rocks the size of loaves of bread and, cradling several in his arms, carry them to the stone boat where he let them roll onto the pile with authoritative thuds. My brother and I amused ourselves through the long day with bickering and bantering but my father worked in silence. When my brother complained of the futility of the task my father only gave a slight smile. "Stones are the first crop of the year," he said, never pausing.

He was most at home in the fields alone with his work. My mother prodded him out to the regular seasonal social gatherings and did her best to get him installed in a group of men where a bottle might make furtive rounds. A nip or two might help you feel more at home. Listen to what they're talking about and add something of your own, she instructed him. Perhaps on that one day at the picnic he had a swallow or two more than he could manage with grace.

I was a large, square-jawed girl—graceless but strong. My ears were too big and once I entered puberty my eyebrows grew too thick and obdurate hairs would sprout where they shouldn't. There was nothing delicate about me and nothing pretty. One year at a picnic I won some small competition, a race of some sort, I don't remember what, but there at the moment of greatest attention my father's voice boomed out: "That's my girl! A great horse of a girl!" My face burned red as girls tittered and boys guffawed. Everyone looking. He had meant it innocently, blurted it in a burst of pride, as a compliment. Even in my mortification I loved my father so powerfully then for his awkwardness, his embarrassment, his best intentions. "A great horse of a girl." So apt. A portrait bundled up in so few words, sharp and crisp as a poem. For years afterwards I heard "Whoa, Nelly" called after me from around corners and behind hands. Clip-clopping noises as I passed. But who among us hasn't suffered some childish cruelty? It teaches us kindness and compassion, endurance and understanding. I was not crushed by the slings and arrows of childhood taunts—not at all. As I grew I prided myself on my neatness and bearing and native intelligence. Jane Eyre was a plain girl, intelligent and determined, and wasn't she the hero of her own life? All the heroines I loved advanced by dint of their wits; indeed the vanity of beauty could easily turn a girl shallow and silly and lead her astray. I prided myself on my common sense. And I kept my personal expectations well in hand. But vanity wears many guises. It is wily and in the end it entrapped me.

I married Ewan MacLaughlin of my own free will. He, like my father, was quiet and awkward. But I construed far too much from this surface similarity. As time would tell, Ewan was not a kind man.

I FIRST MET EWAN MACLAUGHLIN ON A WINTER EVENING. I had begun the evening in my room as usual, arranging my students' lessons for the following day. Shortly after nine o'clock I descended to the kitchen to warm a cup of milk. I had stirred in a dollop of honey and was on my way back up, but as my foot met the bottom step my landlord, Reverend Robert MacLaughlin, called to me from the parlour, a note of pleading evident in his invitation.

"Penelope!"

I poked my head around the corner.

"Penelope, do you know my brother, Ewan?"

"Yes, of course." For the past few years I had boarded with the Reverend MacLaughlin, his wife Alice, and their little ones, Jessie and Robbie. I knew the Reverend's sullen older brother operated a mill way up the Gunn Brook. Very occasionally he would arrive on business, eat a swift and laconic lunch, and leave. I don't know if I had ever heard him speak.

"We've seldom seen you alight for so long in one place, Mr. MacLaughlin. How fortunate you could spare the time to visit."

"Ewan, you'll remember our beloved schoolteacher, Miss Penelope McCabe?"

The miller bobbed his head. His eyes sought the corners of the room. "I had business appointments. For the new mill. There were delays." He frowned at this, ran his fingers lightly along the edge of the table where he had a series of diagrams spread out. "I've calculated the volumes of the garners and the hoppers," he said, perhaps continuing an earlier conversation.

The Reverend had placed himself between me and the doorway, silently encouraging me farther into the room. "My brother is planning to build a new mill up the Gunn Brook."

Ewan MacLaughlin was not tall, barely an inch or two taller than me, but solid, sturdy, in a compact package. He had wide cheekbones and a stalwart jaw; the kind of man one might well expect to find chiselling stone. His sandy hair, with its thrifty little waves, appeared guiltily playful matched with such a serious countenance. His eyes were a dark blue. I placed him at perhaps forty years of age. I stepped towards the drawings spread across the table, reached out and touched the image of a waterwheel. It was a work of art, precise in its depiction but also capturing a sense of the wheel's movement and momentum. Above it were others I did not fully understand but supposed depicted the various stages of the wheel's construction. Each was the product of great care and craftsmanship. "Mr. MacLaughlin, am I to understand you drew these with your own hand?"

"My hand, yes. Guided by the Lord."

I looked at him in earnest, amazed first by his handiwork and secondly by his pious response.

"And you intend to construct this mill? With all these workings?"

"This is my plan."

"I believe you have impressed our schoolteacher, Ewan."

"Yes, indeed you have, Mr. MacLaughlin. I don't believe I have ever seen such strength in intricate drawings."

"Construction notes. Miss McCabe."

"Is this…? I'm afraid I don't…What is this section here?"

When the miller spoke about his proposed mill, his awkwardness fell away. His voice became sure and clear, his focus on the task at hand. He worked his way through the drawings from the dam to the grinding stones, referring to each illustration in its turn, explaining it with clarity and confidence. With each step his eyes lit up afresh then turned serious. When the parlour clock struck ten we simultaneously turned to it in surprise. The Reverend had long ago abandoned the scene.

"Oh my, I'm afraid I've taken up all your evening with your brother. I'm so sorry. You so seldom get time together."

He said nothing and we stood there in silence as the mantle clock ticked off the seconds. Then, in a move both sudden and slow, his face brightened in a diffident smile. "The evening was not wasted," he said.

Such eyes he had—clear and sharp. I felt suddenly uneasy as though I had forgotten something important, and my skin grew uncomfortably warm. Tongue-tied, I searched the corners of the room for something to say. When I looked back, the miller was examining the palms of his hands. Then he jerked his head towards the window although there was nothing to see but the reflection of the room looking back at us.

"Thank you so much for your explanations. It was an honour to see your work, Mr. MacLaughlin."

I curtseyed. For some reason I could not begin to fathom, I actually curtseyed—as though the miller were the Duke of York. Befuddled and embarrassed I fled. Had I said goodnight? Had he? I don't know.

Combing out my hair for bed I twice dropped my hairbrush and I caught my nightdress on the bedpost from clumsiness. A rare and stabbing awareness of my female body overtook me. But for what reason? There was no reason. In the dark, in my bed, I ran my hands along my body under the covers, smoothing my nightdress, pausing to feel the weight of my own hands, smoothing again. Oh heavens. Had I actually bobbed in a little girl's curtsey? He had looked towards the window, perhaps he hadn't seen. My mind's eye snagged on his drawings and there it rested, safe. He captured perfection in ink lines, used words like vector, velocity, logs bottled and dovetailed. Beautiful words, familiar but exotic. Not for a moment had he doubted that I could follow his explanations. Pride riffled over me like a breeze.

The next morning I woke to the first light in the east and the rhythmic thunk and crack of firewood being split in the yard below my window. The looming duties of the day chased away any idle foolishness. I dressed and began my preparations. At the back door, on my way to the privy, there was Mr. Ewan MacLaughlin—cleaving his brother's stove wood! I touched my hair and smoothed my dress. He immediately set down the axe and stepped into my path.

"Miss McCabe."

"Mr. MacLaughlin."

"Miss McCabe, may I write to you?"

"I beg your…? Oh. Write … well yes, certainly, Mr. MacLaughlin. We're always happy to have news from up the hillside I'm sure."

He nodded and gave a curt bow and strode off. I sputtered something about his wanting breakfast but he had already climbed up into his waiting wagon. He snapped the reins and rolled off out of the yard, leaving me gawking.

At the end of the afternoon with the children dismissed and the fire died down, I sat in my cooling schoolroom. No reason to linger, but there I sat. May I write to you, Miss McCabe? He had smiled at me for one brief moment in the parlour, one small splendid, startled smile and now here I was poking at foolish thoughts that felt as though they had been tossed into my head by some woman I did not know. It humiliated me to find myself distracted by so little. The man would have forgotten he had spoken to me by the time he passed the north falls.

I was not a complete innocent. Shortly after I had begun teaching up the shore a lame and tongue-tied cooper with breath like a rotting fish barrel asked me for a picnic and because I couldn't think of how to refuse him without rudeness I conceded. No sooner were we settled than we were beset by hornets and he ran off to the stream leaving me to manage as best I could. Luckily, he did not bother me again. Anyway, with my father as sick as he had been then I could not have thought of giving up my teaching post for anyone. I had little enough to send home but without my help I hate to think how my parents would have suffered. After I had left there and come to the DesBarres school, droopy old Eli Pettigrew came knocking on the schoolhouse door. He was nearly as deaf as the door itself and I had to holler out my rejections at the top of my voice, much to my humiliation and the neighbours' amusement. The following year Tom Hart had asked to take me walking. He was a widower with five children and was desperate for help. He said as much. Perhaps to explain why he might be interested in me. He was a handsome fellow with a quick wit, but the tavern was his first love and he often smelled of drink. In any case, before I could gather a thought he married a girl from upriver—half Indian and barely Christian from what I heard. I received no further attentions. I had not resigned myself to a life as a single woman because I preferred not to consider the subject at all. But there were many girls who had passed under my tutelage at school who were now married with broods. Who could fail to notice it? I have many children, I told myself. A whole schoolroom full of adorable children.

The week after Ewan MacLaughlin's visit a letter arrived for me. I received occasional letters from my brother, who had gone to sea after our mother passed on. They were sent from far-flung ports, the most recent from Kingston, Jamaica. However, this letter had not come off the coach with the official mail but had been delivered by a traveller to Corrigans'. My landlady, Alice, raised an eyebrow but was too polite to inquire directly.

"A note from a past student, I suppose," I said, giving it a carefree glance. I tucked it away to read at my leisure.

Dear Miss McCabe,

I am busy at my stone as well as at the saw. There is cash money in the toll wheat, which I am at some now. Also, I have oats of my own from my north field. Corrigan is after me for oatmeal as he cannot get better anywhere else. I am sawing pine for Sutherland's. In return they are making the windows for my new mill for which you saw the plans. The base of the shelling spindle is heating terribly. The bearing must be redone and so I will look to it tomorrow. Since it is Sunday and I cannot do anything too useful I am writing to you. This past week the plasterer came to crave his $27.40 for his work on this new house that I built for the wife I hope to have soon. I paid him although he was a sorry tool for the job. Today I have set bread. This is no breach of the Sabbath as it is no work to me as it would be to a woman; rather it is a kind of rest. I will put a drawing here since you like to look at them. This is the front aspect of the house, now complete.

Please tell me how old you are. Also do you come from a good family and do you attend my brother's church?

Yours truly, Mr. Ewan MacLaughlin

An odd letter, certainly, but I was touched by its obvious groping for topics and its social blundering. I had a teacher's urge to slide in next to the writer and praise his stronger sentences then isolate the worst faux pas and work them into something finer. The lines and margins were perfectly straight and his penmanship was excellent, his letters small, controlled and even. The space at the bottom of the page was given over to a precise line drawing of a house with its porch and two dormer windows, everything in perfect scale and symmetry. Then to balance the look of the letter as a whole he had added a trim design (of same gingerbread pattern from the porch!) in each of the upper corners. One could not help but appreciate the artistry of the work as a whole although the text itself was far from poetic. I touched the straight ink lines, unsettled and afraid.

What did I know about this man? The Reverend's family stories were always happy ones, idyllic even: adventures at school and summertime outings. He spoke of his brother Charles who was one year his senior, and often of their mother, but little else outside their education. Charles and Robert were the youngest, the babies of the family, and their mother had been adamant about their schooling. Their father had been a miller in Breton Crag village, Cape Breton, but the two of them, Robert and Charles, were to rise above the milling life. The only story the Reverend had to tell about his brother Ewan was their reintroduction as adult men. The Reverend had spent several years after his ordination in a parish in York County, New Brunswick, before settling into life in DesBarres. His wife's family came from Fredericton and he did not discourage the assumption that he did as well. Perhaps because of this, nearly a year passed before the merchant Henry Corrigan thought to ask the Reverend if he were any relation to the new miller, Ewan MacLaughlin, up on the Gunn Brook. The Reverend admitted that he had a brother by this name who was a miller, but in Cape Breton. Nonetheless, he asked the merchant to send word the next time the miller visited the store. Of course he recognized his brother on sight. Despite Robert's dramatic and near-Biblical re-telling of the story of the long-lost brother, he included nothing of Ewan's past, how he came to be on the Gunn Brook, how they had lost touch in the first place, or anything about his brother at all. In fact, they rarely saw each other and barely exchanged more than greetings when they did.

Dear Mr. MacLaughlin,

It was lovely to receive your recent letter with the exquisite little drawing of your house. I can see you are kept extremely busy with your affairs. How difficult it must be to run your saw and millstones and to plant fields besides, not to mention making progress on your proposed new mill as well. I can only say that if your new mill is half as lovely as your drawings (as I am sure it shall be) it will be a magnificent structure indeed. Each new advancement or acquisition in relation to its construction must heighten your anticipation.

I confess I was astonished to hear of your bread-making talents. I hope I will not be telling tales out of school to say you far outperform your brother in this realm, as I believe he would be hard pressed to bake a potato in a campfire.

In response to your question, I can tell you I am a member of your brother's congregation and so am in a position to vouch for his abilities. However I am told you have never heard him preach. I suggest you might manage your affairs in town in such a way that you can remedy the situation. I am sure you would be proud to see how he represents your family from the pulpit. Your reverend brother and Alice provide me with convenient and serviceable accommodation here. It is a joy to have the little ones about. Young Robbie proudly escorts me to school each day. He is such a bright little boy and quick with his studies. Your darling niece, young Jessie, made us laugh this morning with her serious little face. She has been absorbed lately with a new litter of kittens she discovered in the stable. She is very concerned for their welfare. At her porridge this morning she was determined to learn what preparations were being made for the kittens' educations and begged me to take them to school with me so they could learn their lessons.

As you so kindly expressed an interest in my family I can tell you that I was raised the oldest of two children. My father, God rest his soul, farmed near Clifdon until poor health forced him into town. He was taken soon afterwards and we will miss him always. It was a happy home although, as with many, not without hardship. I taught two years in a country school by Clifdon and then five years up the shore before I was able to secure this excellent position here in DesBarres. Over the years I was fortunate to be able to provide at least some meagre aid to my family in this way. My father's illness put a great strain on my mother and she outlived him by only a couple of years. I am glad to say that with my brother's help I was able to keep her with me through her final days. My brother has chosen a life at sea and is now a bosun on a merchant vessel. I am startled to find myself in my sixth year here in DesBarres, settled in snugly, as you know, in your brother's household. As you asked so fearlessly, I shall respond with equal courage and reveal that my age is thirty years.

Now you must tell me how you came to be milling so far from your native home, which I know from your brother was on the island of Cape Breton. I have heard nothing of your early adventures, or your more recent ones for that matter, except that all DesBarres enjoys your fine oatmeal.

As I still have lessons to prepare for tomorrow I must leave this letter now. Everyone, even little Jessie and Robbie, sends best wishes I am sure.

Sincerely, Miss Penelope McCabe

THE FOLLOWING WEEK AS I TIDIED THE SCHOOLHOUSE AFTER THE children had left for the day, I looked up to see Ewan MacLaughlin standing in the doorway.

"Mr. MacLaughlin!"

He nodded and removed his hat.

"Won't you come in out of the cold?"

He edged past the threshold, and although I waited for him to state his business, he said nothing.

"Good afternoon," I managed finally, although the greeting seemed awkwardly out of place by this time. "To what do I owe this pleasant surprise?"

"I've come calling, I suppose."

I could not think what he meant. I cast about for an idea of how to converse with this ill-at-ease man standing in the middle of my empty classroom. "Do you have any prominent memories of your own schooldays, Mr. MacLaughlin?" I ventured.

"The Lancasters and the Yorks."

"What do you remember of them?"

He then delivered a short, factual speech on the topic. Perhaps this start built his confidence, as it appeared to loosen him somewhat. We spoke just over half an hour but it seemed to me a dizzying amount of ground was covered. The conversation was as exhilarating as it was difficult. He asked blunt questions but meaningful ones. Do you believe God has a purpose predestined for each of us? Which are our greatest duties on earth? What strengthens a child? What weakens a child? Which are the most commendable branches of study? The man seemed unable or unwilling to skim through the usual social banter. Well, what chance did he have to practise the niceties of polite conversation, living alone as he did? And wasn't it better to address matters of substance than engage in parlour chatter at any rate?

Finally he said, "If you like me well enough you ought to call me Ewan."

When he turned abruptly to leave I was taken by surprise and said he could not leave without his supper, surely. And at this time of day should he not spend the night at the manse and set off fresh in the morning? He would not hear of staying and claimed he had only stopped in briefly after completing business in town.

During supper that evening, as we exchanged tales of our days, it dawned on me that Ewan had not visited the manse at all. No one mentioned him stopping in for his dinner earlier in the day: not the Reverend, Alice, the children or the serving girl. I opened my mouth to relate the visit and unorthodox conversation but turned back, something inside me reluctant to share.

The predominant feature of Ewan's next letter was an intricate rendering of a cook stove. I could see him at a table with his ink well, his lamp and my letter by his side, struggling over his composition.

Dear Miss McCabe,
  I took up milling here after I was no longer needed in Cape Breton. My father's mill passed to my oldest brother so I came to the mainland with my trade. The land I now own I bought with my own labour. I had no house for a wife before now so this is why I am yet single. This drawing is of the new stove I bought for the wife who will get this house. I paid a full $35 for it as it is the most modern to be had and a good design. It was shipped up from Amherst. I have used it a little myself to try it out and I figure it does all right. When I come in to Corrigans' with my next load of meal I will buy you a present.
  Yours truly, Mr. Ewan MacLaughlin

I sat on the edge of my bed reading and re-reading the letter and biting my fist to stifle my laughter. Only a couple of days earlier I had discovered at school a secret love note, lovingly crafted then carelessly left to wander astray (for such is the way with children). Eleven-year-old Eddie Joudrey intended, and then forgot, to pour out his heart to his ten-year-old sweetheart: *I want for you to mary me some day. I will by you a present becaus I have lots of money what I got stakin wood. I mean I got FIVE cints and all for spending. PS This is a seacret note.*

I could imagine Ewan screwing up his courage to ask some local fellow what to put in a second letter to a lady now that he had exhausted all he had to say in his first. There was no mistaking his intent now. Or was there? I would go over what I knew and where my assumptions might be leading me astray.

THE NEXT SUNDAY AFTERNOON EWAN ARRIVED TO CALL. He had made the journey of some thirty miles that morning and he meant to pass only a few hours in town then return home that evening. He had no other business, of course, it being the Sabbath. When I expressed my incredulity he looked confused and a little hurt.

"I've come courting," he said, as though this diminished the distance. Or the Sabbath. "I've come to take you walking." Speechless, what could I do but fetch my coat and hurry out after him? After my beau. The thought of the word made me smile, so incongruous with Ewan's sober demeanour. Courting!

Ewan fumbled in his pocket then and pulled out a copy of Elizabeth Barrett Browning's *Last Poems*. I had admired the slim, leather-bound volume at Corrigans' but could not justify the extravagance for myself. The thoughtfulness, the insight of the gesture moved me deeply. I was as much out of my depth as he was. Courting. "But what brings you so far afield?" I asked. "There must be many deserving young ladies closer to home who'd be anxious to have a handsome miller." I felt exposed, vulnerable and afraid.

"Those girls are young and skittish, running here and there. Lazing about, off to Scotch River to gossip every chance they get. Who knows what nonsense they have in their heads. A woman has her business at home. A woman must have sense."

He looked at me with a steady eye and I had to turn away. He did not want the young and pretty. He wanted me. What more did I need to know? For all my supposed sensible level-headedness it was this vanity that sealed my fate.

He delivered me home again and had to be begged to take a bowl of soup before he set off back up the mountain, all the way in the winter dark and cold.

THERE IS LITTLE MORE TO SAY. Ewan came by once more. On a fine March day, with the sun's heat promising spring and the wind no more than a wisp, we walked out beyond the church where the foot traffic was sparse. Ewan opened his coat to the warmth. Out of town we strayed off the path and stepped into the woods for some shelter from the world. Up into the woods. The wonder of it, this lair of temptation, this home to ruin and sin and here was I, the schoolteacher, alone with a man. To think I, of all people, could find myself so near scandal! I trembled there between two worlds. Ewan and I stood close together, trying on each other's breath. He set his hand upon my shoulder—a large and meaty workingman's hand. The skin rough and dark from years of dressing millstones. His mettle. He touched my neck. Then, as carefully as one would stroke the down of a chick, he touched his thumb to my cheek. He undid the buttons on my coat and rested his hand on my waist. Then he lifted his hand to my breast, held it. I was wearing my best winter dress. It had ruffles down the bodice. I remember this, the ruffles between the warmth of his hand and my breast. Both hands then, breasts, waist, abdomen, hips. He took the measure of me and I seemed to hover above myself, watching him pass his eyes and hands ever so slowly down my body, waiting for him to snicker or turn away, a great horse of a girl. But he did not. I felt I had left the pull of the earth, as though in mid leap, and could put no name to this feeling of both terror and giddiness. His mouth covered mine and his body pressed against me. My arms were around him although I did not remember placing them there. The whole of a man, flesh and bone, all of him—this was the other world.

When we stood apart again, he looked off into the trees. "Whoso findeth a wife findeth a good thing, and obtaineth favour of the Lord," he said, earnest.

"Yes."

And so it was agreed.

I thought that I would complete my teaching year but Ewan grew insistent that we must marry right away. God had guided me to him, he said. He had prayed and God had answered his prayers. I must settle into my new home in time to plant my garden. I must see spring in my new home. The banns should be published in his brother's church right away. By next winter I would bear his first son. I laughed light-headedly at his sudden ardour, the way he expressed his hopes in sentences of such certainty. I pleaded that I needed some time to prepare. I needed a proper dress at least. And I would need to outfit my kitchen and pantry. Ewan was to send me an inventory of what he had and I was to choose any supplies I would need for my household from Corrigans' General Store. He would arrange with Corrigan for payment. The first week of May was our compromise, a Thursday as was customary.

With ewan's commitment, the world seemed to alter; its axis bent a few degrees perhaps. Everything seemed fresh, seemed to reflect light in a different way. I felt a new poignancy in the men and women I met each day. The depths of all they felt, and had felt, glimmered around them now. Even the relationships between people and animals, people and inanimate objects, seemed to take on extra meaning. When I walked among the townsfolk carrying the knowledge of my engagement, I felt myself among them in a way I never had before.

When I entered the store searching for lamp wicks, Henry Corrigan turned his warm eyes on me and came out from behind the counter as he often did to greet his customers. Unlike his father, who saw the store only as a way to make a living, Henry loved the business. For him each customer carried with them needs that ran much deeper than their shopping lists indicated. Mrs. Reid came to the store for flour and a spool of white thread but what she needed was reassurance that people's pity had not diminished her in some real, inescapable way since the death of her husband. Jerry Tupper wanted a skein of rope but needed to know there remained a possibility of adventure beyond his life. William Holmes wanted nails but also assurance that his children would love him despite his many weaknesses. With Henry at their elbow, customers often found themselves standing in front of some piece of merchandise they had not realized they had been yearning for. Indeed by the time Henry had finished his greeting we had come to rest at a set of handsome but serviceable kitchen cutlery. Beside the cutlery sat a beautiful crystal saltcellar. Henry picked up a spoon and polished it with the corner of his handkerchief. For all the intricacies of Reverend MacLaughlin's work it occurred to me for the first time that Henry Corrigan, with his quiet discretion, probably knew more secrets than any clergyman.

Every item in the store now held the question of its usefulness to me personally. The lamps, the washboards, the flatirons, clocks, brooms, hinges, sleigh bells, rope, axe handles had become potential parts of my household. And if not my household, then that of someone else who felt deeply, who had begun their lives in love and optimism with a new partner. I looked over the new bolts of material on the counter, gauging their strength and their delicacy between my fingers. There were several pretty cotton prints. I must write to ask Ewan about the number and placement of windows in the house. Such a lovely deep blue raw silk. More practically, a strong hearty tweed for a going-away suit perhaps. I passed my eye over the small selection of books that Henry Corrigan kept and noted, of course, the copy of *Last Poems* that was missing. I realized the gift did not represent Ewan's powers of imagination nearly so much as it did Henry's acumen. I smiled thinking of poor Ewan's torments in seeking help over the problem of a gift for a lady and I loved him all the more for his determination and perseverance.

I did not see Ewan again over the four weeks of our engagement. But I was so busy I hardly noticed his absence during the days. And at night I had my new situation to contemplate. I was to be a wife. I conjured him beside me, creating a man from all I did not know.

We were married in the Presbyterian chapel at four o'clock in the afternoon on the first Thursday in May. The year was 1875. Reverend MacLaughlin performed the rite and Alice served us a nice wedding supper. I had made the cake myself. Ewan had packed the wagon before the service and as he was anxious to get on the road we did not tarry long. He would not hear of spending the night. The evening was clear and cold. We set off down Main Street then turned inland setting our backs to the strait. The wagonload was heavy and the road mostly uphill but the horses were steady. As we made our way a canopy of stars emerged to adorn the night. Beside me, strong and silent, my new husband held the reins.

This is the story of how you were loved. All that came before, all you saw and heard, all you lost and lived without, this will be the truth to carry you, Granddaughter. Your brothers can walk into a world built for men. They will become men with wives to make them kings of their homes and to carry their pain and produce their joys. Truth would only slow them down. But you, my granddaughter, this is yours—the story that made you.

CHAPTER TWO

I AWOKE ALONE, DISORIENTED, WITH THE MORNING SUN BRIGHT on the bare, freshly painted walls around me. The tweed of my travelling outfit draped over the foot of the bed dispelled my confusion. I was a married woman in my new home. Beside me the quilt lay wilted on the mattress. I slid my hands across to the empty space where my husband had slept, seeking the lingering heat of his body, but it had dissipated.

"Ewan?" My voice sounded hollow in the emptiness of the room. Yes, I remembered. The bit of lace I had sewn at the neckline of my new nightdress felt so delicate beneath my fingertips. I slid my hand down from my neckline to my breast. I remembered the weight of his body. I touched the vague heaviness he had left between my legs. I was married.

"Ewan?"

I climbed out of bed and dressed quickly in the cool of the morning. My husband's wedding suit sprawled on the chair and I gathered it up in my arms. The wardrobe by the window was simple but elegant. Like everything around me, it was new and freshly painted and as I ran my fingers along its edge I wondered if Ewan had built it himself. When I opened the door I was surprised to find it completely empty except for a row of wooden hangers. I hung up Ewan's suit and my travelling clothes side by side, smoothing them with my palms. By the wardrobe there was a washstand, complete with water in the pitcher, and a bar of soap. Besides his chair, Ewan had a simple table with a single candle and a bible on it. My side of the room was less sparsely appointed. My dressing table had four delicate drawers, a charming little stool, and a looking glass. Ewan had brought in my trunk. I had no memory of him carrying it in from the wagon; perhaps he had wrestled it up the stairs this morning? It looked a great awkward load for one man. Through the large east-facing window I could see the sun had been up for an hour or so. Ewan must have grown tired of waiting for me to wake and had simply gone off to work. I looked out across the yard and the laneway to a small barn that may once have been a rude house. I moved to the smaller dormer window, which faced the road and offered a panorama of trees, dipping into a ravine then rising up the hillside beyond. Both windows needed curtains, and the furniture could use a runner or a doily or two.

Just beyond the washstand was a door and I had no idea where it led. How odd it was to be standing in a house—my own home— which I had yet to see. One small lamp had lit our way through the house last night but even had it been daylight I would have seen little. With the excitements of the day, the jostling three-hour trek by starlight had left me exhausted. Now my mysterious new home lay waiting for my explorations. I stepped through the door into a bright nursery with a protected nook for a crib. The room was barren but its emptiness spoke of hope and promise and I was delighted with the clever little space. Across the hall I found two more bedrooms both similarly vacant. I walked around each room and inspected the view from each window, admired the painted floorboards, the smooth sills, the well-planed wall boards ready for paper. The front bedroom seemed the slightly bigger of the two and had a dormer as well as a gable window. This will be the girls' room, I thought, and imagined creamy wallpaper with patterns of pink roses dancing along it. I smiled at my own foolishness and addressed myself aloud in my most serious schoolmarm voice. "Mrs. MacLaughlin, perhaps you would do better to attend to today and leave tomorrow to God."

I suddenly became aware of my ravenous hunger. I would investigate the kitchen next.

    I made my way downstairs to find a large and sunny kitchen with three windows where I could monitor both the barnyard and the road while I worked. On the kitchen table lay brief note: *Northwest field. E.M.* I turned it over and back, looking for what? Some sort of embellishment? Smiling, I folded the note—the first from my new husband—and tucked it into my sleeve. The smartest cook stove you could ever hope to see dominated the kitchen. I ran my fingers along the chrome, explored the warming oven, the firebox and the reservoir. There was a pot of porridge on the back of the stove. The stovetop was warm but the flame had long since been reduced to embers. Ewan must have breakfasted hours ago. The wood box was piled high and the basket next to it brimmed over with kindling. I built up the fire and set the kettle on for tea. Off the kitchen I found an excellent pantry lined with shelves and cupboards and drawers. Each door I opened offered me the fresh smell of newly milled lumber. There was a built-in bread box, a handy pullout flour bin mouse-proofed with a tin lining, and many other novelties in the nooks and crannies—even an icebox awaiting summertime! All that was left to be desired was a stock of food. A few sparse staples were crowded into a corner of the pantry as though they were afraid to intrude. There was flour and meal from the mill of course, and a small jug of molasses, a string of onions, two smoked trout and a small bucket of salt beef. I was immediately grateful for the fresh meat and the few spices and other basic supplies I had brought out from town. A basket with half a cabbage and a few potatoes led me to think I might check the cellar for vegetable bins. I ate my porridge with a spoonful of molasses then set to roast several pounds of the beef I had put on Ewan's account at Corrigans'. I poured myself a fat mug of tea and set off to further my explorations.

    I found I was mistress of a parlour, large and bright with a moulded tin ceiling and elegant wooden panels crowned with a chair rail. I perched on the beautifully upholstered sofa and gazed at the matching chairs I knew had come from Sutherland's factory. The delicate tea table had been burnished to a fine luster and in the corner sat a glass-door bookcase with a little key poised in the lock. A good many trees had been felled and sawn in the mill, a good many hundredweight of grist ground, to pay for these furnishings I wouldn't doubt. This room, perhaps more than the others, pleaded to be completed with a woman's touch—a rug, draperies, a vase of flowers and a watercolour or two to warm the walls. That I would have the rest of my life to make this room my own filled me with a sense of joyous adventure.

By the back door I discovered a small room just big enough for a monk to hole up in. A narrow bed, one tiny table with a candle, a razor and shaving mug, and beneath the bed a sort of wooden locker with Ewan's clothing and a few personal effects: a pen and a box of nibs, a pot of ink, a book, two handkerchiefs, a tin of boot black, a bit of sealing wax. Propped in the corner I recognized the roll of Ewan's construction diagrams. This was where Ewan had tucked himself away in his bachelor days—like a little mouse in the skirting boards! I realized now that I had seen nothing of Ewan's in any of the other rooms. Except for the building and finishing of the house I don't believe he had set foot beyond the stove in the run of his daily life.

Out the back door was a little vestibule area with a bench, a mat for boots and pegs for coats. Beyond this, the woodshed and Ewan's workshop. Then the granary. Across from the house sat the barn of rough, old-fashioned construction. It looked as though it may have been Ewan's first home. I made a note to ask him about it. As I explored the yard, I found Ewan's little garden plot and saw immediately how I could expand it to take advantage of the south slope for early planting. Behind the house I looked out over the pasture and the fields. The silence of the countryside, after my decade in town, startled me with its breadth and depth. I revelled in it; I basked in it. On the rise behind the back field I could make out Ewan and the horses pulling stumps. I must check the cellar at once and take stock of provisions for his dinner.

I had never been in full command of a farm kitchen. The domestic sphere had not been my primary preoccupation for many years. But I could certainly manage to rustle up a decent meal to feed my new husband. As I suspected I found a store of winter vegetables in the cellar along with several heaping baskets of apples. And so I set to work. At noon I snugged everything—meat and gravy, potatoes and turnip, and biscuits and apple pie and a can of hot tea—carefully down into a basket I found hanging in the pantry. Picking my way along the ploughed field I felt myself back in the happy days of my childhood, carrying the dinner basket to my father in the fields. Once, in the early days of her marriage my mother must have delivered this workaday picnic to her new husband and sat with him, smiling, in the field. In later years I imagine she must have watched from her kitchen window as her children took on the loving task. Just as some day I would watch my own little ones set out on the journey—the bearer of rest and refreshment. As I approached, I watched Ewan work—steady, sure and unrelenting. As I drew close enough to hail him he looked up from a stump, the sweat glistening on his brow, the brief smile turning his features momentarily boyish. Ewan's smiles, always fleeting as though accompanied by some small pain, were all the more rewarding for their sparseness. Throughout the day I would keep the memory of his smile with me. I brought a blanket to keep the dampness at bay and while I spread it out on the ground he tended to the horses. I handed him a mug of tea and unpacked his dinner. As we sat together he watched the stumps beside us as though gauging how best to liberate them.

That afternoon, shortly after I returned from the field and was busy unpacking my kitchen crate and organizing my new pantry, Mrs. Delilah Cunningham arrived with a pail of milk. The Cunningham farm was a quarter mile downstream and our closest neighbour, she informed me. Mrs. Cunningham scanned the kitchen in a way that put me in mind of a hawk on a limb. She had an unfortunate hooked nose and piercing eyes. She seemed to be about ten years my senior and was plainly dressed but clean and neat and appeared to be holding back great reserves of power beneath a patina of exhaustion.

"I thought I'd come to say welcome, ya know. In the general run of things I send one of the youngsters up with the milk, but where you're new and all … here I brought this bit of cheese for your supper. As a present, ya understand. I always sent milk up here, for Merton, ya know. And then the miller. My boys are always happy for a bit of work at the mill. Harry too." She spoke pointedly, either stopping abruptly at the close of each sentence or somewhere in the middle.

"You'll see me when it's time for the babies 'cause I'm the one you call to tend—to cut the cord and all. I've seen just about every baby on the Scotch River Road into this world." Once she had said her piece she looked around, apparently stumped for further conversation. She accepted my offer of tea but fidgeted in her seat.

"So you have several children, do you, Mrs. Cunningham?"

"I have six children. And since God's blessings cannot be stopped I may yet have that many more. My oldest, Donny, is good to work, now. So is William. I know he's small yet but he can work, Lord yes, like a wonder. And Sarah, she was down to Sutherland's, helping to feed the men, ya know, and she was the best they ever had. They couldn't believe how young she was, working like that, ya know. Mr. MacLaughlin never wanted help with his cooking and cleaning. I don't know why. How can a man do without cooking and cleaning? It ain't right. Any road, you're here now. So that's all right, I suppose."

She ground to a halt at this point. When I quizzed her about the neighbours she was happy enough to lay out who kept a bull, who bred piglets, who maintained beehives for honey. "There's not much traffic up here. There's nobody further up the road except the Browns. The soil gets too thin beyond that far hill. Everybody else is on the Scotch River Road below. I sends up the milk here every other day—and a bit of butter too. I sends one of the young ones up with it. The miller's got a bowl of nickels somewheres—in the pantry I believe…" She turned her head to stare at the pantry door.

"Oh, I see. Perhaps I can take a look." Indeed Ewan did keep a small jar with a few coins in it in a little cupboard behind the door. When I produced the nickel Mrs. Cunningham smiled and nodded her head as though I had passed some rigorous test of domestic suitability. Indeed she immediately popped up out of her chair and put on her coat.

Next came Abby Brown, the only neighbour farther up the road. I heard hooves and the clatter of wheels in the dooryard and poked my head out to investigate. I found a woman in an alarmingly advanced state of pregnancy struggling down from a buggy and balancing packages around her swollen belly. I rushed out to greet her and help her down but she waved me aside with a merry laugh.

"If I can't manage around one of these by now there's no help for me," she sang, cradling her mound of unborn child. "I dismayed of Mr. MacLaughlin ever finding the wit to marry and here look at the prize he's hauled home. Welcome, welcome you are, dear."

I laughed at the sheer energy of the woman foisting a pound cake and a pot of jam towards me.

Abby paused a moment gazing across at the stable. "It still looks odd to see poor Merton's house dragged over and made a horse barn." But she turned away in half a beat. "I must bring you some lavender! There's a perfect place right by your door there. I'll send little Frankie down with it as soon as the weather's fit. And I've got lily of the valley too, if that's your fancy. Oh, I can see this place now with a woman's touch." She squeezed my shoulder. "High time for it too!"

Once inside I put on the kettle as Abby lowered herself onto a kitchen chair. "Ah, what a lovely stout house you've got here. Just grand! You'll have it ringing with bairns in no time. My poor old place—the youngsters have it tore up like an old woodshed. That lot of mine would have Job swilling rum with the devil within a week. The little hoodlums!

"Now tell me what's true and what's a lie and what's yet to be said. Honestly, you could set a turnip on a stump and get more news out of it than you could pry from Ewan MacLaughlin with a crowbar! If it wasn't for Elsie Murdock's sister living in DesBarres and hearing of the banns there's not a soul here would ever have heard of Ewan's marriage or wife or any of it and..." she leaned in with a conspiratorial whisper, "there'd be no pound cake today! Now, I understand you're from the graded school in town? Are you lonely for all the little ones you left?"

"Yes I am, a little," I said. I had not realized until that moment that I was. "If I can be lonely for them and happy to be here at the same time." Abby listened with the same bright intensity she brought to her speech. She admired the gingham I had spread out on the table for my kitchen curtains. She peered this way and that and asked what plans I had for the rest of the house. I prepared the tea and sliced the cake and suggested we take our tea into the parlour.

"Oh heavens, there's no need of ... or perhaps just for a peek."

I led the way. Abby stopped at the parlour door, her easy flow of words suddenly dammed. She proceeded gingerly into the room. She eased herself into the upholstered chair and let her head sink back onto the fabric, her eyes closed. "Listen to that. Nothing but the sound of the buds popping."

"Yes, it is lovely and quiet here."

"I wouldn't mind a day or two of this before the new bawlin' begins." She winked and rubbed her belly lovingly. "That Peter of mine what a racket he makes! So help me God, he only leaves off throwing things long enough to find something to kick. Smashed a pane right out of the kitchen window with a stone last week! Well, I sent him off to find a windowpane bush since he's so convinced that glass grows on trees. 'And don't come back 'til you've got a nice one,' I said to him." She laughed. "Oh, but we've all got our time for quiet and our time for fun, don't we?"

Abby had a wonderfully kind face with eyes that snapped with brightness and good humour. She had fine wrists and high cheekbones and hair that gleamed in the light with a reddish tinge too bright to be called auburn. There was music in her voice.

"It's a wonderful time, isn't it? Spring? My Frank is just itching to get at the fields. A day or two of fine weather will do it, he says. Have you got your garden plot picked out? You say what you need now, because I've got sage and savory and horseradish to fill a ditch."

We chatted away, her giving me the lay of the land, as she called it.

"I'll just freshen up the pot," I said when we'd drained our cups.

"No, no, my dear, I mustn't linger." Abby leaned forward and lowered her voice in mock conspiracy. "I'm on a spree today because my sister's here to help with the new baby—this little monkey was to have been here last week! So I've slipped off to see you properly welcomed and left her at the mercy of the mob. Do you know what my Nancy Ann got up to last week while I'm hauling water and Harriet is busy tipping my fresh laundry in the dirt by the line? Grabbed a hold of Frankie's school pencil and got a wondrous work of art all over the wall! Now even supposing they leave the four walls standing, by the time I get back they'll be one of them either bleeding or busting the furniture—likely it'll be my sister!"

Abby hauled herself up adjusting her belly and toddled back to the kitchen. "Awful nice to meet you," she said. "Come and see us real soon—meet the brood. I mean it. Come to see the new baby. I'll be mad if you don't. I'll send the youngsters down with news. We need to get you set up properly here. You find yourself short of anything, you just give us a holler. Don't you be a stranger now."

She climbed back up onto the rig and clicked the pony into a trot. I watched her from the dooryard and returned her wave as she set off up the road.

EWAN HAD LITTLE TO SAY OVER SUPPER THAT NIGHT. A habit of his lonely life, I supposed. I tried to draw him out but he only grunted. It was understandably difficult for him to elaborate on a day of stump-pulling. He intended to devote the next month to field-work, he said when I asked. He had been sawing lumber in the mill before we married but he had had his fill of the yakking and yawning from the canter and deal piler.

"Those idlers are sorry tools. There'll be no more lumber sawn once I'm done with the Old Nag."

"The Old Nag? Is that the mill you have now?"

"Yes. The old make-do pile of jury-rigging."

"You won't keep the old mill for sawing after the new grist mill is built? Where will people saw their lumber?"

"They can build themselves a pit saw. It's no affair of mine. I mill flour and meal. That's enough about that."

I left this topic alone and tried another tack. "Abby Brown was by to welcome me. She's a wonderful lady."

Ewan chewed as though dinner were yet another task in the day's routine.

"Do you know Frank Brown at all?" I persisted.

"Farmer. Of sorts."

"Mrs. Cunningham was by with a pail of milk. I gave her the nickel she said was due. I hope I did right."

"You'll have a cow of your own. That Sutherland from over the brook ought to have brought it by now. Still in bed, I suppose. We don't need the Cunninghams traipsing through here now."

"A cow! Why, that's a happy surprise, Ewan. Thank you. I'm anxious to see her. What's she like?"

"A cow."

I tried again. "Abby said the old barn used to be Merton's house?"

"No talk of Merton!" He punctuated his point by thumping his near-empty tea mug on the table, and was out the door and into his workshop in what seemed to me one fluid movement.

"Ewan?"

A doubt, soft and silent as a single falling leaf, fluttered through me. For the first time since our engagement I felt the whole of my decision. The breadth and weight of marriage, the irrevocable vows, my reliance on a man I knew so superficially, filled me. I set my hands flat upon the table in front of me and steadied my breathing. You have done well, I told myself. You have followed your heart. You will have friends—you have one already! You will have neighbours to visit and work and socialize with. You will have a family, a full and happy life. Marriage is as new to Ewan as it is to you. I talked myself back to confidence. "You will walk with purpose," I said aloud with mock sternness. And I strode from one beautiful room of my new house to another coming to light finally in the little nursery off our bedroom. Yes, I had done well. I would be a good wife and I would transform Ewan into a good husband.

THE PHYSICAL INTIMACY OF MARRIAGE SURPRISED US BOTH I think. At times I wondered if I would be swallowed by the strange intensity of it all and I believe he felt the same. That night, after he had spent himself, he rested his head on my breast. I ran my fingers through his hair and felt a renewed certainty in my new life.

"Do you like being married?" I whispered in the dark.

At first he did not answer.

"Ewan, do you like being married?"

Finally he responded, his words spare and thrilling like ginger on the tongue, "Yes. It is God's will."

THE NEXT DAY EWAN ROSE IN THE DARK WELL BEFORE DAWN, breakfasted on the stove-back porridge, harnessed Billy and Pride and, in the dark, the three of them made their way across to the clearing at the far edge of the field. They waited, hindered by darkness, in the morning chill. Ewan, like everyone else, was waiting for the fields to dry sufficiently to be worked. Until then he was busy pushing back the boundaries of the wilderness, hauling out the stumps of the trees he had felled for lumber. I could imagine him sucking his teeth, trying to draw first light over the horizon, enough so he could see to fasten his chain. At the first ray of dawn the horses leaned into their collars, their shoes digging into the earth, kicking up little chunks of mud. Ewan put his shoulder to the stump straining as hard as the beasts, hollering, "Haw there, up there, get up. Up!"

When I brought him his dinner at noon I suggested he might like to come back to the house to warm up, but he met this idea with scorn. "There's no greater sin than the waste of good daylight," he said.

That evening I waited for him to come in for supper. When the biscuits were done I wrapped them in a towel and set them in the warming oven. From the window of the west bedroom upstairs I could just glimpse the silhouette of the horses against the fading pink of the sunset. An hour later I still had not heard them return. Wondering slipped into concern, then worry. Just as I became convinced of a calamity I heard the jostle of horse and chain in the yard. Then the glow of the stable lantern pricked a hole in the darkness. By and by I heard Ewan scrape his boots and I felt the brisk breath of evening as he came into the kitchen.

"You must be hungry. You must have had a hard time seeing out there—I was just about to go after you with a light!"

He hung up his coat and pried off his boots while I poured a dipper of warm water into the wash basin for him.

"The horses will be glad of their blankets and their oats, I would say."

The stew had filled the kitchen with its fragrance. Truth be told I would have been happy to fill my bowl long ago. I set a bowl before Ewan and put the biscuits beside the butter Delilah Cunningham had provided. "We'll have our own butter soon enough," I said cheerily. "I hope you like the stew. I haven't much in the way of herbs but there'll be lots this summer once I get the garden in."

Ewan tucked into the stew and biscuits well enough, which was its own sort of compliment.

"You got a good day put in today."

"Stop talking."

I thought perhaps he had heard a noise outside and was listening to hear it again. I listened too but heard nothing. I waited expecting him to resume conversation but he did not. Finally I asked, "Did you hear something?"

"I've heard nothing but your yattering for the last two days."

"I beg your pardon?" I stared at him; hurt puddled below my heart and indignation rushed in to battle it. But I thrust my intellect forth to intercept my feelings. Ewan did not recognize the harshness of what he had said. He needed help to refine his everyday manners. I raised my eyebrows and placed my hands on my hips hoping to give him clues he could pick up on himself. But he simply continued eating.

"What could you possibly mean by that, Ewan?" I kept my voice as even as possible as though I were asking where the garden hoe was stored.

His brow wrinkled in annoyance but still he said nothing. I cast about for clues. Could he possibly have taken my comments about the butter and the herbs as criticism? "Have I said something wrong? I'm sure I didn't mean to."

"Silence at the table. That's God's way. With quietness they work and eat their own bread."

God's way? He got what he asked for. Confusion trumped my sense of affront. I would need time to consider my response. Immediately after he finished his dinner he stood and left the kitchen. I cleaned up the table and the dishes while I waited for him to return, but he did not return. Eventually I ventured out looking for him and found him in his shop hunched over his workbench with a mallet and chisel. Two lanterns burned above him, dispelling any shadow. He looked up, slowly took in my presence as though his eyes had to travel a great distance from his workbench to me.

"I wondered where you'd got to." He said nothing. Blank stare.

A sullen farm boy! All of a sudden I was back in my classroom facing down some smirking lout who had been sent off to school to keep him out of trouble after the farm work was done. I did not try to hide the pique in my voice. In fact I turned on my no-nonsense tone. "How much more work do you intend to do? When will you be coming in?"

"I will finish three more cogs after this one. I expect the time will be approximately 10:35."

He returned to his work, once again completely absorbed. I opened my mouth then closed it again. He did not respond to my annoyance, neither invited me in nor dismissed me. But he had answered my questions. This information I carried back to the kitchen with me and I sat by the stove with it while I hemmed the new curtains I had measured and cut that day. I had been a good teacher. I attended closely to my craft; I learned and grew in the thirteen years I spent at this occupation. After a few years I was able to teach children who I would have despaired of earlier. I believe most young people left my care not only better scholars but more open and confident in their dealings with others. Surely I could learn to understand and guide one man. To explore and comprehend, this was my first task. I would not waste my time worrying over my own over-sensitive feelings. I sat plotting my course until it was time to set the porridge oats to soak, bank the coals and retire.

I WAS SURPRISED BY HIS DAILY DEVOTIONS. As I sat at my dressing table each night combing out my hair Ewan knelt by the bed, his eyes closed and his hands clasped like a child's, and he prayed in a low rolling voice. The first night I saw this I felt the perfect heathen. Occasionally I would sit in contemplation of the Lord for a few minutes at the end of my day but I had not kneeled by my bedside since I had left my childhood home. More surprising yet was finding Ewan unprepared for church on our first Sunday morning as man and wife. He changed into clean Sunday clothes after he fed the horses but then he simply took down his bible and sat by the window with it open on his lap. After he had been so diligent in seeking my opinions on church doctrine it had not occurred to me to ask him about his religious habits. Despite his apparent piety and his asking about my allegiance, Ewan never attended the little Presbyterian church we had passed down on the Coach Road.

"Gossip and vanity," he said. "People minding other people's business. Ladies contemplating their neighbours' new hats rather than the gospels." He would have none of it. "Go if you want," he said to me but in my confusion and disappointment I did not. I had imagined that on Sunday I would be making my first foray into public society on my husband's arm. I would see in broad daylight the homes and farms we had passed in darkness on our wedding day and I would be able to take stock of the people who made up my new world. And of course, they would all see the miller's new wife. Suddenly the distance to the church seemed too great a journey and more than I could manage on my own. Perhaps later on when I'd got my bearings—next Sunday or the week after. As I sat with my own bible I found myself thinking of the new gloves I had bought for my trousseau and my regret at not being able to wear them now. Perhaps Ewan was right. Vanity and gossip. And what foolishness to dwell on trivial disappointments. I rallied my spirits and decided to use the leisure of the day to attend to neglected correspondence, to send my thanks to the Reverend and Alice for their help in our wedding arrangements. At the end of the missive I signed my new name, still a stranger to my own hand—Mrs. Ewan MacLaughlin.

CHAPTER THREE

Abby's Peter arrived after breakfast first thing on Monday morning. He was bright eyed and befreckled. I pegged him at about six years old. He stood at my door armed with his introduction and his instructions.

"My name is Peter and I've come with a message. My Mam says the baby's born and it's a wee girl and fine as the spring. And she said for me to come ahead to you before school and bring the news 'cause it's not every day a fellow like me gets a brand new baby sister to look after."

"Why thank you, Peter. How thoughtful. Come in, come in and tell me all about her." Peter and I were fast friends by the time the two older Browns, Frankie and Harriet, showed up to pull him away to school. We all introduced ourselves before I tucked some extra molasses cookies into their lunch basket and waved them off. Then I set off in the opposite direction, up the road to see the new baby for myself. I passed Mrs. Cunningham on her way home. Frank must have gone for her help sometime during the night.

Delilah Cunningham shook her head in the same resigned fashion she used to welcome me on her visit those few days ago. "Whatever else may be her sins Abby don't dally about squawkin' when it comes to having babies. Tie the cord and make the tea and home for breakfast." She gave me a self-satisfied nod and brushed on by.

Abby's sister was there and busy with the toddler and the breakfast dishes. "Go on up," she said, indicating the stairs. Abby looked exhausted but glowing.

Frank sat by the bed holding the infant. I stepped back, embarrassed to intrude, but he stood, beaming. "Come on in. I'm just on my way off to the fields. I'm embarrassed into it with all the work Abby's done already this morning."

This was my first meeting with Frank Brown and it formed the image of him that always stayed with me. With a pleased-to-meet-you he set the babe in my arms and was gone. The baby, with her full head of hair, lay washed and shiny and snug in a bundle.

"Meet Lily," Abby said.

In the following days I often dropped up to the Browns' for an hour or so in the afternoon to see what use I could be. Abby drew all her children to her, gave them all turns sitting with and holding their new sister. "What's good advice to give to her?" Abby asked them all. "Could be your best chance to have her listening."

"Don't stand right behind a horse, 'specially if you're hollering."

"Always do your schoolwork."

"Don't try to drink sap out of a cold pail."

"Kiss Mam every day."

"Always be good."

"The best food is warm bread with strawberry jam."

"If it's really cold, put your clothes on under the covers before you get up."

"She don't need to put clothes on—she's a baby!"

"Yeah, but this is advice for later when she's bigger, right, Mam?"

"Don't throw rocks."

This was the sort of family I wanted for myself. Ewan might need more coaxing and cajoling, more careful thinking and delicate handling than an ordinary man, but seeing the Browns I was sure we could build a home as strong and warm ourselves. Once we had children Ewan would learn along with the young ones how to be loving and caring.

Abby had begun to wash the spring fleeces before her labour began.

The tubs were all out and the first batch of fleeces set to soak. As she resumed some of her regular tasks around the kitchen Harriet and I picked up the fleece-washing job where it had been left. I had never done this work before which made Harriet the teacher and delighted with her elevated status. She was a serious girl with big brown eyes and a high forehead. The raw fleeces stuck to my fingers, gritty with dirt and oil. "Pull out all the dirt you can, Mrs. MacLaughlin, and take out the second cuts—they're nothing but a torment later on." We picked away and piled up the fleeces waiting their turn in the soaking tub, rinsed and re-rinsed those in the rinsing tubs and prepared the clean ones for drying. "You mustn't be stirring the water up into a tempest now, nice and easy does it," she told me as we submerged the wool. Abby came over to admire our work once we had all the wool set out on the racks to dry. After a quick cup of tea and a moment with the little one I set off home filled with confidence and optimism to make Ewan's supper.

It was my job to try to make Ewan all he could be. His old habits would have to be altered now that he was a married man. I would work with him firmly and gently. I would begin by giving him a choice: would we speak during dinner or afterwards while he drank his tea? We would be a family and I would see to it. Over the next week I set out a series of experiments to probe my new husband's conversational potential. My initial observation proved telling. Ewan would answer a question put to him directly. The more specific and concrete the question, the more readily the answer was forthcoming. For example, how much land did you clear—twenty-seven square yards. How many stumps did you pull to accomplish this—nine. Questions about the future could come back in the form of a prediction based on past experience or some apparent law but not in the form of wondering, dreaming or imagining. But his tolerance for conversation of any sort was low. And his desire was lower yet.

"How much land did you get seeded today?"

"Open your eyes and look if you want to know what I'm doing."

"You've been too solitary, Ewan. You need to practise a little conversation. We can start by sharing our days. Five minutes, then ten, then fifteen—soon we will have a rudimentary conversation."

"Don't be an ass."

"You may not speak to me like this, Ewan…"

But he was up and gone to his workshop and I was left stewing.

He was captive during his noon dinner at least. He could hardly leave the field the way he could the kitchen. I decided to try to broach the subject of a small flock of sheep. His eyebrow lifted in interest.

"How many do you want?"

That's all he said. Before I knew it I had half a dozen bright big ewes in a pen by the cow. See how receptive he can be, I told myself. How many women would love to have such a husband! By the time the spring grass was up I had seven pretty lambs cavorting alongside their mothers. Within a month of my marriage I was as busy as any farm wife in the province. What had I done with my time in town, I wondered as I bustled around tending to cow and calf, chickens, sheep, and my new garden.

I WAS NOT TO DO BUSINESS IN SCOTCH RIVER. I had not been forbidden to do anything since I was a child. Even as my hackles raised, I gathered all my patience and restraint and focused my attention on the source of the Scotch River problem and away from my awakened temper. Apparently the merchant there had insulted Ewan in some profound way that Ewan would not elaborate upon. I tried to cajole the story of the insult from him thinking I might be able to mitigate the problem, to clear up misunderstanding or negotiate around hurt feelings. But no. No truck nor trade, no buying or selling from his household would flow in that direction. Furthermore, it was Ewan's opinion that strolling about the streets of town was a shameful waste of time and the providence of wastrels and gadabouts—throwing good daylight back into the face of the Lord. I tried to reason with him. There was no profit in my keeping a cow if I couldn't sell my butter. Scotch River lay only a few miles to the east whereas DesBarres was a three-hour plod in the opposite direction. It simply wasn't practical. How could I sell my eggs? How could I pick up everyday articles, a wooden spoon, a pound of raisins?

"I'll make you a wooden spoon," he said.

"And the raisins? Will you make them too? And sugar. And linen when you need a new shirt?"

"Corrigan can send them up the Coach Road."

"Not all that way! What do you mean?"

"Nettle," he said. "And no more about it."

I was to call on the woman simply named "Nettle." The woman was so like a nettle in every way the moniker seemed more of a taunt than a name. Her voice was raspy and sharp as nettles and her eyes, just as pointed, glared from under a rat's nest of hair. It was impossible to say how old she was, her skin deeply pockmarked with scarring, a drooping eye and her right hand no more than a claw (burnt away, according to some accounts).

What I knew of her came from Abby and what Abby knew of her came mostly from the mists of rumour. She was the sole survivor of a house fire that had taken her parents, all of her siblings, her looks and her right hand when she was a girl. The fire had been spectacular, flames leaping so high above the trees that the parson called out to pray for their souls could not approach for the heat but could read scripture by the light from three farms away. Men sailing a sloop across the strait had seen the blaze thirty miles off. Flaming bodies were seen falling from the upstairs windows like so many flankers. There was no end to the tales: the family had kept a goat in the house; they had kept a crow in the house. There had been smallpox caught from carousing with Indians. The mother had spoken a foreign language, beguiled a neighbour's horse and made it lame. Nettle had escaped the blaze because she had second sight. No, because she had kindled the fire herself. No, she had been meeting a lover by moonlight on the night of the blaze and had not been there at all. There had been unpardonable evil in the house; the house had been full of turpentine, full of rum, full of straw where they all slept in a pile, full of sin. The shack she lived in was where she ran to on the night of the fire and had refused to budge since. No, she had built that cabin herself from stolen lumber, from lumber bought from the avails of unspeakable acts. She had given her right arm for it. No, she traded her arm for the second sight. She had been a beauty once. A woman alone—well, how do you think she lives? Carters and drivers stopping day and night. Her large black dog could curse you with a look.

What I knew to be true was that she lived in a ramshackle cabin—little more than a shed—and that her personal history was regarded as a canvas for the communal imagination. The shack was tucked in behind a scraggly line of scrub alders and spruce, a quarter mile beyond the church. A dog met all visitors with neither a growl nor a wag but with a clear, cold gaze and if necessary, one sharp bark. I learned, just as Ewan promised, that for a small fee Nettle could see any letter or parcel or bag or barrel of goods transported in or out, up or down. It was true that many carters and drivers stopped here. She knew them all.

An old metal hoop and a stick hanging from the front eave of the shack made a sort of bell that summoned her out into the light of day. We took the look of each other, standing there in the barren patch of dirt that passed for her yard. I stood with my basket and my hesitation, she with her nettle eyes and her great black dog.

"The new miller's wife," she said and turned away before I could collect myself to speak. She beckoned me through the low door of the shack and I followed her into the gloom, blinking in the murkiness. A shallow apron of space along the front of her rude home was crowded with crates and baskets and casks. The place smelled of stale bread and unwashed clothes and a privy too close. There was the sniff of malted barley and of scandal beyond that. Nothing in her "store" belonged to her. Everything was on its way somewhere else.

"Ye'll never lose a thing ye hand to me. I've done with losing. This bundle for Corrigan, is it? Come back in three days."

I handed over my butter and eggs and my list of supplies: a spool of blue thread, a milk crock, cheesecloth, fancy molasses, an ounce of cinnamon. In all honesty I hoped the trade would be lost or stolen or damaged and then I could rightly complain to Ewan that his plan was not only ridiculous but also unworkable.

But true to her word, every ounce of butter, each egg, arrived at Corrigans' fresh and intact. Henry Corrigan had attached a record of our transaction with the package he sent back up. All was in order. Goods (even cash money, Nettle assured me) flowed in and out unmolested and undiminished. Preposterous, ludicrous, ridiculous the arrangement remained, but it was possible, manageable. So while other women turned east on the road to Scotch River, I turned west to Nettle's lair. While others smiled and chatted, compared stories of their gardens and their stock, showed off their children or their produce, I ducked into Nettle's hovel and bore her cocked eye and sour breath.

EWAN MOVED SEAMLESSLY FROM ONE SET OF TASKS TO ANOTHER. One July day he paused long enough over his supper plate to say, "The men come tomorrow."

"What is this, my dear? Which men?"

"MacIsaac from over the river. And the papist from beyond the gulch. That papist owes me for lumber and he wants more yet. He's strong, so he claims. He's big anyway. He can sleep on the cot there." Ewan bent his head to indicate the small room off the kitchen. "But if he starts clacking his beads he can go right home again."

He spoke as though we had been discussing the arrival of these men for weeks, but this was the first I had heard of anyone coming to stay. "What will they be doing?"

He looked up at me in surprise and incomprehension. Then annoyance. Had he married an idiot after all, his eyes demanded. "The dam. What do you think?"

"There is no need to use such a rough tone, Ewan. I've mentioned your tone of voice before."

"We've been waiting for this since the day you got here. The dam, the dam, the dam! My new mill. The river is low."

The river is low, he had said at yesterday's dinner. Before we were married he had said he would begin construction of the dam when the river was low. The river is low was not idle conversation. All through the spring farm work, the making and stowing of the first cut of hay, he was waiting for the summer sun to draw down the flow of water so construction could begin. Of course he was thinking of the dam—he never ceased thinking of it.

"Of course. They come tomorrow to help you begin the dam. Did you send for them?" But of course he had sent for them, otherwise they would not be coming. "I mean, who sent them word to come? When? I didn't know you had arranged this."

"That Cunningham boy took the message. Yesterday."

"Ah." If I did not pay closer attention Mrs. Cunningham would know my business before I did. "Well, we shall have company to dinner then, and a guest to stay. I must consult with the servants about preparations."

Ewan gaped at me, alarmed, stricken. Again I had to correct myself. Ewan, for all he understood of cogs and levers, could not understand a joke. The truth of this observation crystalized for me in this moment. His gruff manner, his uneasiness with light conversation—he was afraid of what he couldn't understand, that was all. My annoyance slipped away. "A little fun, my dear. Don't worry, there are no servants. These are working men, I know. I'll make up the cot off the kitchen. Tomorrow is a big day—the day construction begins! This will be the first time I'll be preparing meals for more than you and me. We'll have to see how your new wife fares, won't we?"

Ewan nodded, uncertain.

"I'll get your tea," I said.

THE PAPIST'S NAME WAS MICHAEL FLANNERY ALTHOUGH EWAN didn't use the name—didn't seem to call him anything at all from what I could see. Michael was a pleasant enough fellow and a good worker, if a little rude in his habits. Even Ewan grudgingly admitted he had no complaints with him. Michael worked like an ox then fell into bed after dark with barely the energy to wash his hands and face. But he was up again before the sun, porridge eaten, and down the hill to the dam alongside Ewan. Duncan MacIsaac was the older of the two though not yet thirty. He had a wife and baby and a small stony place of his own not two miles along, across the river. He arrived after breakfast each day to join the work.

Once I finished with my milking and my pies and my butter in the morning, I set about preparing and packing up the dinner. At noon I arrived and laid out their picnic on the bank. Michael was always happy to see the lunch basket and gave me the sunniest of smiles. "Ah, Missus, I could eat a sheep and a goat," he'd say. The men pulled off their sodden boots to let the summer sun get at their feet. Ewan chewed his meat and slurped his tea, never taking his eyes off the dam, as though their morning's work might run off if left unguarded. He returned to work still chewing the last bite of his pie and the hired men had no choice but to follow.

I lingered on the bank a few minutes each day to watch their progress. My husband was bending a river. With silence, strength and sweat they erected the dam before my eyes. They began with a short wall which I thought impressive enough, but this was just the start. It was tied with cross logs into the higher fore-wall several yards downstream—making what seemed more a box than a wall. As they progressed they hoisted each massive log higher, rolling them up skids. I watched Ewan chop swift, clean notches and dovetail each log in place. As the walls grew they dumped tons of stone in behind them, sometimes two or three of them wrestling stones the size of bushel baskets. Their backs and arms strained as men's backs and arms had strained since the beginning of time. Building.

One day I stared at the gorge trying to visualize the future that Ewan saw. I guessed at the new water levels, trying to identify which trees would be flooded, where the edges of the new millpond would come. For a fleeting moment I felt I had grasped it all but then it flew off again, not finding a steady enough perch in my mind. He holds it all in his head, I realized. To him it's as easy and natural as breath. Here, at work, Ewan was perfect. Here the power and grace of his body melded in harmony with his intellect and his spirit and he attained a beauty almost painful to behold. I packed up my dinner basket trying to settle the quiver in my body.

THAT NIGHT, I WATCHED HIM IN THE MIRROR AS I SAT AT MY dressing table brushing out my hair. I waited until he rose from his childlike prayers before I spoke.

"You look so impressive working there in the river. Strong as horses. I never knew before how handsome a dam could be—such a beautiful crisscross rhythm to it. Is it going up well, do you think?"

Ewan frowned. "That MacIsaac is a sorry tool. He wanders in with the morning half gone and he's the first one to the lunch basket. Eats like a Mohawk and whines to go home at seven o'clock with the sun still blazing full."

"Oh now, Ewan, you know he has work of his own waiting at home."

"I don't pay him for that. I won't pay him a full day's wages for less than a day."

"Already it seems as though the dam were always meant to be there. Does it look as you thought it would?"

"Aye. How could it be otherwise when I do the thinking and the building both?"

"Not everything turns out just as we imagine it, surely?"

"The Lord gives us the strength to see His will and do His work. Diverging from the Lord's perfect path is a sin."

In the years to come I would often remember this pronouncement. That night, however, I was too tired for puzzles. I set down my hairbrush and joined my husband under the summer quilt.

FINALLY THE DAM WAS COMPLETED. MacIsaac pocketed his earnings and escaped home, relieved to be out from under Ewan's critical eye, I'm sure. Michael, the popish boy, stayed to help Ewan prepare the foundation and put everything in place for the frolic.

It was painful to watch Ewan suffer from the idea of the frolic, his brow furrowed so deeply I was sure his head ached. People everywhere! I imagined he felt them like lice on his skin and in his hair, itchy and dirty. But there was no other way, with the massive sills and posts and beams to be erected and all the mill workings waiting for the building that would house them. His lumber, his doors and windows, staircases, kiln tiles, hinges and hardware were collected and organized. Sheathing board was piled at the site in a stack the size of a cabin. Ewan would have to see his own way to the inevitable—the date must be set.

In the meantime I prepared myself. This would be no ordinary frolic. I discovered that before Ewan had arrived on the Gunn Brook people had had to truck their grain fifteen miles to a mill and even then they returned with an inferior product. There was great rejoicing when Ewan set the current millstones into Merton's old sawmill. The news that this basic jury-rigged facility was to be supplanted with a new, scientifically designed mill that would be the envy of the district had the air crackling with anticipation. Everyone would want to claim their part in building the structure that would house the fancy new mill. Abby warned me that the miller's new wife and her new house would also be up for inspection. I was like a child given the starring role in the school play: thrilled by the prospect of the adventure but terrified I would not meet the challenge. Even before the date was set I began to marshal my resources. Abby promised me all her help and made sure I knew to get a jug of rum from Nettle. Abby spoke to Irene Sutherland, who had a wonderful ice house and loved to be in charge of making the ice cream. I learned the names of the fiddlers who must be asked. Mrs. Cunningham called by to give me strict instructions about trestle tables and how to avoid burning the edges of my pie crust (information she seemed certain that I needed) and to tell me she was prepared to sell us—at a price more generous than anyone else would consider offering—a young pig to roast.

Finally, when there was nowhere to march but forward, Ewan spoke. Out of the blue, as I was collecting the supper dishes he said, "The twentieth."

"Ah. For the frolic, of course." I could not hide my pride. See how quickly I had learned to anticipate and understand my husband's awkward speech?

"Hum." He ducked his head in half a nod.

"Wonderful. I'll have young Donny Cunningham deliver the message down around the road and beyond the schoolhouse, shall I? And I'll tell Abby to pass the news, and that fellow who cants for you at your old mill—what's his name? I understand he's a sociable fellow. Shall I have them spread the word?"

"Yes. They better not stay all night, carrying on."

"Oh, but they will, my dearest. And they will have a grand time. It's essential for your business that they do. Why would they come to work if they have no spree at the end of it? In fact, the better fed and watered and entertained everyone is, the less likely they are to notice you at all. No one will be looking for you once the music starts. The day will come and go and you'll be no worse for it. And think of the mill!"

Ewan grunted.

I spoke to Michael. He and the one-armed carpenter from Randal's Crossing would do what they could to direct the work and try to keep Ewan from the worst effects of social interaction and the assembled men from the worst effects of Ewan. Then all my concerns were directed at my own preparations.

The miller's frolic was the largest and grandest that could be remembered in the district. No less than seventy men crawled over the mill site. The huge joists and beams, a foot in breadth and depth and more than thirty feet long, were set in place while joiners pounded pegs. They cut in braces at every corner to bolster the structure against the constant strain of the mill's motion. Boys fetched and carried. Hammers rang with a din that could be heard up and down the gorge, a concert of drumming. Saws chewed through hemlock boards wide as a man. No sooner was a board laid on the decking than it was nailed into place. The planking, sawn at the old mill, closed in the floors and walls, capturing the smell of the woods, the warm tawny air that mixed with the smell of sweat. The rafters were hauled into place and the roof sheathed. Boys nailed row after row of shingles onto the exterior walls. Men fitted the windows and doors and laid the cast-iron floor tiles for the oat kiln.

The builders hollered and laughed. They shouted teasing insults at each other recalling every triumph or mishap from previous frolics. Lads on the threshold of manhood surreptitiously sized up the abilities of their contemporaries and weighed them against their own: how many swings they took to sink a nail, how many planks they carried at once, how quickly and snugly they fit boards into place.

There was not a woman for miles who could resist the chance to explore my house for herself. Precious few people had seen inside. And who knows what tales and idle notions had swirled around the new wife—an unknown entity entirely, with no relatives in the area. Throughout the day women arrived with stews and pies and loaves of bread and baskets of sweets. So many introduced themselves I could not begin to keep them straight. Some smiled as warm as could be: "What a smart kitchen and look what you've done with it." Others tighter about the mouth: "Haven't you done well for yourself with house and mill and all." Some jolly with optimism: "Think of the smart modern mill we'll have next fall." Others sly with their compliments: "I understand he's ordered a French buhrstone, only the finest, yet isn't it shocking the things some people say about him?" Abby sorted out the women, setting some to tasks and encouraging others out to the yard. On occasions when a stranger seemed particularly pointed, Abby invariably appeared by my side, and I knew I was being protected. I was happy to keep my mind on my duties, greeting, thanking, flattering, managing food, ever aware of the many eyes upon me.

Outside, clumps of women, safely out of earshot, bent their heads towards each other in conference. Children chased each other around the yard, the older ones pointing to the stable and whispering to the wide-eyed younger ones until rumours of ice cream pushed all else aside. Once the men began straggling up the hill from the mill, food was set out on long trestle tables beside the house. Heaping plates were ferried around the yard by an army of children. Mothers called incessantly to their oldest daughters as young men winked from the cool patches of shade beneath the maples. Pots of tea were boiled, tobacco smoke mingled with the perfume of a summer evening, laughter bloomed everywhere. From a clutch of folks by the corner of the stable a lone fiddle sent out a jaunty reel. Like tossing a crust to a barnyard chicken, the bait brought a flock of fiddlers, seemingly from nowhere, into the circle. Someone hauled a squeezebox from under a wagon seat. A piper joined in and the dancing began.

As daylight began to fade and the music swelled I packed a basket from the feast tables and slipped off in search of Ewan. At the top of the hill I stood in wonder gazing down at the three-storey building that had risen from the foundation that day, whole and complete and waiting for the shafts and gears that would transform it into a mill. It had all the balance and grace I would have expected of my husband's design.

"It's beautiful," I said aloud to the endless sky, and I hugged the supper basket to me, rocking myself gently back and forth. I caught a movement in the upstairs window and waved. Ewan showed himself then, his face behind the pane. For a moment I simply stood and looked, then I stepped forward, to the new building with my husband's supper.

Not long after the frolic the harvest began trickling in. This would be the last harvest ground in the old mill and everyone commented upon this as they brought in their first sacks of barley and oats, then wheat and corn. By next fall the new mill would be operational. We had three fields of our own to reap and stook and gather in, so through the beginning of the season Ewan ran from the reaper in the field to the mill trying to manage both operations. Donny Cunningham and I followed the reaper building stooks. Then we followed the wagon, pitching and stacking. There were no pies and no raisin puddings on these days—it was all I could do to keep stew in the pot and bread on the table. Load by load we filled the granary.

By the time the threshers came through Ewan was at the millstones all day. He took his meals in the Old Nag and when custom was particularly heavy he lit the lamps and worked into the night until all the day's grist was ground and bagged. Whenever rain forced a pause in harvesting, and his grinding was caught up, Ewan stole a few lamplight hours for his new mill. His workshop bulged with parts and pieces for his power train. Load by load he carted the makings of the mill's machinery down to its new home. I could see that he felt the elements of power there, hovering like souls waiting to be born. Imagined lines would be transformed into shafts, tangents into belts; Platonic circles would come to life in pulleys and gears.

As winter closed in Ewan set his ice axe by the door at the Old Nag. Darkness swallowed up both ends of the day leaving only a few squinty hours of sunlight. He ground in the old mill when he had to, worked on the new mill when he could. On Christmas Day he raised the giant spur wheel into place. By New Year's all four stone nuts were mounted and the spindles set with their hackle screws ready to accept their millstones. He installed the cup elevators he had made according to the most modern design. Automatically they would carry wheat and oats and fodder from one stage of processing to the next. On the top floor he installed a winch for a rope hoist and cut trap doors in the main floor and upstairs floor, one immediately above the other, to allow sacks to be hauled up the entire height of the mill. All his hoppers and garners and chutes delivered grist directly to the required stones or shifters or shakers. So elegantly designed was the mill that one man could easily manage the entire operation on his own.

"Our sons will tend the kiln fire, work the sluice gate, sweep the floors. Then they'll learn the stones." So Ewan declared, his eyes coming to rest on my womb. "The mill will be their toy."

On the first day of February, although my flour bin was half full and I had not asked for more, Ewan arrived home, emerging from the darkness with a small flour bag swinging at his side. He placed it on the table with a poof.

"From the new mill?"

"Yes."

"Oh, Ewan." I dipped both my hands into the bag and let the whole-wheat flour run through my fingers. "It's lovely."

A stranger might have missed the glint in his eye, the twitch at the corner of his mouth. "I'll bolt a batch of that through the silk tomorrow. You'll have white flour," he said.

That night in his prayers he thanked God for his new mill. I felt the shape of his pride—a summer egg, protected with a shell of humility, wrapped in a transparent blanket of assurance, shielding the perfect orange yolk of pride. When I awoke in the morning the bed was empty beside me as usual. Ewan was back at work.

CHAPTER FOUR

A YEAR AND A HALF HAD PASSED SINCE OUR MARRIAGE AND no sign yet of a child. A full journey around the sun and more—two springs, two summers, and soon two harvests. I counselled patience for myself but this advice grew increasingly difficult to bear. I heard Ewan at his prayers at night, kneeling by his bedside. During the first months of our marriage I had closed my ears to this moment of intimacy between man and God but soon shed my scruples. Clearly, these would be the only intimacies I would know. At first it warmed me to be included in my husband's prayers but as time wore on I heard a different message.

"Make my wife worthy of Thy blessing. Show my wife the path of Godly labour. Forgive her sins and make her worthy of Thy service. Make her diligent. Reward my labours with a son."

I delighted in Abby's children, watched them grow, chatted with them as they passed my door on their way to and from school, gave them pennies or treats for small chores. Abby and I visited back and forth whenever our work allowed during the week and often on Sundays. The Browns provided tenderness and joy in my life but I could never come away from them without the tugging of that persistent ache for a family of my own.

When the leaves began to turn and the water ran high again, the fall crop began to arrive at the door of the new mill. Wagons lined up from early in the morning, farmers leaning against trees, smoking pipes, enjoying the holiday of talk and leisure and the luxury of the newest, most modern mill in the district. Determined to enjoy a walk in the fine fall weather I packed up my baskets for Nettle and set off down the road. I had several cheeses and a basket of eggs bound for Corrigans' store and I expected to retrieve a spool of wicking, a can of kerosene and some new dyes I had ordered.

Nettle sat sunning herself on the stump outside her cabin and grimaced, as usual, in response to my greeting. Perhaps it was the fine day or my familiarity with our routine but seeing her there by her hovel, my curiosity bubbled out.

"How is it you came to be … in business for yourself like this, Nettle?"

"A body's got to make their way in the world."

"But out here … on your own. People say—"

"I'm no different from the rest of you. We're all Fortune's fools. One day I had a man and the next I didn't."

"A man? Are you a widow then?" I appalled myself with the surprise in my voice and immediately tried to cover my rudeness. "What happened to him?"

"You leave me to my worries. Tend to your own man." She stared at my womb then into my eyes until I blushed in shame. There was nothing more to do but follow her into her shack where she bustled about, exchanging our parcels and calculating our business with no further interference from me. But as I turned to leave she spoke again: "I'm in the business of keeping things tight and passing them on, and I hold secrets close. Mine and others'. You never know when some bit of knowing will come in valuable." She spit into the muddy corner of the shack, pulled a hank of flesh off a smoked fish hanging on the wall, stuffed the greater part into her mouth and passed the rest to her silent, waiting dog.

In spite of the birdsong and the brilliant autumn sky and the invigorating walk home, Nettle had unnerved me. All the more because I couldn't precisely say why.

On the last day of October we woke to the whisper of drizzling rain on the dark windowpane. By dawn the drizzle had settled into a steady rain and the air was heavy with the assurance of a good long drenching. No grain would be coming in today. Ewan had been waiting for just such a day to tend to the cleaner above his shelling stone. It was too finicky, too likely to clog if not watched closely. Ewan had thought he had fixed the problem once before but when it re-emerged he took it as a personal affront. He trained his attention on the offending part. Because he would be back and forth to his shop, in and out all day with his mind occupied, he hired Donny Cunningham, as he had in the past when he was particularly busy, to mind the kiln.

And so Donny happily stayed home from school to earn fifty cents for feeding the fire and keeping an eye on the temperature in the kiln. No custom—no farmers, nothing rolling down the hill except rivulets of rain dashing for the millpond. I can imagine Donny stretching out into his day of solitary leisure punctuated only by Mr. MacLaughlin's intermittent presence. The sack hoist was great fun. It was simply a rope on a winch. Two sets of trap doors, one directly above the other, opened up the vertical space from the meal floor in the basement all the way up to the top of the mill. The hoist could as easily carry a man as a sack. Indeed Ewan had ordered a little metal stirrup from the smithy, knotted it to the end of the hoist rope, for just this purpose. From down on the meal floor Donny could set his foot in the stirrup, and hang on to the rope like a sailor in the rigging. The mechanism that controlled the winch could be activated from any floor by pulling one of two light ropes that hung down the length of the mill. One engaged the winch and the other disengaged it. When Donny engaged the hoist, up he went, not fast, but still with the thrill of outside propulsion. With his free hand he could push open the first set of trap doors above his head and emerge onto the main floor. Onward and upward he would likewise fold open the second set of trap doors and then swing out onto the top floor, disengage the winch, send the hoist rope down, and run back down the two sets of stairs for another ride. Ewan would never have approved of swinging on the hoist for fun, for playing pirates—swinging from the rigging with a kindling cutlass capturing chests full of gold.

At first Donny would have kept a sharp lookout for his boss, but vigilance wanes. As the afternoon dragged on he likely lost track of where Ewan was. He tended his oats, set the broom aside and leaned back against the wall, watching the spur wheel rumble along on its perpetual journey. No doubt his mind wandered to some pretty girl he had had his eye on. In some clumsy scenario she smiles at him, picking berries maybe and beckons him somewhere unlikely—a make-believe copse by an implausible waterfall. However it was, at one point Donny reached up and grabbed the rope above his head. Intending what? Intending nothing. Intending only to swing his weight on it, idly. Only to hang on to it the way he might a low branch overhead. But he failed to look up, failed to note the creaking of the bollard far above his head announcing that Ewan was, at that very moment, riding the sack hoist from the ground floor to the upper floor.

When Donny reached up and so idly grabbed the rope that disengaged the winch, the wooden fingers that had been carrying Ewan's weight through the air were released. The sky fell in a rush, in a smack that knocked Donny off his feet like a shot steer. Everything in a single unintelligible instant—a thunder of confusion, a scatter of pain, a snap like a floorboard giving way and a great weight pinning him to the floor. Sudden darkness and a bellowed curse from God himself. Donny must have scrabbled to extricate himself, scrambled to his feet, gawking as the heap of sudden weight reconfigured itself into his boss.

"Mr. MacLaughlin!"

I was at my churn when Donny burst into the kitchen with no breath to speak but with eyes wild with terror. "…accident." I dropped the dasher and tore past him not pausing for coat or bonnet, my skirts flying out behind me. I had no idea what state I might find Ewan in. The notion of Ewan diminished in any way was simply inconceivable. Donny trailed behind me, hobbling and gasping, clutching the stitch in his side. I flew down the hill, half sliding down the steep path over the bank, then the slap of my boot soles on the wooden step of the mill.

"Ewan?"

"God damn it to hell!"

I nearly laughed from the relief of his being alive, lucid and strong enough to bellow. And from the novelty of a shouted profanity erupting from the hole at my feet like Satan calling from the underworld. Ewan's curse hauled me from panic down to a searing, rational fear. I thundered down the stairs and there he lay crumpled, his right leg splayed off unnaturally, his face scarlet, his eyes as fierce as the Devil's. He tried to stand, got halfway up and toppled over.

"Don't move, Ewan. Don't! For God's sake, stay down!" I gave instructions to Donny, now cowering at the top of the stairs. "Cut me two splints, this long. Bring me two long-handled tools, like a broom or shovel, bring me a stack of flour bags. Bring me cord or a rope of some kind. Run."

Ewan had fallen two full floors. That his leg was broken was self-evident. There was a gash on his head and blood. I fashioned a stretcher out of flour bags, a gaff and an iron rod. I do not know how we wrestled the livid, railing Ewan and his twisted leg onto the stretcher and up the stairs. I know that by the time we reached the road Ewan had gone silent and where his skin was not crimson with blood it had drained as white as the flour bags he lay upon. I remember the sacks of pain where my lungs had been and the rhythmic hollow explosions of blood in my veins. Finally we reached the house and set the stretcher on the cot in the room off the kitchen.

"Saddle up Pride—she's the faster. Go for the doctor. Go!"

We are all Fortune's fools. For a moment I stood idle, unsure of my next step, but fear threatened to drown me. I fetched warm water and began dabbing at Ewan's wounds. Blood had caked in his hair, stained the shoulder of his shirt, speckled out everywhere. A nasty bruise was rising on his forearm but no blood from the leg.

"Ewan?"

He would not look at me although his eyes were open. He blinked. His right hand he kept opening and closing in a fist.

"Ewan, can you hear me?"

"Aye."

I wrung the blood from my cloth and wiped his face. He stared at the wall. Suddenly terror flashed in his eyes and his entire body tightened in a gasp. His mouth shaped into a shout but no sound emerged, as though he were falling all over again. Then he settled for a few minutes.

I eased the bloody shirt off him, used it to staunch the still seeping blood. A whispered chant seemed to rise out of him and hover. I lowered my ear, strained to hear. A request? A prayer? No.

"…second, their velocity is always in proportion to the time of their fall and the time is as the square root of the distance fallen, third, the spaces through which they pass are as the squares of the times or velocities, fourth, their velocities are as the square root of the space descended through…"

Mrs. Cunningham filled the doorway, clicking her tongue, as usual. "Always a foolish amount of blood from a head wound." She was swift and efficient. "Scissors," she said. "We'll need to cut them trousers off him."

When the doctor arrived he shooed us out of his way. There was barely room for one by the bedside in the tiny room. I stood in the doorway trying to gauge the frown on the doctor's face as he checked the bandages then focused his attention on the injured leg. "He broke the bone for sure. But he didn't break the skin. That's a help anyway." He straightened and looked around the cramped space. "We're going to set that bone now." He pulled a flask from his medical bag and held it out to Ewan. Ewan waved it away.

"Ah, you'd better," the doctor said. "The hollering can upset the ladies."

"Won't upset me, I'm sure. Nothing I ain't heard before," Mrs. Cunningham said.

"I was thinking more of his wife."

"Just set the damned thing and never mind," Ewan ordered.

"I'll just leave the bottle here then." The doctor set the rum on the bedside table, beckoned to Mrs. Cunningham, and stationed himself at the foot of the bed. Then he turned to me. "Best you wait in the kitchen."

I opened my mouth to argue but nothing came out.

"Shut that door behind you."

"We're ready," I heard him say to Mrs. Cunningham presently. "Hold onto him tight."

I waited for the screams of pain but none came—only the huffing of the doctor straining overlaid with the steely silence of Ewan's will. Finally the doctor emerged from the room sighing and rubbing his shoulder. He seemed suddenly old and tired, worn down from the weight of decades of bearing bad news. "Alright. I need a fresh pail of water, then come in here and I'll show you how to make a nice snug bandage."

I stood at the end of the bed while the doctor splinted the leg and wove a soaked bandage around it all. Ewan stared straight up at the ceiling, his arms rigid by his sides and skin white as lime, while the doctor worked.

From time to time the doctor spoke to Ewan, gauging his responsiveness. Ewan answered in monotones. My fear crackled over everything and wooziness forced me to the chair.

Finally the doctor finished and called me out of the room with him. "He'll be on his back for a while now," he said. "He's not to move. You watch for fever and call me if he gets hot. You can give him a couple of these pills every day. And a bit of rum for the pain if he'll take it. Missus there," he jerked his head to indicate Mrs. Cunningham, "she'll likely have him doused up with twig tea and old roots before I get past the crossroads. See she doesn't poison him."

I untied the handkerchief I'd tucked into my apron pocket and held out several dollars in coins, willing my hand to stop its quivering. "I can get more," I said.

He raised an eyebrow in surprise, perhaps taken off guard to see cash money up so far into the country. "This is plenty for now. Let's see how he comes out." Then realizing how this sounded he softened his tone in contrition. "Now don't you worry, Mrs. MacLaughlin. I've seen lots worse than this. Bones heal themselves. We couldn't stop them if we wanted to and it's a good clean break. He'll knit up, you wait and see. The thing is to keep him still. He's not to move off that bed. He's not to move in it, either." The doctor fit his hat firmly on his head and bowed slightly. "I'll call back up in a day or two."

Ewan lay with his face to the wall. After a while I offered to read to him. A few passages from the Bible, perhaps? He would not hear the word of God but he allowed me to pass an hour or so stumbling through his Oliver Evans *Miller's Guide*. The laws of spouting fluids. The laws of motion and rest. It seemed to calm him. He drifted in and out of sleep.

"The seven essential properties of bodies: extension, figure, impenetrability, divisibility, mobility, inertia, attraction." I heard him at it the next day, lists running like grain through fingers: simple, knowable, soothing. Not a prayer, not a plea, but an incantation, a touchstone, immutable and true. "Five kinds of attraction between bodies: gravitation, cohesion, magnetism, electrical and chemical. What are the eight laws of falling bodies? Number one: they are equally accelerated. Number two: their velocity is always in proportion to the time of their fall, and the time is as the square root of the distance fallen. Number three…" I listened to him clutching at this perfect world of the mind, reaching out to these absolutes.

It took very little time before Ewan's incapacities turned him wrathful. Early mornings were the worst. I steeled myself before poking my head in the door. "How did you sleep, Ewan? Your tea will be ready in a jiffy. And your oatmeal."

"Why don't you get out of bed when you should? There's daylight all around. God's not going to favour a lazy slattern! I never saw a woman sleep so much as you! Idler! Layabout! Barren as a mule and no wonder!"

It was the frustration of captivity that made him so wild, I knew. But this did not assuage the hurt. I knew there was an element of truth in what he said, not about my indolence, which I knew was an unfair charge, but true that he expected more of me. True that he blamed me for my childlessness, my failure to produce in good time.

"I see now how my seed falls upon stony places." As soon as I was sure the fire had caught in the stove I grabbed my milk pail and fled to the barn where I wept into the flank of my gentle cow.

Twice each day I had to check Ewan's brow for fever. It was like plotting to corner a pig. Approaching him set him off roaring, no matter that I had not even touched him. If it had been a painful thing, if I were required to bleed him, for example, I could imagine him thrusting his arm towards me impatient for the blade. But a touch, the heaping of the vulnerability of affection upon the vulnerability of incapacity was too much for him. Tea he would take, and cod liver oil. A hot potion of comfrey with a splash of medicinal rum he would accept from time to time, but the rum bottle by his bedside he never touched. I pulled back the curtains I had stitched for the little window only last year, rubbing the cotton between my thumb and fingers. Sunshine always strengthens the constitution, I meant to say, but as I turned to him the slash of raw pain that contorted his face as the daylight hit strangled the words in my throat. Daylight equals man plus work. The untouched porridge I had dished up for his breakfast hit the wall, splattered, the bowl smashed, milk dripping onto the floor.

His outbursts, though fierce, were set in a bleak landscape of silence. He seldom slept but slipped into bouts of unresponsiveness. Sometimes when I approached, his eyes had glassed over so wholly I was seized by the fear that he had died and had been lying here a cooling corpse as I went about my work. I would rush to touch him, feel the life in his skin and he, roused from his comatose state, would rage. "I never saw a woman sleep so much as you."

Abby came down with baby Lily and little Nancy Ann. She nestled the baby in my arms and unwrapped the dishtowel protecting warm sweet buns that released a bloom of cinnamon that nearly made me cry with the comfort.

"Don't you worry now. Dr. Thomas is not like a lot of them. I'm not saying he doesn't do his share of clucking and rubbing his chin and charging you two months' egg money for the joy of watching him, but he's a fine bonesetter. His father was a bonesetter in Wales. Did you know that? So he learned the trade proper before any of that other poking and prodding and whatnot. Well, you know Jake Hollis. He broke his arm as a young fellow. You'd never know that today, would you? And Joe-Iron MacDonald with his leg—not even a limp. And Belle Matheson had two fingers set. And that fellow down by the ford, oh there's no end to the folks Dr. Thomas has fixed up their bones strong as new."

Abby had us all settled at buns and butter and tea in no time. She carried Ewan's in to him before I realized she had done it. Truth was, once I settled at the table with Abby's baby, with the toddler at my feet and Abby bustling with such constancy and confidence behind me, exhaustion descended in a dead weight on my shoulders and I could not have faced him.

"Where's my wife?" The demand filled the kitchen. I stiffened. Abby's response was too muted to make out but it sounded cheerful enough. And before I could pry myself off the chair Abby was back.

"Don't get up, my dear. He's right as rain." She leaned over and whispered in my ear. "Men. They're worse than youngsters when they're sick." She laughed and added, "Sometimes even when they're not sick!"

I listened for the crack of the plate against the wall but it did not come. I cringed in anticipation of one of his cruel outbursts but perhaps he was aware enough of outside company to restrain himself.

"He hollers out, and will hardly eat a thing. Sometimes he says things..." I whispered, desperate to confide but horrified by the betrayal of relating Ewan's wild behaviour.

Abby set off into a peel of laughter. "See? Sounds like a babe to me! He's only blowing the poison out of his system. Spouting like a whale. Don't you take mind of *anything* he says now. You just tend to your work, talk cheerful to him and laugh at what he answers you—like it's all jokes and fun." She nestled in beside me and squeezed my shoulder, whispering now. "He's going to be fine. All the men are like that. You know we can no more pass our patience over to the men than they can pass the strength of their backs over to us. They can't help it any more than we can."

Then Abby was up and at the firebox with the poker, her voice back to its cheery normal. "Tea, buns and a nap is what's for you, my girl. Me and the babies are here to see you get it before we go home again."

"Fill the wood box," he hollered in my face when I brought in his supper. "It's all but empty. Nothing but chips!"

I retreated and brought in an armload, but it did little to appease him.

"There's not more than seven sticks in that wood box! Six more likely."

Perhaps physical distance gave me courage, perhaps exhaustion eroded my better intentions. My hurt flared to anger. "How would you know? You can't see around corners!"

"Count them," he demanded. "How many?"

There were six. I moved several sticks heavily in the box, then moved them again making the box sound full.

"Fourteen!"

"Liar!"

He had been counting every armload in from the shed, every soft clunk into the firebox. For days, I suppose. Likely every footstep as well, every moment I sat in a chair, every click of a spoon on a pot. Keeping track—the empty box weighing on his mind always.

"Fill the box!"

"I'll fill it when I want!" Even as I spoke I was shamed by my childishness, my fatigue, my inability to follow Abby's wise advice. But even ashamed I remained stubbornly unrepentant. Angry. "There's fourteen sticks," I repeated. "Three quarters full."

I stalked to the bedroom door intending to shut it tight, but Ewan, goaded on by my childishness, lunged sideways as if to stand. He twisted, half caught himself on outstretched hands as he hurled to the floor. The splinted leg, a beast with its own will, gathered momentum and followed his torso out of bed. The leg clattered down on top of him. He cried out once in pain then lay silent and still where he had fallen. I ran to him, shrieked at the contorted huddle on the floor. I knelt beside him, reached out gingerly to touch him and saw his face streaked with tears of frustration.

"Ewan," I whispered. "It's all right. Sh-sh now, don't cry. It's all right now."

I had to fetch Mrs. Cunningham to help me heft him back into bed, limp as a sack of corn. When I brought him a mug of tea he turned his face to the wall and would not eat or drink or speak for the rest of the day. I filled the wood box to overflowing. When daylight slipped away and I appeared with a lamp he spoke his first words since his outburst. "No light."

"Ewan, you must have a lamp. I thought perhaps I could sit a while and read to you. A piece from the Bible maybe. Or Oliver Evans, if you like."

"Leave me."

That night I crawled upstairs and sat by our bed numb from desperation. I found myself staring at the empty spot where Ewan would kneel for his nightly prayers and I knew the place must be filled. I crossed the room and sank down, clasping my hands and reproducing the words he might have said as closely as I could imagine them. Praying for my husband. "Our Father who art in heaven … make my wife diligent. Make her exalt Thee with her labour. Make her worthy of Thy blessing. Forgive her her trespasses."

CHAPTER FIVE

EWAN

T HE NIGHT SILENCE PRESSED IN ON HIM AS HE LAY IN the room off the kitchen, his body submerged in pain, his leg throbbing. He shunned the candle, preferring to hide in the dark. Ewan's own father had died of a broken leg—suffered blood loss, then infection and fever. How did your father die, his wife had once asked. He was felled by a tree, he had said. Where was the point in yattering on? Gone is gone.

In fact, a sudden gust and a bounce off a snag and his father had been pinned, his leg crushed by a great hemlock. Ewan's brother had run for help and it had taken six men to lift the tree to free him they said. The men carried him home. Ewan and the younger children had been at school and arrived home just as the wretched procession was making its way across the barnyard. Ewan stood there chewing on his mitten as the troop of men passed in front of him. He remembered the parallel poles of the approaching stretcher. There was blood and—he was sure he had seen this, visible in the slanting afternoon light—jagged bone poking up. He did not remember his father's face. He remembered the terrified silence of the house and the barred door of the bedroom where his father lay. Children were banished, questions forbidden.

Ewan had no memory that predated his place in the mill—the broom, sacks, barrels, the warm smell of smoky wool when he buried his nose in the crook of his arm, the way the dust settled like a fine mist on his eyelashes and the fine hairs of his arms—all these things had always been. There must have been a first time Ewan had raised the sluice gate in the flume but he had no memory of a time before he knew the raspy slide of the little door within its wooden track. There was no time he could not hunker down by the edge of the millpond and scoop up a pail of water. Always he had shovelled oat husks into sacks as large as himself but still light enough to drag out of the mill and up the steps to the waiting cart. His first clear memory was of scooping up a small sack of fine white flour for a man in a shirt with a collar. His father took the sack from Ewan and was tying it up when the man turned and appeared to address Ewan himself.

"And how is Mr. Dusty today?"

The man stared right at him. Ewan looked around. There was no one else. Ewan knew the answer to the question "How are you?" because his mother had told him the answer. It wasn't a real question like other questions; it was just to see if a person knew their manners. The proper answer was "Fine thank you, ma'am," or "Fine thank you, sir." But Ewan did not understand who Mr. Dusty was or why the man had mistaken Ewan for him.

"I'm not Mr. Dusty. My name is Ewan MacLaughlin," he said.

In his memory there were people everywhere all of a sudden, just like in a dream, looking at him and all laughing for no reason that Ewan could see. Farmers laughing. Everyone, even his own father, laughing at him. And there he stood, confused, with a gurgly feeling in his stomach.

Ewan could never tell when laughing would start: at school, at the mill, anywhere. Sometimes people laughed at a lie, sometimes at a truth. Sometimes people laughed when things did not go as they ought. Or sometimes if things went exactly as hoped for. Ewan tried to categorize and predict but still laughter caught him by surprise. One day a boy or girl might speak to him as though they were friends but then the next they could as easily turn on him, their laughing mean. Ewan wanted predictability. He wanted the world to unfold as expected.

He was not like his brothers Sander and Hector who were always anxious for things to go askew. In the winter they stole each other's mitts and filled them with snow; in the summer they wrestled in the millpond, each trying to manoeuvre the other's head below the surface, half drowning each other. One brother would burst to the surface gasping and furious. Hacking and red-faced he would lunge at his tormentor who would take off up the bank laughing like a maniac, keeping several paces ahead of the breathless pursuer. Then at the next opportunity they would be back at the game again. Once they rigged a pulley in the barn and hoisted the young calves into the mow. One toppled off the platform, broke its back and had to be slaughtered. Despite the loss of a good calf and the whippings, that night in bed they brushed their welts with their fingertips and laughed themselves silly. They hoarded little piles of pebbles around the mill and barn to ambush the squirrels and birds in the trees. They kept up a running competition with an inconsistent and illogical scoring system recorded in notches on a barn beam. The tally did little to record hits and kills but rather evoked the kinds of sabotage and squabbling they both delighted in. Their tussling braided into their laughter and back out again. Ewan watched. He worked and he waited.

The shirts and trousers that Sander and Hector did not wear out came down, in time, to him. He loved the way these hand-me-downs enveloped him with the essence of his brothers. He rubbed his hands up and down the length of the sleeves and along the thighs of the trouser legs trying to absorb his brothers out of their clothing. Perhaps the intricate warp and weave held the secret information. How could they speak so easily about nothing at all and end up happy? How could they carry on so foolishly, tightly together, until they looked like two halves of the same animal? They could bump shoulders or hips or grab the other by the back of the neck with no more notice than scratching their own elbows. Ewan kneeled by his bed saying his prayers as he had been taught.

Hector slipped up behind him and pressed his hand down on Ewan's head until it hurt. "Offer your labours to the Lord," Hector said, rolling his R's ridiculously in imitation of the minister. "What have you done today with the hands God gave you?"

Sander climbed onto the bed and hiked his nightshirt up to his waist, "Oh Lord, I have pulled the blessed bone You gave me until it gushed forth in a mighty froth. Glory be to the Almighty!" Hector strutted across the room. "Oh heavenly angels, spread your wings for me!" Hector and Sander laughed until they held their sides and tears ran down their cheeks. Ewan crawled into bed and pulled the covers over his head. He closed his eyes and listed his chores silently to God.

When Ewan was twelve years old he had been whipped in school for idling, for daydreaming. He was to have been writing a composition about the Lancasters and the Yorks. But two rows behind him the boys in the upper class were being introduced to the principles of geometry and Ewan could not keep his ears to himself. Geometry—the word itself sounded like a magical incantation. A point. A line. Common words, yes, but Master was transforming them into tools to unearth some deeper meaning. No previous teacher had ever spoken like this, Ewan was sure of it. But this schoolmaster was exceptional. Master had been to school in Edinburgh. In addition to his regular teaching duties he offered lessons in Latin and navigation on Saturday afternoons for an additional fee. There were vague claims he had been an adventurer of some sort. In Africa perhaps. Rumour had it he was convalescing from some condition not spoken of. The left side of his mouth he propped up in a permanent sardonic smile at once inviting and dangerous. He amused at least himself with his rhetoric and most of the time seemed on the verge of some hilarity discernible only to the most sophisticated, or such was the tacit message. Half the population thought him ridiculous and good for nothing more than teaching, and the other half fought to feed him Sunday dinner and hear him string his lovely words together and imagine all the things their sons might learn from him. At school Master goaded and bullied with apparent good humour, his perpetual smirk interrupted by occasional terrifying flashes of temper.

"A circle is a set of points equidistant from a given point," Master declared. Ewan teased these words, turning them over in his mind, trying to decipher them. A point? A point. He had seen his father attach a string to a nail to draw a circle on a board. Ewan had done this himself and had admired the perfect circle: Did the master mean the point was the point of the nail? And equal distance? He marked a dot in his copybook, drew a crude circle around it, imagining a string to steady his hand. He drew in one tentative radius. Every radius must be exactly this length. A string would make it so. Of course he had known *how* this worked but now he saw *why* it worked. Behind him the master continued with his lesson.

"A perfect circle exists only in space, gentlemen. Geometry is an art of the mind. It lives with God in a realm of metaphysics that few of you cherished sons of stone and lichen will ever glimpse. Nevertheless, feed upon this pearl, my churlish charges…"

A perfect circle exists only in space. In the air? Ewan struggled to follow the master's ongoing instructions. Fix upon a point in space. Ewan was unsure but focused on the upper right corner of the framed portrait of the Queen. Now, envision all points that are exactly one foot from it. When he pictured it, the circle emerged perfect and precise in his mind. He imagined another—two concentric circles. Exquisite. He drew a second wobbly circle in his copybook and stared hard at its obvious lopsidedness. But the master was right. Even if he had a nail and string the result would only be better, not perfect. When Ewan raised his eyes again all of creation lifted off the page. His scalp tingled, he felt lightheaded, his breath stilled in his body. Yes. A circle was an *idea*. Any drawn shape was only a crude representation. The beauty of the perfect idea welled up underneath his heart like a moth fluttering its wings. That he might have seen and used and identified circles and never have understood their essence, their perfection, struck him as profoundly sad and it seemed a matter of extraordinary luck that he had stumbled across this information. Ewan's heart beat faster, a breeze passed through him blowing bits of his insides up into swirls. A line is the shortest distance between two points. Yes, exactly. He stared at the window, a rectangle. Where the sun slanted across the floorboards, a triangle. The corner of the room where two walls met the ceiling, the desks, the slates, the water bucket—all shapes fashioned in the image of a mathematical ideal. The globe of the world sat on its own special table by the window. Ewan stared, his fresh understanding enveloping it. Turn a circle in the air and it becomes a ball with a single, dead centre point deep inside—all points in every direction equal distance from a given point.

Gradually Ewan became aware of a vague whistling and laughter all around him. Master stood beside Ewan's desk, with his arms folded, bouncing on the balls of his feet and looking about, whistling as though he had not a care in the world other than to pass the time 'til supper. All the children stared, giggling, waiting for Ewan to notice he was being made the centre of attention. Ewan looked up, his face burning.

"Oh look, children, Master MacLaughlin has returned from his fantastical cerebral ramblings. With all this time for leisure perhaps, young sir, you would like to read out your composition for us all to enjoy? I am sure that with all your contemplations it must be an excellent one."

Ewan sat frozen.

"No? Well, let me see." The master held up Ewan's copybook, soiled with two lopsided circles but not a single word beyond the title. "Now don't be fooled, scholars. What we have here is a cunning visual representation of the two warring houses of England. But which wayward circle do you suppose, children, is meant to be the 'rose' of the Yorks and which to be of the unfortunate Lancasters? Which is meant to be white and which red? It is in this distinction that we will discover the thrust of this young philosopher's argument." The children readily joined in the mockery, relieved not to be the butt of scorn themselves. The master built their laughter to its apex then turned suddenly, slamming his fist on the desk, inches away from Ewan, his face black with anger. He abandoned his terrified pupils amid the very laughter he had engendered, turned on his heel and stalked to the front of the class where he grabbed the switch that stood in the corner. "Ewan MacLaughlin, come here."

The news that Ewan had been whipped at school flew home as though on the wings of birds. Daydreaming. His mother was rendered momentarily motionless at the charge. She had been halfway across the kitchen, a pail of lard in one hand and a bowl of apples in the other, and she had stopped at the news. She had set down her load and this Ewan remembered sharp and clear—her stillness, her emptied hands, her standing stock-still with that look of utter disbelief. He had committed a crime so heinous it had the power to disrupt the progress that was the very essence of his mother.

"Ewan. Daydreaming," she said, half a question, half an accusation as though she could not quite comprehend the iniquity of it. "Ten days," she said when she regained herself. She resumed her work but as though her burdens had taken on the new weight of disappointment. Ewan's true nature had been revealed. She sent him off to fetch a hardy switch.

Each day for ten days Ewan's father applied the rod with calm concentrated dedication to task. On the Sabbath his father had to slip off his Sunday jacket and set it carefully on the back of a chair before taking up the necessary work of the beating. On the tenth day, after the tenth switching, his father made quick kindling of the birch branch and stuffed it into the firebox before he turned to his son. "Now, have I got your attention?" he asked.

The master stayed only six months at the school. With his leaving, instruction reverted to the hands of the more usual sort of girl. There was no further talk of geometry. Ewan kept what he had gleaned and what little he wrested from his older brother who had been in the upper class, but this information was pocked full of holes and often skewed as Hector had little aptitude and no interest in circles in the sky and fiddling with protractors. But perhaps it was the master's teaching that prompted their father to return from the merchant's with a book: *The Young Mill-Wright and Miller's Guide.* He handed it to Hector. Had the master taught him how to read this? he asked. It was not long before Hector had tossed the book aside onto the windowsill where Ewan picked it up. Oliver Evans, Engineer. This was where Ewan first saw an industrial drawing. Here geometry was pulled down from the air and used to figure and to design. Water falling to a waterwheel was represented as a tangent. The arc of a cog intersecting with the arc of a gear could be symbolized with circles. All this could be calculated on paper then brought to life through wood and iron. This was how building was thought about. Engineer.

In the cracks of the day between chores, in the walk to and from school, in the quiet pools of wakefulness before sleep or sometimes waking in the middle of the night, or on Sunday afternoons, young Ewan let the lines and vectors and ratios, the perfect geometry of the mind wash over him. But it was far too easy to be carried away calculating ratios and find himself distracted from work—standing by the wood box with arms half laden, staring idly into space. More than once he narrowly escaped detection. Ewan learned he must always be on guard against his filthy daydreaming nature. He learned to hide his sin and never to let the pace of his work slacken, never allow mathematics to push its way in and allow him to be caught inattentive.

AND THEN CAME HIS FATHER'S ACCIDENT. There he was being carried in on a stretcher and set up in the room off the kitchen. The doctor. The whispers. The next morning their mother picked Ewan's schoolbooks off the kitchen table and tossed them on top of the cupboard. "You're done with these," she said. Ewan was not sorry to leave behind school's silly girls and stupid, bullying boys. Since Master left they'd learned nothing of any use anyway. Their mother turned fiery eyes on Sander and Hector. "Go back to the woods and find that tree that fell on your father. Chop it into pieces the size of my shoe—I want to see it burn in the stove. You—" She turned back to Ewan—"there's a grist of oats to be dried. You mind the kiln."

Ewan made his way to the mill. After he spread the oats over the kiln floor and lit the fire he wandered beneath the great spur wheel and stared up into the wooden cogs. At fourteen years old this was the first time he could remember standing here completely alone, no one between him and the machinery of the mill. Although it was not his business to grind, he opened the sluice and set the mill running. Without a soul to discover him or correct him or interrupt him he stood staring up at the gears with his arms dangling, measuring with his eyes, imagining the workings as drawings like those he'd seen in his father's book. He imagined the drawings as conceptions, his mind ranging, stretching, dancing amid the infinite possibilities of the theoretical world. He stood still while the kiln fire burned low with inattention, with floors awaiting sweeping and a stack of sacks needing stitching. And as he stood idle in the mill with his head in the clouds and his hands hanging empty at his sides, his father, lying up in the house, died.

THREE SONS FOR THE MILL: SANDER, HECTOR AND EWAN. Three daughters for the house: Mary, Agnes and Catherine. This was God's will. The girls learned what they needed from their mother. Their business was their own and of no concern to men. They nattered away like hens—if there was meaning in the chatter it was nothing to Ewan. They cooked and cleaned and provided what was needed.

At the tail end of the family, after a short hiatus, with their mother well into her forties, Charles and then Robert had been born. Their mother had declared three sons were enough for any mill and she would have these two for herself, one for the clergy, one for a doctor. She had set up a table and a shelf for a library in the parlour. She had had the girls light lamps and keep a blaze in the parlour stove so the younger boys could tend to their books in the evenings. Even before they had started school their mother had had them at slates and bought them copybooks to practise their letters. Copybooks! By the time she had sent them off to school they were already reading one-syllable words and reciting, already adding apples and oranges. Robert and Charles had been declared too delicate for the boys' room and instead had shared the small bedroom at the top of the stairs. Robert and Charles had not been called to the mill. Or the fields. Or the woods. In fact, they were of no account at all as far as Ewan could see.

But then came the accident. Their father broken and buried. All was disrupted. When the family touched earth again on the far side of the funeral their mother's resolve was redoubled. Tribulations or no, she would see her two youngest sons properly educated and thrust up into society. She had Sander, Hector and Ewan for the mill. Boys yes, but at nineteen, eighteen and fourteen they had the basics of the trade. From their father they had learned to swing an axe, an adze, a pick. They could repair the dam and dress the stones. They could dry, shell, grind and sift well enough to make a start. They had learned the value of daylight and needed only to develop a devotion to task. This she could provide. Experience would teach the rest. As for the girls, she sent Mary off to the Boston States to send home a monthly pay packet. The younger two girls, when not at their studies, swept, scrubbed and churned until they reached the age where they could be sent out to teach at any school that could send fifty dollars home. She bought another cow, bred the young heifer and expanded her laying flock. She kept bees and sold honey. The back pasture could support a few sheep. She worked beside her sons in the fields wringing out every possible head of grain for flour or meal. She squeezed and hoarded money, kept it trickling in from every possible source. Robert and Charles spent their evenings at their books in the parlour, unmolested by the industry around them.

AT FIRST THE BOY MILLERS FOUND THEIR WAY BY STEPPING carefully into the footprints their father had left for them. They worked as though under the eye of their father and this gave them courage and direction and the patina of certainty. While their connection with the world of men seemed oddly kinked without their father, their connection with the world of boys had been severed. Sander and Hector enfolded Ewan into their world as their father would have directed. The three of them shovelled and hauled grain and meal and flour and bran. From wagons to the kiln to hoppers to barrels and sacks and back to wagons the three of them inhabited this island all their own. What Ewan remembered of those early days was the smoky warmth of the kiln, the toasty smell, the mild stinging of his eyes. Three shovels scraping the iron of the kiln floor or the hardwood boards of the mill floor and the whoosh as the kernels ran together. Rhythmic scrape and dump, a river of grain, his brothers there beside him, Hector's periodic little cough, Sander whistling almost imperceptibly through his teeth.

Sander greeted the farmers. Hector weighed the grain. Ewan worked the figures and kept the accounts. Every Saturday night Ewan laid the books before his mother for her perusal. She set her hand on his shoulder and nodded her head. "God knew your father's journey would be short. That's why He sent you for the mill. That's why He made you a good worker," she said. For a quarter of an hour every Saturday evening Ewan sat by his mother basking in her full attention and her approbation. On Sunday mornings he sat with his family in the MacLaughlins' pew and listened while the world's workings were elucidated in the immutable laws of God. *Neither did we eat any man's bread for nought; but wrought with labour and travail night and day, that we might not be chargeable to any of you. If any should not work, neither should he eat.* On Sunday afternoons Ewan sat with his father's copy of Oliver Evans's millwright's guide. Like God, everything Oliver Evans said was true, and if Ewan did not understand a law or a passage he had only to reread, to attend more closely, and the meaning would become clear. *Every body in a state of rest will remain so and every body in motion will continue to move in a right line until a change is effected by the agency of some mechanical force.* What he read on Sunday trickled through his bloodstream and was absorbed into his flesh through the week. *With quietness they work and eat their own bread. The velocities and powers of spouting fluids, under equal pressures or equal perpendicular heights and equal apertures are equal in all cases. I must work the works of him that sent me while it is day. If a body be struck by two equal forces in contrary directions, it will remain unmoved.* And so Ewan's world was built, law by law, truth by truth, until it ran predictable and straight.

As the miller boys hauled themselves through one complete cycle of the seasons they grew the confidence of young men. Their father's voice faded. They naturally slid towards the inclinations of their characters. Perhaps if Ewan had been subtler, less direct, more patient, less exacting, they could have rolled along. Perhaps if Ewan had paid homage of some sort to the superior position of his elder brothers, or perhaps if these two brothers had not been so neatly matched, Ewan could have made himself respected, even indispensable. No one could deny his mechanical prowess. When some piece of machinery needed fixing or replacing Sander and Hector could do only what had been done in the past. They had little ability when it came to solving novel problems. Ewan criticized. Then to counter Ewan's arrogance, Sander, bolstered by Hector's loyalty, felt compelled to present some alleged innovation of his own. When Sander put forward his inevitably ridiculous proposal, Ewan said nothing—he simply stood quiet, letting the silliness of the idea fill the space between them. Then Ewan repeated his brother's words with great care, as if to underline them, looking into the middle distance with impassive eyes. He would turn his back and set about stitching sacks or sweeping, or some other such menial task, leaving his older brothers to institute the ludicrous plans. When the results fell flat Sander and Hector would throw down their tools in humiliation and head to town on some flimsy pretext. Ewan was always careful repeat this pretext word for word to their mother to explain their absence. Then Ewan fixed up their mess, adding some small improvement that the older brothers would ridicule from spite. With every repetition of this cycle Ewan found himself thrust further and further from the brothers he loved but could not touch.

Ewan kept a close eye on the mill's power train, the belts, the dam and the wheel. He kept a running tally in his head of the number of hours each stone operated between dressings, monitored their grinds and kept them all sharp. By the time he was seventeen he could dismantle a set of stones in the morning, dress them, reassemble them, and have them balanced and running before dinnertime. Sander stopped objecting to Ewan acting without his say-so in this regard but he did not allow unauthorized tampering with the mill itself. How could he? If he did, soon he would be running a mill he could not repair or understand.

For the most part Sander and Hector tended to their business under their mother's watchful eye but occasionally they would cover for each other allowing one of them to sport off to town or down the road to see a girl. From time to time they would risk some caper together setting off "to the woods" and returning with string of trout they would fry up or hang to smoke in the kiln. Or Sander would liberate the clandestine pack of cards from its hiding spot in the buckwheat sifter, blow the bran off it, and tuck it into his shirt pocket. Then he and Hector would head for the blacksmith's forge. When Ewan frowned, Sander turned on him. "What's the matter, Sour-pickle-face? We need a new rod for the shaker. It's gonna be a heavy sonofabitch. Hector's gotta help heft 'er, right, Hec?" The two of them trotted off laughing, leaving the grinding to Ewan.

When, up at the house, young Charles and Robert finished at the local school there was money for tuition and board in town, for the school clothes, and books, for violin and elocution lessons, for a Latin tutor. Then on to their professional educations. Finally the matriarch saw Robert inducted into the ministry and the following year Charles established in a medical practice. She died three weeks later, exhausted and utterly content. Sander married almost instantly and brought his new wife to live in the house. Sander's wife changed things around and put things in the wrong places. She didn't make oatcakes the way Ewan's mother had. Hector set off to Boston for long-dreamed-of adventures. Before the summer was over all the girls had married the sweethearts they had kept waiting and Sander's wife was expecting their first child.

And there stood Ewan. In the middle of all this upheaval Ewan got up every day as he always had and raised the sluice at first light. Ewan replaced the teeth in the stone nut that Sander had let drop into the spur. Sander's son was born. The baby bawled all night so no one could sleep. Ewan replaced the over-heating gudgeon Sander had made such a mess of. Sander spoke longingly of Hector and wondered would he return to the mill once he'd had a go at Boston. Ewan said the dam would be due for an overhaul next summer. Sander said no, it was the wheel that needed attention first and he had a great idea for a new wheel. Ewan spat out of the side of his mouth onto the ground, which was more of a response than the idea warranted.

By mid-morning Ewan was halfway through shelling a grist of oats. Sander was leaning back against the doorframe speaking to a couple of farmers in a voice meant to convey information over the farmers' heads and straight to Ewan's ears. When Ewan passed by with a sack of meal for a customer Sander proclaimed they would be building a new waterwheel. He had heard of a twelve-foot wheel in Inverness and he meant to build one of that size here to increase their power. Ewan told him not to be so thick and he turned away to readjust a stone that Sander had just lowered. He had told him half a dozen times already that his waterwheel plan was inane—it was plain, clear mathematics. Perhaps it was the snicker of one of the farmers, perhaps it was lack of sleep or simply the moment the camel's back snapped. Perhaps Sander had been preparing for the showdown all along. Whatever the case Sander lunged at his brother, hauled him through the door and shoved him into the dirt outside the mill. Ewan, taken by surprise, scrambled to his feet.

"I own this mill!" Sander backed him up against the wall shouting into his face. "It is mine, not yours. I am the oldest son, not you. It was left to me. Do you need to see the deed?"

Ewan had never imagined the ownership of the mill, never questioned it, never conceived of the mill being owned at all—no more than he would have conceived of the clouds in the sky being capable of being possessed. He scrabbled to recover from the ambush, taking refuge behind his mask of cold disdain.

"What are you waiting for?" Again and again his oldest brother yelling, red-faced and spitting, bubbles dancing at the corners of his mouth. "What are you waiting for? Why are you still here?"

"Where else would I be? Someone has to run the place."

"You think you're so damned smart but you're the dullest wit I ever saw. Open your eyes. Who wants you here? Nobody. Mother kept you here until she got the youngsters straightened away. The youngsters are set up. Mother is gone. Look around you! You think I want you here looking down your snotty nose at me all the time? Telling me what to do? What's the matter with you, little brother? This was Father's mill, now it's mine, when the time comes it'll be John Alex's. You want me to write that up in the account book for you?"

"Mother would never have…"

"Mother is more than a year dead and you're still running to her like a babe on the tit!"

"You couldn't manage a week without me."

And that was a mistake because that was when Sander hit him. Sander was taller, quicker, angrier and much more experienced at tussling. Ewan managed to get in a few pokes amid the rain of savage punches. Then everything shifted with a crack to the side of his head. He could hear Sander panting. Small stones pressed themselves into his cheek where he lay on the dirt. A sticky wetness covered his palms that covered his face and he recognized it as blood from the metallic taste in his throat. His body curled in to protect itself. The kick in his back exploded as a visual thing, a yellow star of pain. He smelled earth and blood and a wild sharp tang that may have been fear. One ear roared with blood. The other frantically hunted sound. Sander panting above him, yes, then gathering breath and shouting in gasps and sobs. "Stupid. Little. Shit." A kick punctuating every word. Sander crying like a boy, like he had cried the time he had drowned Ewan's cat out of spite. As though he, Sander, was the victim and not the aggressor. As though Ewan had driven him to heights of cruelty he could not possibly have reached on his own.

Then Sander's voice moved away. The farmers who had been excited by the prospect of a fight at first had stepped back quickly, embarrassed by the flood of passion. When the kicking began, two moved in to pull Sander away.

But Sander kept hollering. "Go! Take what you want! Take a horse. Take what you want, just get out! Go! Get off this place. Don't come back. Leave me alone, God damn you!"

Ewan did not remember climbing to his feet. Perhaps he had been helped. He remembered the smear of blood along the sleeve of his shirt, the filthy ochre pool at the cuff with a trail up to his bloody nose. He remembered the way his hands shook when he held them under the water from the pump. He remembered the cold black rage he carried with his flour sack through every room of the house. He picked up and discarded ten items for each one he stuffed into the sack. His father's two books he took. Socks, a string of sausages, a shirt, a pencil. Blasphemous. Scatter-brained. Lazy as a mat. No head for machinery or numbers or anything at all. A tin bowl. Cheese. Three candles. He stuffed two saddlebags full of tools from the workshop, passed through the stable, chose Billy, the strongest horse, handfuls of oats. Idiot. Brute. Couldn't run a wheelbarrow—see him try a mill. Useless. He saddled up, flung his luggage aboard under a hasty loop of rope, up and gone. Hell-bent for leather.

Ewan finally reined in the horse and slid down out of the saddle, the gelding lathered and heaving beside him. The poor animal's load hung askew—sacks and saddlebags, a shovel handle stuck out at a ludicrous angle. A shovel. What did Ewan want with a shovel? What did he own that needed shovelling? After thirty years, he had nothing but a sack of tools, a horse, a small bundle of clothes and less money than a girl would pin into her hem on a journey to Boston. He took the load apart and re-packed it properly, pitching the shovel into the woods. They continued westward on the road, both walking now, farther west than Ewan had ever been. The bridge of Ewan's nose carried the crack of impact and a bruise stained his jaw. His knuckles ached with the memory of his few flailing punches.

When night descended Ewan led the horse off the road and they slept in the woods, but exhaustion offered no refuge. The moment sleep overtook him a horrible drowning nightmare crashed over him, the waves swelling up behind him and he couldn't catch hold of anything. The water tore him back and held him under and just as his lungs were about to explode he was thrown up again. He grabbed at the bank but again he was dragged over and away, his fingers raking over tree roots and stones, leaving streaks of blood. Water everywhere pressing and hauling until he sputtered awake gulping damp fall air and listening to his heart hammer. Before dawn he fed his horse a handful of oats and they continued on until they came to the road's end, the island's rocky edge. Here, at the edge of the known world, a pier pointed into the choppy waters of the strait towards the mainland of Nova Scotia. In the distance he could see the ferryman making his way towards him.

CHAPTER SIX

FOR SEVERAL DAYS THEY TRAVELLED WEST, EWAN FEELING a fugitive, hunted, simply unable to stop. He would ride, then walk, then ride again. Prosperous farms, forges, tanneries, labourers' houses, manufacturing businesses, churches, schools, woods, streams and roads. He turned away from towns and villages; he chose narrow trails that climbed hills with thin soil and scrubby trees. He tried to find some order in his thoughts but his head felt empty. He could feel the contours of it, a bowl of nothing but axioms and articles. *When two or more forces act upon a body, in such a way as to destroy the operation of each other, there is then said to be an equilibrium of forces.* Soon his sparse supplies would be gone. He must form a plan of some sort. *Non-elastic bodies are those which not only change their forms, when struck, but remain permanently altered in this particular.* He met a brook and followed it northward in the declining light of the evening. The brook widened suddenly into a millpond. Indeed, there up ahead a raggedy sawmill listed into the bank. Although the air carried the scent of fresh sawdust, he could see no activity anywhere. Ewan unburdened the horse and let him drink while he looked around thinking he might find a bed of sawdust for the night. Then, in the slanting rays of the day's end, Ewan saw the shadows. It was a mirage, surely. But no, as he approached the shapes gained solidity. Millstones—just lying there in the grass by the pond, out of the way of spring high water. "Ah," he said, surprising himself with the sound of his own voice. "Ah, stones." He knelt by them, his hand drawn to the pattern, settling his fingertips into the grooves, following the stitching from the eye to the skirt. He hooked his arm through the eye and held the stone firm. Just like in the dream, waves of dread crashed and tugged but he held fast, hugging the immovable stone. Even as the darkness of the evening thickened, he could not let go.

When Merton picked his way down the path from his cabin in the morning to check the water level he spotted the horse and then saw the man sleeping on the hard millstone. Outside—with the relative comfort of the mill just across the yard. Merton picked up a pebble and tossed it onto the stone near the sleeper's ear.

Ewan struggled upright, groggy from thin, fitful sleep. He hobbled a few feet but his right leg, numb and cold from lying motionless on the granite, threatened to give way. His right arm had gone wooden and when he rubbed it he felt the pattern the stones had set into his flesh. The two men regarded each other.

"Morning," Merton said, gruff and wary, then shuffled over to the brow where he bent and splashed water on his face. Behind him the little mill leaned into the bank. It was a lazy-looking affair, a lonely, neglected shack. A couple of dozen logs floated in the millpond. When Merton stood, massaging his left temple carefully, he turned and struggled to bring Ewan into focus. "Don't suppose ye've got the day to spare, to cant a few logs?"

Ewan did not know what to say that did not lay bare all that had been taken from him. Here he stood, a vagabond at worst, a common day labourer at best. Ewan had worked for wages before, when the opportunity arose. Good work for good money. But this sudden necessity for it appalled him. His answering the offer set his indigence before another human being—acknowledged it, established it.

"Supper and a bed—ye and yer horse too—and fifty cents. I'm not a rich man."

Ewan did not reply because he could not round up the simple

necessary words and drive them through the desert of his mouth into the air.

"Sixty cents then. And breakfast in the bargain. Ye can cant a few logs, I suppose?"

"I've got the millers' trade," he managed.

"That so?" Merton turned towards the mill, quick to take this as a yes. "Ye can set yer horse up there."

Everything about the little mill had the air of making do, of a lick and a promise, of minimum requirements. So Ewan was surprised when he flicked his thumb alongside the saw blade testing its edge and found it keen. He looked around for a peavey and found one tossed in the corner. He corralled the logs in from the pond to the brow and one by one set them on the carriage where Merton pinched them snug with the dogs. Once Ewan had a few ahead he darted to the far side of the saw and hauled the sawn lumber away to stack it on the small square of land Merton referred to as the yard. The harder he worked the more tension he drew down through his arms and out of his body. Bark and slabs from the previous job had been left where they fell. While Merton squared his logs Ewan began hauling the pile away. When he caught up with this task he took a bucksaw down off its peg and began sawing the slabs into stove wood, the seesaw work lulling him. Then back to the millpond to cant another log. In this way Ewan kept his body moving and straining all day, his mind tricked into stasis.

"Ye can climb around and shut the sluice gate, I suppose?"

Ewan looked around him searching for what had gone awry. The angle of the sun had sharpened but there were at least two hours of good daylight left. Merton disengaged the blade, turned and hung his leather apron on a nail. Ewan did not question the order, simply shimmied out along the dam until he could drop the gate that diverted the water flow and halted the waterwheel.

"Come up to the house, now. I'm drier than Lucifer's coal dust."

Merton's cabin was small but tight, built of sawn beams and planks, a strong stone chimney and two grimy glass-paned windows. The floor was rough wood sanded smooth by foot traffic in paths around the table, the filthy cook stove and the bed at the far end of the cabin. There was also a small stand with a washtub, two chairs, a shelf and a row of clothes hooks, mostly empty. The cabin smelled of indolence, of bedclothes gone too long without airing, of damp wool and pork fat. The sweet tint of rum in the air was overpowered by the stale heaviness of over-indulgence. The only freshness rose from the sawdust that settled over coats and trousers, hair and eyelashes, carried in the nostrils.

Supper was boiled potatoes and salt pork. As for dinner conversation, Ewan could not have asked for better. Merton asked no questions, exhibited no curiosity. As soon as they finished Ewan washed their plates and forks and the potato pot, although with the ring of scum encrusted in a collar around the top of the pot he gathered this was not part of the general domestic routine.

When the clean pot was set on the table Merton spoke. "There now. There's no need for ye to be running off in the morning. There's another great pile of logs across the dam to be sawn once we finish up with those in the pond."

Ewan watched the man light a lamp in the gathering gloom, its sooty chimney almost opaque. He watched the man measuring the silence, then peering up at him from under spiky greying eyebrows that made Ewan think of a great horned owl, Merton's eyes fixed on his in a gaze halfway between a challenge and a question. Obviously Ewan had nowhere else to be.

"Alright," Ewan said, looking away in shame.

Long after Merton blew out the lamp and went to bed Ewan sat at the table in the dark. He held his head in his hands and repeated the Lord's Prayer over and over, not audibly but not quite to himself either. The mindless familiarity of the chant offered little comfort but remaining upright meant he didn't have to lie down on a pile of straw in the corner like a dog. And it meant he didn't have to close his eyes and dream the rushing torrent of water into his lungs. Exhausted from labour and worry, he eventually pried off his boots, lowered his body to the floor and drew his blanket around him. Twice he woke gasping for air and wet with sweat, his heart crashing wild like an anvil falling down stairs. Finally, he crept out of his nest, pulled on his boots, and scrabbled out the door and over the road. The stars and the moon gave off what light was to be had and Ewan picked his way along the path. Tingling anxiety mounted and he realized, quite to his astonishment and shame, that he was afraid to find the millstones gone. Washed away in the night. A ton of Scottish granite was going nowhere but as he descended the slope his pulse quickened and his breathing grew shallow, anxiety mounting towards panic. His eyes scanned for the circle of black in the grasses as he groped his way towards the spot, reached out, ah yes. His palms found the surface; he fit his fingers into the grooves. He sat a moment while his body returned to normal, while his anxiety flattened and slipped sideways into a profound embarrassment. Even with no one to witness the depth of his emotion, shame lapped over him. As soon as first light allowed the grey of the granite to ease across the stone and the path to separate itself from the obstacles on it, Ewan got to his feet and hurried back up the slope. He tended the horses in the stable. Merton had a fine-looking young mare of his own. Pride, he'd called her. A few scrawny hens rousted on a rafter overhead but he could find no cow or pig on the place. There would be no sweet milk to lighten their porridge.

Ewan clanked the stove lid when he lit the fire. He was careful to clatter the kettle a few extra times, set the frying pan down flat with declaration, but Merton only turned over on his tick, moaned and pulled his blanket over his head. Ewan liked to be ready to work as soon as he could see. When he was a boy his mother was driven to fury by morning laziness and set upon occupied beds with a switch. One morning when he had given in to the warm pillowy comfort surrounding him and drifted back to sleep he was reawakened by her heavy footfall on the top step. In desperation he rolled from beneath the covers and sank to his knees on the cold floor clasping his hands, closing his eyes in feigned prayer, sure she could not attack him in communion with God. She set about his head and back with the switch, laying into him until welts crisscrossed his back like a herring net. "In daylight you pray with your hands laden, you scamp, you idler. Pretend to give thanks while you spit God's good daylight back in His face!"

Ewan filled the water bucket, the wood box, and split a bundle of kindling while he waited for the porridge to boil up. There wasn't so much as a heel of bread that he could find in the house. When Merton finally found his boots he sat into the table with a fresh mug of tea warming his hands and a bowl of hot oatmeal. He lifted an eyebrow in Ewan's direction.

"If ye weren't so ugly ye'd be as good as a woman."

"Aye, and what would you be good as?"

There was no further conversation over breakfast.

"That's Joudrey's pile there now," Merton said at dinnertime. "The rest is mine." It was clear enough that Merton was amazed and delighted to see the fine stack of deal in the yard, bark carted away and slabs cut and piled. Here he was the boss of such a fine establishment that he impressed himself. "John Peter's got a pile of logs up the hill. I didn't know when I'd get to them but we could start in after dinner."

Dinner was fried potatoes and eggs. They sawed all afternoon. Supper was potatoes and a bit of cheese.

"I'm not sleeping on the floor like a dog. Some of that lumber in the stable could make a loft there."

Merton shifted uncomfortably in his seat. "What's this, now?"

"There's time yet before bed."

Before Merton's eyes Ewan raised a loft in one end of the cabin above Merton's bed. "Hold this," he said to Merton as he set the header in place. He hammered the decking boards down and fashioned a quick ladder from scraps. He swept sawdust and scraps off the floor and dumped them into the stove, carried the tools back to the barn and climbed up to bed.

The next evening Ewan fashioned himself a rough mattress of boughs and straw. The next evening he took a few coins down to the nearest neighbours' for a cake of lye soap, a small sack of flour, and a bowl of yeast. Cunningham was their name. He arranged with the woman to fetch over a bottle of milk for them every few days, and perhaps a bit of butter. He put one of Merton's delinquent-looking chickens in the stewpot. He set bread to rise before he went to bed. The next morning when he ventured out to inspect Merton's patch of oats he tripped over a cabbage in the grass and so discovered the vegetable garden. In the mornings between dawn and when Merton made his way down to the mill Ewan weeded and hoed. He scrubbed the windows and every washable surface in the cabin. He shovelled sawdust into a cart and hauled it away, shovelled up bark and debris until space opened up that Merton had forgotten existed. Every morning Ewan knelt by the millstones on the stream bank, leaned his body into them. Sometimes he could get through the night now with the drowning nightmare visiting him only once. Maybe twice. He slept for several hours at a stretch.

On Sunday morning Ewan lay in his bunk with his hands behind his head, the roof boards slanting above him, and waited for dawn light to flood the cabin through the now-sparkling windows. He rose and washed his face and shaved with warm water. He poured the last of the sweet milk over his porridge. Merton snorted in his sleep, grunted and resumed a low snore. After tending to the horses Ewan took a flask of tea down to the pond. He sat on the millstone staring at nothing. He missed his brother, his mill, his predictable life, so powerfully his lungs ached. The leaves at the tops of the trees had begun to redden and the crops would be coming off the fields all over the province. Sander would never get all the harvest work done without him. Who knew what a mess he would make of it. Sander would have to send for him. Sander needed him.

Merton eventually hauled himself out of bed and, finding himself alone in the cabin, brewed himself a pot of strong tea. Bread and butter waited for him on the table. His cabin glistened, a loft had been built, there was soup on the back of the stove, wood box and water bucket filled, and the animals tended. The garden was hoed. A week's worth of lumber had been sawn in two days and the mill looked in better shape than it ever had. It was true that Merton had to learn to duck his head so as to avoid the loft floor, but the header beam was proving a diligent teacher. It was true the man clattered the stove lids with a little too much insistence way too early in the mornings. It was true that Merton himself was drawn into more work than he would normally like and that he felt the ache of over-taxed muscles. But Ewan knew what to do without being told. He worked by daylight and lamplight for nothing and still he craned his neck looking for more. Indeed Merton could see the desperation in his labour and since someone had to benefit from the man's need it might as well be him as anyone.

It being Sunday and the indisputable day of rest, today there seemed no downside to having the young man at all. Merton gathered up his trouting rod and wandered downstream to the most propitious of the fish pools. He dug up several fat worms, impaled one on his hook and snuggled down on the bank in the September sunshine, completely content. As he waited for his prey he contemplated his newfound fortune. And plotted how best to keep the goose laying the golden eggs. That afternoon Merton sat on the stable doorstep whistling and gutting two fat trout. The barn cat sat at a safe distance, just out of kicking range, howling with impatience. Merton flicked a fish head on the tip of his knife, catapulting it in a high arc and sending the cat into an athletic back flip snatching the treat in midair. He laughed through his stained teeth, sat and watched her gnawing at the gills with feral greed. Ewan appeared over the rise and Merton waved him over.

"Watch this now." Merton flipped the second fish head into the air but the cat never looked up from her first prize. "Ah well. Never mind. How's this for a grand dinner? Loaves and fishes for yer Sabbath, eh?"

Ewan's eyes settled on the ravenous cat. Inside the skull the pink tongue worked and worked until Ewan could almost feel its rough scraping on the insides of his own ribs. Completely hollowed out.

Merton grinned as he fried up the trout, which they ate with the fresh bread and butter. When they finished Merton pushed his chair back and tamped tobacco into his pipe, as happy and satisfied as he could remember. Despite the day of rest his new housemate looked as rigid and troubled as ever. Merton fetched two tin cups and poured a shot of rum into each.

"Here, this'll make you smile at yer troubles."

Ewan stared at the cup.

"It's good for what ails ye."

Ewan looked up at Merton's crooked-teeth smile. Rum. Fishing on the Sabbath. "You're not a papist, are you?" Ewan said.

Merton laughed. "Of all the things I am not, papist is first amongst 'em. Ye're a man with troubles, I can see. Have a dram for your comfort after a good week's work."

Merton sighed and took a great gulp of rum. "I suppose I got to get those millstones set up. I been trying to get at it these two years now. People been at me for it. I guess I could make a start on it now."

The lazy fool. "Have you got bearings built for that, or a stone nut? You'd need a spindle, a gimble bar, a bridging box. I've seen no signs of the trade around here. Have you ever dressed a stone or balanced one? Ever milled a sack of grist?"

Merton tried to look indignant but ended up with more of a grimace on his face. "Now, now. Ye're a good man to help, I suppose. If ye can stay on it'd be a help." Merton gauged his labourer's reaction. Careful that his flattery did not to stray too far and tip his hand. "Ye're a clever sort, I know," he added, mumbling and fixing his eyes on the corner of the floor as though it were not an admission he made lightly.

Instantly Ewan was thrown back into confusion. Angry, proud, resentful, relieved. All these feelings made him dizzy, ill. If he stayed with Merton he would have lodgings and board. He'd be hidden from home yet not irretrievably far from it. More importantly he would have work for his back and his brain to keep him from losing his mind.

"I got a shaft. A couple of pulleys," Merton said.

Ewan reckoned he could set those stones into the power train of the sawmill. It would not be such a great puzzle. "We'll look at it tomorrow."

"Good man." Merton splashed another ounce or two of rum into his cup.

Ewan stood and turned away leaving his mug untouched. He climbed the ladder to his loft with his candle. At the bottom of his pack, wrapped in a rag of cloth, lay his late father's entire library: a copy of the King James Bible and *The Young Mill-Wright and Miller's Guide*. He set these on the little stand he had made to hold his lamp. Perched like a gargoyle at the edge of his bunk he hunched over the manual and began to plan out the best way to set the grindstones into the sawmill.

That night his nightmare softened to a disturbing dream. Although water swirled up all around him it never submerged him as he clung to the stone on the bank. When he rose in the blackness before dawn and revived the fire in the stove, he found a new energy in his anticipation of the project.

AMID EWAN'S JUMBLED AND CRAZY BAGGAGE WERE A PEN AND NIBS but no ink, a bouquet of pencils from long-stemmed to stubs but no paper. He rummaged around and did the best he could. In the evening he sat at the table with the lamp at his elbow and the *Miller's Guide* open before him, beginning his calculations. *Multiply the revolutions of the waterwheel per minute by the number of cogs in all driving wheels successively and note the product. Multiply the number of cogs or rounds in all leading wheels successively, and note the product.* Merton sat in the dim corner of the cabin watching Ewan completely entranced in his figuring. *Divide the first product by the last and the quotient is the number of revolutions of the stone per minute.* Ewan checked back and forth between his notes and the text, tapped the end of his pencil absently on his teeth, made his calculations and altered the sketch in front of him. When he looked up from his work he was amazed to find it deep night. Merton's breath rustled the dark with a raspy half-snore.

In the early mornings before Merton managed to haul himself down the hill to the mill Ewan stood with his hands on his hips staring at the space he had chosen for the stones, imagining measurements and ratios. In the evenings after dark the plan took shape in front of him on paper. Then there was Merton's pile of shafts and pulleys and gears and scrap iron to be sifted through. He was transported so completely by the enterprise that when sadness found him in cracks of time between chores Ewan felt the shock of it like he had just fallen out of a tree.

THE FIRST TIME MERTON HAULED A LOAD OF LUMBER DOWN TO SCOTCH River he was gone for days. When he finally managed to crawl home he had nothing to show for it but a headache. Ewan stared in disbelief. Merton had squandered not only his own wages but Ewan's as well. Ewan split half a cord of firewood then found the contrite-looking Merton slumped at the table with his head in his hands.

"How much land you got here, Merton?"

"Oh, you know…" He waved his hand ineffectually in the air.

Ewan did not repeat his question, he simply leaned back, folded his arms across his chest and waited.

"I'm not a wealthy man, if that's what you mean."

"No. I don't see how you could be unless there's a wage for lying in bed or swaying between public houses." Ewan felt his mother by his side, setting out the plans as she always had. Imagine this, she would say, and there would be no imagining about it. "Imagine this, Merton. You spend your money however you want. Just give me a dollar a week and my room and board. Then you credit me sixteen additional dollars every month towards that piece of woods that you're doing nothing with—that lot that runs down to the brook. Once the stones are operational we'll grind or saw depending on the business. Lumber and shingles sales are yours but two days a week I have use of the mill to saw my own lumber. When I'm grinding, half the milling fees are mine on top of my wages."

"What!" Merton winced as though he'd been struck, but a dollar a week in cash was a pittance to pay for labour like this. Any idiot could see that. With Ewan he'd sawn more logs in the last week than he would ordinarily in a month. And Ewan would add a grist mill and run it too, leaving him to rake in the profits. The plan was better than Merton could have hoped for. If Ewan wanted land he must be meaning to stay. The golden goose building a nest right under his roof. "That's an awful pretty deal for you, I'd say. A big fat wage and milling fees too! And good, deep farm land all lovely with trees."

"Feeling yourself short of trees, are you?"

"Ach, never mind. I'll take the deal. But you buy that land acre by acre, starting at the back of the farm. The world's done enough to kick an old man around—ye might as well have yer go as well."

"Next time you head to town for a tub of rum, you fetch us back a proper ledger book and a pot of ink so we can keep this all good and square. Maybe bring us a hunk of fresh meat and a bit of tea before we catch the ship fever."

Ewan began piecing the new stone together. Once ready he made his way to the blacksmith's forge with his bill of iron. He endured the curiosity of the smithy and the gathered men. Ewan MacLaughlin, he said. Miller by trade. Fittings for Merton's new stone, he said. He concentrated on his work. He did the best he could with Merton's millstones although they were not high quality stones and the mill had not been designed to accommodate them. Despite this, it was not long before Ewan had jury-rigged a reasonable system and had the first flour running through the stones.

As Ewan surmised, Merton proved unable to distinguish between the improvement of his living conditions and the gradual disintegration of his real wealth in the form of land. In the ledger book Merton's wealth trickled into Ewan's account. The more Merton enjoyed cash money through Ewan's labours the less inclined he was to work himself. "I'm not as young as I was," he would complain in the early mornings, trying to rub the rum headache away. "When my back was young I could tote a tree this big around," he would say to Ewan, his hands cupped in the air to demonstrate a mast-sized pole. Merton hired a younger man for canting and Ewan sawed while Merton warmed his bones and tended to his rheumatism in the mornings. Ewan took down the trees, yarded the logs, sawed them, sold them. In the spring he harnessed his horse to the plough and sowed his first patch of oats. There were moments when Ewan saw his life with great clarity. The Lord had led him out of bondage. His blessings came in such cruel guises he had railed against them: against his brother, his expulsion and his aimless wandering. Now, like Jacob in the Bible, he had contracted his labour in order to achieve his destiny. He would have a mill of his own.

Ewan cleared the land as he bought it. The fifty-acre tract he meant to own crossed the road and ended in a lovely sweep down to the brook where the gorge formed an ideal plot for a new mill. Here he would build a proper establishment—not a clunky and awkward combination mill like Merton's Old Nag—but a brand new modern grist mill. He wasn't worried about Merton. Without him, Merton's business would simply shrivel up and blow away.

But over the years Merton found one excuse after another to sell land only down as far as the road. Ewan built fields first and then began to build the kind of house that befits a miller and his family, like the house he had left in Breton Crag.

"I know ye want to build a new mill in the fine pocket downstream.

Go ahead. I'll sell you the land once yer done. It would do ye as much good as it would me. Ye'd have a fine mill to work in."

"Do you think I'm daft? Sell me the land first."

"Start yer mill. I'll sell you the lot next year."

Ewan wasn't going to build on another man's land. He worked and waited. Inevitably Merton had nothing left except the tiny plot where his cabin stood and the waterfront land below the road.

"I'll take that plot of land now," Ewan said.

"I can't sell that. I'm an old man. It's all I've got left. I'll die in the poorhouse!"

Negotiations swirled around in a fury, Merton determined not to give up his excellent position and Ewan determined to get the land he had worked towards for so long. Finally, one exhausted evening, they settled, the answer oddly simple. Ewan would become Merton's sole heir. On Merton's death all would pass to Ewan—the coveted land along the brook would be his. And everything else as well: the Old Nag, Merton's cabin, tools, horse and tack. Everything. Both their futures were assured. They saddled their horses and set out to have the Scotch River lawyer draw up the documents. All signed, sealed and delivered.

THREE WEEKS PASSED. THE DEVIL PROVIDED THE DRINK THAT BROUGHT Merton home barely sensate. The Lord provided the industry that had kept Ewan milling shingles late into the night. The Lord called Ewan down along the brook to stretch his legs before heading to bed, to settle after a hard day, before sleep. Despite the faint moon and skiffing cloud lingering from the day's rain, despite the gusty wind, God called him along the brook. The path along the bank was slick and he nearly slipped. He picked up a sturdy stick from the bank to help steady himself. The Lord led him to the rock shelf just above the north trout pool. It was not the best trout pool but a popular one because of the way the rock jutted out like a balcony a couple of feet above the water's surface. Boys more interested in lazing and boasting and smoking tobacco than in catching fish idled endless hours stretched out on this rock with lines dangling in the water. Ewan stood there breathing in the night air, watching the swift-moving shadows—clouds revealing then obscuring colonies of stars. Ewan remembered thinking, I must go home to bed. Yet he did not move. Another minute or so passed before he heard the traveller. Above him on the road he could make out the shape of Merton heading home from Scotch River, barely clinging to the saddle. Stinking drunk. The mare made her way by moonlight and horse sense—the only sense between the two of them. The verge would have been slippery with mud from the evening's rain. Ewan did not see what spooked the mare, perhaps a rabbit, or a bobcat, sudden from the bushes. Or perhaps the Lord had sent an angel to startle the horse. Ewan only saw the mare balk, her precarious load topple out of the saddle and over the bank where it tumbled a short way and came to rest. Perhaps if Merton had been just a little drunker, he would have passed out where he fell. Or if he had been a little closer to sober, if he had taken just a couple fewer drinks, he may have been able to crawl back up to the road. But as it was he kept clawing at the earth, struggling upwards but falling back, the steep slope drawing him farther and farther down towards the brook. Ewan lost sight of him for a moment but could hear his slurred cussing and stumbling, branches snapping and leaves shifting underfoot. And then there he was again, slipping backwards, grabbing at a tree that grew crooked, elbowing out from the slope. His grasp slowed his descent but did not stop it. Finally he came to rest on the rock balcony, his head bouncing drunkenly. Blood, yes, but not enough. The man flopped back splayed out on the stone at Ewan's feet, arms thrown wide. He sprawled so close to the rock's edge that one leg dangled over, the sole of his boot nearly skimming the surface of the water.

"Get up, Merton," Ewan said, calm and clear. The wretch opened his eyes. A smirk. The man drunk to helplessness on rum that Ewan's labour had paid for. Ewan advanced, held out his walking stick towards the prone man and nudged him. He nudged him again, pushing him a few inches closer to the edge of the rock. Ewan watched as the man struggled through his fog to focus on Ewan's face, to recognize, finally to understand. In panic he flopped around a moment like a seal before a final nudge from the stick sent him over the edge of the rock, splashing into the water.

The pool was no more than waist deep, the water cold but not frigid, the rocks slick but not impossibly so. Any man ought to have been able to stand and wade to shore. The cold ought to have sobered anyone. Merton scrabbled to find footing, slipped, thrashed, went under. He resurfaced, gasping, fell again. Ewan stood back away from the edge. *Justice and judgment are the habitation of Thy throne.* The Lord would choose to take or leave him. The thrashing slowed. Nothing further broke the surface to catch the scant moonlight. Ewan turned and walked home to bed. In the night it rained again washing away all traces of the comings and goings of men. In the morning Ewan found Pride with her empty saddle askew, cropping grass by the roadside. But Merton did not come home.

THIS WAS ALL LONG PAST, OVER THREE YEARS AGO. Now Ewan lay in the house he had built on the land he had earned and cleared with his own labour. He ran his hands up and down his broken leg. His blessings had always come in such deep, perverse disguises, but labour always brought forth reward. Always. He would work. Ewan felt his resolve awaken with such strength and clarity he knew God had stretched out His hand to him. His own mortal weakness had pulled him to despair and nearly beaten him but now he could see the way. Of course he would work. Had the Lord not provided for him so far? Had he not suffered his seven years of servitude to be rewarded? Did he not own land and a house and stable and a brand new mill worthy of his trade? In need of sons, had he not prayed for a wife only to have the woman placed before him? Where were his sons? The Lord asked only for faith and labour. How ludicrous to imagine this was not possible. His mind raced, tumbled, somersaulted over itself, his blood, pumping through his body, alive with resolve. He would work.

CHAPTER SEVEN

PENELOPE

THE NIGHT BROUGHT ME LITTLE REST. In the cracks between fretting when I escaped into sleep, dreams hunted me down, hauling me to Ewan's body, his casket, his graveside. And there was Nettle stretching out her withered hand towards me. We're sisters now, she said and when I tried to speak and explain how this was not so, my words were snared in my throat. At first light, exhausted from struggle, I dressed and braced for the day. Normally, no matter how quiet my tread, Ewan began his bellowing as soon as I set my foot on the first stair. But today silence met me. This was another dream surely. But no, the stairs beneath my feet, the kitchen floor, the stove and table and porridge pot all carried the unchanging solidity of wakefulness. My heart hammered. As I approached his door I heard a single word. "Penelope." I had not heard him speak my name in—it seemed like years. There was no tenderness in his voice (tenderness would have terrified me) but neither was there rancour or frustration. His voice was clear, steady and pointed.

When I opened the door I barely recognized the invalid I had left the night before. His eyes, snapping clear, met mine.

"I need my measuring rule and pencils. Bring me paper. And your breadboard. Be quick."

He ate several thick slabs of bread and jam with his tea and porridge. I fried up a pan of sausage and made him a pumpkin pie. Whenever I peeked in he was scrawling lines and equations with his pencil, or holding his measuring rule out in front of him as though it were a rare species to be studied, or staring intently into space. He used up all my correspondence paper then called for sheets torn from the back of his ledger book, then more—he did not care where from. He produced drawings, crossed them out and made new ones. The next afternoon he intercepted me as I passed his door on the way to the cellar with a bushel of parsnips.

"Have that Cunningham brat carry this bill of iron to the smith. Tell him to make me these parts. The specifications are clear. I don't want any of his usual slipshod business. I want this done properly, so help me God."

He called me ten times a day to fetch him tools and wood and bolts and Lord knows what else. I gave his linens and blankets up for lost the first time he dumped out a box of bolts and screws and fanned them over his lap. Before he was done he sent young Donny to the forge three times and to the harness-maker and all the way to the foundry. I felt badly for the boy, cowering under Ewan's glare, but really he was the least of my worries. As for myself, so long as Ewan was occupied I was content to see him one day sawing and sanding and spewing sawdust over the room, the next riveting leather, then metal work, then back at paper and ink.

One day Donny arrived back from the smithy with a pair of wheels on his shoulder and various rods and pieces protruding from the top of a sack. I had understood from Ewan's drawings and hammerings that he intended to set the wheels under his body but the day for that seemed impossibly distant. I was certainly unprepared the following afternoon when he summoned me to help him out of bed.

Ewan's contraption featured a hammock-like seat rigged with straps and buckles on an iron framework. The framework protruded out where a sling hung to support his leg. Two large wheels framed the seat and in front, a half-size, articulated wheel was attached to a sort of rudder. Tool baskets of various sizes and shapes he had tucked in here and there around the chair. I stood back in the doorway of the little room making placating noises, praising his efforts but insisting we must wait for the doctor and perhaps in a month or so…

Even as I spoke I could see him gauging the distance between the bed and the cart. "Help me or I'll jump for it myself and bugger the pain."

Of course he would. There was no question. There was no place to begin an argument or a negotiation. I folded a blanket into the seat at least. It was all the concession I could wrest from him. Ewan was all concentration and instructions; his eye fixed on the goal. He would carry as much of his own weight as he could on his good leg and I was to heft the broken one into place. The manoeuvre was far from smooth. I tried my best to keep the awkward limb in line with his body but he had to wriggle somewhat to get himself settled into the seat. He blanched in pain, tiny beads of sweat emerging on his forehead, but he did not waver. I fussed with the blanket while he recovered himself but as soon as he had caught his breath he grabbed hold of the wheel rims and propelled himself through the doorway and into the kitchen like a bird through an open window.

"Help me to my shop. I have to get some tools together. I need to screw some boards onto those brackets. In there by the bed, see? Bring them along. That's the ramp. Get the wheelbarrow."

He sent me down to the mill first with the wheelbarrow to set up the ramp he had made for the mill steps. By the time I returned he was beside himself with impatience. He had wheeled himself to the door of the shop, his tools stowed in the various compartments of the chair, but he could go no farther. The contraption could wheel around freely on even floors but Ewan was at my mercy when it came to navigating steps or the ruts and bumps of the uneven ground beyond. I took up my position behind him and wielded the contraption across the yard, along the road, down the mill lane and finally, after more than a three-week absence, up the ramp and into his mill. He wasted not a moment in celebration.

"Go down to the meal floor. That stone over there. That's the one I want you to engage. Pull out the wedge and make sure that nut has settled snug into the spur. Then come back up."

"Ewan, I don't … I can't…"

Ewan pushed himself forward but too fast and slapped his leg on the oat vat. He gasped in a pain but paused only a moment.

"Ewan, let me help. Where are you going?"

"To the desk." He waved me off, eased himself around the corner, but over compensated and had to pull himself to a stop before his broken leg caught the corner of the wall. He needed to conceive of the shape of his body differently. I could see him already drawing the new shape in his mind. At the desk he scooped up his time book and pencil. "Look." On a blank page he drew the clean lines of a shaft and a toothy representation of a wooden stone nut. "Here. You'll see a wedge in here, look. You'll see a bar on the floor. Push that nut up a little so you can pull the wedge out. Then that nut will slide down on that shaft." He pointed to the far corner of the mill. "That stone. Just tug out the wedge. That nut'll snug down. Go on."

Carefully this time, watching how his cart reacted to different pressures, pulls and pushes, he eased his way across the mill floor and around to his buhrstone. What choice did I have? I trotted down to the meal floor and located the proper spindle. On the floor directly above my head I heard the wheels of his cart roll up to the vat. I followed his instructions, wrestled with the bar until the wedge dropped free and the stone nut fell into place just as Ewan had described. I stood there a moment staring at what I had done, certain yet at the same time unsure. Ewan's voice cut short my dithering.

"Now go around outside and open the sluice."

WORD OF EWAN'S RETURN TO WORK SPREAD QUICKLY. The farmers lined up with their wagons loaded with grain, amazed to see him darting around in his contraption. Between the cart and the wife in the mill, there was not a soul within ten miles who could resist the spectacle.

The men did the best they could to welcome him back. "Ah you'll soon be back to dancing just as free and jolly as you ever did." A chuckle all around, a ripple of laughter, a moment of levity meant to bring Ewan into the company of men.

Ewan turned a cold stare on this farmer and I cringed as the man withered into silence. All of these men had joined the frolic that had raised this building last year; all of them had a drop of sweat in these boards. I wished that I had been blessed with the kind of quick wit that could salvage the situation and put everyone at ease, but quips evaded me. In the icy moment that followed I understood with such clarity the fact that Ewan did not have a single friend. Nor was it likely that he ever would. He had never spoken of a childhood playmate, or play at all for that matter. And he never mentioned men he met or served or worked with or hired except to complain about their shortcomings. I suppose I had never organized my knowledge into this single thought before and his isolation chilled me. More than this, I realized that he understood this isolation as a normal state. I could not stop to consider all the ramifications of this with sacks of oats and wheat piling up by the scales and the kiln fire needing tending, but I would hold it in my mind.

"I could spare my oldest lad, if your missus has other work to do," one farmer offered.

"No more boys," Ewan said, and wheeled away.

The men turned back to their own company, laughing and smoking outside the door, safe from Ewan's glare. I could hear them just beyond the window.

"I'll have to get my wife up workin'."

"Maybe you could get her in the harness and save yourself a horse."

"She already eats like a horse."

"Course, you'll want a horse you can drive and ride both."

Great hilarity. Ewan called to me to engage the shelling stone.

Needless to say, my own work was left in a shambles. A woman's work was of no account to Ewan. He was in a blind rush to get down to the mill each day and he was loath to leave it. It was all I could do to wrest an hour at noon to run up the hill to the house and put our dinner together.

As I look back searching for the turns in the path that led us to our troubles I strive to remember these days in their entirety, to judge the good with the bad. And silver linings did peek out from the clouds. Yes, I was bone weary from running up and down stairs all day and trying to squeeze two days' work into one. But between the comings and goings I glimpsed the magic in the workings of the mill. The aroma of wheat and oats and barley filled the air with unexpected warmth even when the temperatures dropped. The French buhrstone with its damsel slapped out a perfect and irresistible "Saint Ann's Reel" which I found myself inadvertently humming from time to time. I loved the tidy order of Ewan's daybook with its weights and measures and accounts. Although I most decidedly did not appreciate being made a spectacle, I admit to a glimmer of pride. It surprised me to discover what a lady could absorb about cogs and belts and pulleys. But then again, why did I expect such a mystery? Why should a woman's mind be so different from a man's? When out from under the gaze of farmers, working alone on the meal floor, I felt the power of the machinery and felt my own strength of mind and body in the running of it.

THE WEEKS STRETCHED OUT, ONE AFTER ANOTHER. Ewan was almost as anxious to get out of his cart as he had been to get into it. As soon as the doctor could no longer guarantee catastrophe if Ewan took up crutches, Ewan summoned Donny Cunningham for the final time and sent him to fetch him some good strong ash wood.

"Now get out and don't come back here—I don't want to see you again," was all he said to the boy once he made sure the wood would serve his purpose.

Ewan spent several evenings building his crutches. Before long he was able to shift himself in and out of his cart. Then he could hobble his way across a floor and up or down a step or two. Although Dr. Thomas continued to counsel caution, Ewan finally forced him to admit that the bone could likely withstand a little weight. He traded his crutches for canes. One morning when I was weighing out some barley he made his way down the stairs and engaged a gear. I didn't see him until he had made it, leaning heavily into the stone foundation wall by the stairs, nearly all the way back up to the main floor. He waved off my help with his cane.

"Go on up to the house now, I don't need you. And I'll want a proper dinner today."

This was my thanks. Was I supposed to be grateful for my release?

"You're welcome, I'm sure. It was no bother at all."

I might as well have been the oat bin for all the notice he took of me standing there with my hands on my hips. I started across the mill after him to demand a civil thanks at least, but the barley's owner let out a low whistle and cocked his eyebrow. I turned back towards the door. "Oh, weigh your own sacks," I told him and swatted him out of my way. By the titter that rose behind me as I climbed the hill I knew he had heard me muttering, "I'll break your other leg, Ewan MacLaughlin." That'll make a story to pass around, no doubt.

CHAPTER EIGHT

Are you impatient, Granddaughter? All this talk and still there's no sign of even your mother? But this is the way of our stories; they start long before we arrive and continue farther down the road than we can ever see. Listen. Waiting is the longest part of making anything. I had married for a home not just a house, but the only warmth I knew came from the fire in the stove. All this time I waited and yearned for a child to love.

I SOON RELAXED BACK INTO MY OWN ROUTINE. When I pressed Ewan about his leg he admitted to a twinge that buzzed on the impact of each step. He admitted to a heaviness that I suspected came with a persistent ache. His right leg paused in a slight limp but I considered us fortunate to have escaped with only these consequences.

Every day I looked for happiness in my lambs and calves and chicks, in my new puppy from the Browns' spring litter, in Abby's children who swam in the old millpond and regaled me with tales of their adventures. Young Frankie and Peter discovered the treasures of the old millpond and began promising careers as fishermen. I looked up from my garden one afternoon to see them trotting up the lane, smiles as bright as oranges.

"I caught the big one, Mrs. MacLaughlin!" Peter proclaimed. "Frankie caught the little one. We're going to catch some for Mama tomorrow but she said we should practise out on you first."

"What a fine supper we'll have tonight! I'd say those hearty specimens would be worth a nickel a piece plus two ginger cookies."

"Sold to the pretty lady in the apron," Frankie said. Already Frankie showed his father's easygoing nature and quick wit.

Whenever I had a few moments on a summer's afternoon I would skip up to Abby's to see where I could lend a hand. She was expecting child number six in the fall, which made me ache with jealousy in my lonely hours. While in her company, however, she always made me feel as though my own child's conception was imminent, that we were mothers together. She shared her children with me, even when scolding me for my doting.

"Now don't you go wasting your good money giving it to my lads for playing in your pond. Lord knows we owe you strings of fish and more for all you do for the little scamps." She laughed her silver laugh. "They were racing their nickels on the table after breakfast—rolling them on their edges to see whose is first to the string. I told them they better have those nickels in their fists when it came time to buy their copybooks and pencils in the fall or they'd be drawing in the dust with their fingers."

"You know I love to give them little things."

"That's enough though now. You'll have your own little ones to think of before you know it. I asked them how it was right that you pay them for fish living in your own millpond and Frankie—you know that one's always smart with an answer—says it's not for the fish exac'ly, Mama, it's the carting fee to get them from the brook to the kitchen."

COME FALL THE WHIRLWIND OF HARVEST SWEPT UP EVERYONE BUT NO one more than millers. I raced about trying to get the last of the fall chores done before winter set in. I was pleased with the amount of produce I had managed to get to Nettle over the fall, over and above what I put by for ourselves. Our two pigs were slaughtered at last and I was busy with sausage and potage and tending to the ham and bacon in the kiln. I had tallow stored for a batch of soap and then candles to make. The harvest arrived by the wagonload and the mill growled away through every daylight hour.

"I have to go and see about a mill," Ewan said as he got up from his supper one night.

Having been deep in my own thoughts I was more startled by the fact of conversation than the information. "About a mill? How do you mean?"

"Advice on improvements."

"Oh, this is news. Whose mill is this? Did he ask for you?"

"A man named Peter Gilbert who lives in Curry Point. He needs instruction. He won't have anyone but me."

"Curry Point! That's so far away. It would take you all day to travel."

"Better to improve mills too distant to offer competition, I'd say."

"Well yes, I suppose that's true. I don't understand, though. How could you do it? You are so busy."

"It is my Christian duty."

I cocked my head, perplexed. This was a novel interpretation of Christian duty for Ewan. And certainly no answer to my question. "And so you intend to go?"

"Yes."

"When?"

He stood and headed for the door. He shrugged on his coat as he answered. "Shortly. I'll stay a fortnight. Investigate the problem. See what can be done. Set him to work on it."

"Not in the middle of the harvest, surely!"

He shut the kitchen door behind him, leaving me to wonder.

On Sunday, when Ewan was harnessed to the idleness of the Sabbath, he took up the subject as though the conversation had never been interrupted.

"A child could run that mill," he said out of the blue, as though this were the final word in a protracted argument.

I looked up, my mind scrambling to situate the comment. Ewan patted a corner of bread into his broth and brought the morsel carefully to his mouth. "That Curry Point mill?" I asked.

"Mine! My mill. Weigh the grist and figure their fee or their percentage. Collect what is owed, keep one man's batch separate from the next, and maintain the quality of the grind. There's precious little to do—the design being what it is. I ran it lame. I could run it in my sleep."

"Ewan, what are you saying?"

"You're looking at me like I'm mad but I'm not the foolish one. The foolish notion is that all over the civilized world men are tied up running operations that could be easily managed by women and children. Consequently men are kept from work that could better employ their strength and skills."

"What?"

"Have you gone thick? A man and his wife are one. While I'm away you'll run my mill."

"That's the most foolish notion I've ever heard! I'm a woman, Ewan, which you well know. I have my place and my work here in the house. And I'm no miller." I laughed. I can hardly remember it but I'm sure I must have. The idea, if I understood him correctly, was ludicrous, of course. "Don't be so utterly foolish!"

"Foolish? Now you tell your husband what's proper? Is that so? What is wise and what is foolish?"

"It seems I must, yes! If you go, and honestly I don't see why you would, you can hire a man. Hire the sawyer."

"I will not see another man at my work, jabbing and poking at my good mill."

"Better a man who knows the mill than me marooned there to poke and jab! This is preposterous! You can't leave the mill in my hands. Leave it in the hands of someone who knows better. Why would you leave anyway? Here you have your beautiful new mill and you're running off to tend to someone else's work. You have all you could want—why leave it? Or if you're determined to go, then shut your mill for a couple of weeks. Resume work when you return."

"Shut a mill in the fall! Now who's foolish?"

"There is no place for a woman in a mill! I cannot do it. I will not. I have my work here in the house."

His voice turned glacial. "The work you do is running up the road to sit and visit with the layabout neighbours, clucking and laughing and drinking tea. I will not have you defy me. You will do this work and if it pleases God you will be rewarded for it. I will ride over the mountain next Sunday."

I opened my mouth but could not form a word.

"MacCarron's boy will come to help you shift sacks if you like, although I hardly see it's necessary. You're hearty. And the lane's blocked with farmers from sunup to sunset. They can wield a few sacks of grain, I suppose, between their chatter and resting. That MacCarron boy is a lout but I suppose he can mind a kiln."

Frightened now, and desperate, I pleaded. "Ewan, I simply couldn't. The idea is outrageous. What will people say—your wife in the mill! Do you want people saying you can't provide for a wife? And the Sabbath is not to be used for travel. There is nothing necessary in it. Do you imagine for one instant that God will reward your flagrant disregard…"

With one stroke of Ewan's arm the supper, dishes and all, crashed to the floor in a riot of splatter and shards. Suddenly his face overpowered my field of vision, ice-diamond eyes, his nostrils flared like a horse's, a bubble of spit at the corner of his mouth. I tried to scuttle backwards but my chair held me captive until it tipped, nearly dumping me at his feet. He spoke, his lips thin with rage, his voice so low, so gelid, my skin tightened with each word. A hint of beef on his breath. "Don't. You. Preach. To me. God's. Design."

He spun in one movement and walked across the kitchen, his gait stiff as frostbite. When he closed the door behind him, wood approached wood with such terrifying restraint the lone click of the latch cracked the air like bone.

I stooped to clean up the mess on the kitchen floor, my hands quaking so badly I broke a teacup that had escaped the original calamity. The fear of those early vicious days of Ewan's confinement with the broken leg, his wild captive fury, reclaimed me. To be the focus of such rage shrinks the soul. I cowered. The word itself cradled around me. Coward. Indignation rescued me. Listening night after night to his prayers—make my wife worthy of Thy blessing—charges of indolence! Running the roads and gossiping! And now he meant to leave me to run the mill. True the very busiest weeks had passed but there would be steady custom for months yet. What was I to do about my work? Because Ewan believed I did not work did not make it true. And the MacCarron boy would fetch and carry and watch the kiln? This is what he offers me? That boy's father, the lecherous cad, I knew only too well from Ewan's broken leg days. He stood too close, brushed against my sleeve. "You grind wild oats too?" And with Ewan right there in the mill, barely out of earshot. Fresh heat rose to my cheeks. This was not right. Ewan could not make me do this. I would send for the sawyer to come and run the mill. I would hang a closed sign on the door. If he would not listen to me I would call on the local preacher to demand he listen to sense. I would turn away the customers at the mill door or I would make such a poor job of the milling that his reputation would be destroyed.

As I finished the washing up, swept, set the bread for the next day, I ranted myself dry. Night closed in and with it the stark quiet that feeds loneliness. What could possibly have possessed Ewan to come up with such a plan? I struggled to set myself aside and examine Ewan's perceptions, reminded myself how all couples had this duty to understand their mates, but me more than most because of Ewan's awkward deficiencies that seemed inextricably paired with his mechanical gifts. By the window, in the glow of the lamp, I sat with folded hands and plumbed his assumptions. The mill was his. The wife was his. A man and his wife are one. This *one*, as we are meant to discover in our own time, is the husband. I knew how to mill—experience brought about through his suffering. With my efforts added to his he could effectively work in two places at once. These ideas would be self-evident to Ewan and arguing did not alter his truth. Sadness crept into the crevices and niches left by my retreating anger. Make my wife worthy, make my wife worthy—every night in his prayers. I, in my indolence, had not yet brought him a son and I stood there flouting his will. Until I produced the son why would I not be asked to fill the void?

"I do not agree." I spoke aloud and with force, repeating myself, hearing my own voice striking against the silence of the house. "A woman is not a slave to her husband's wishes. A woman has a body and a mind and a will of her own. She has duties of her own and a place of her own."

I thought of the farmers I would see at the mill door, of their heading home with flour and meal and news of the miller's wife working in the mill. Not at my injured husband's side, which was spectacle enough, but on my *own*. Like a man. Shame flushed over me. I imagined the news met with disdain in kitchens everywhere—I never heard of such a thing! We'll all be wearing trousers next I suppose, and felling trees and wrestling oxen as if we don't have enough to do. I could see Mrs. Cunningham striking her wooden spoon on the edge of her stewpot and bristling at the news—It doesn't surprise me to hear her putting herself around like a man. She always thought she was better than everyone else. Or pity—That poor dear! I swear Ewan MacLaughlin would harness a cat if he could catch it. Or—I thank God I have a husband who knows his duty to his family.

"Is this your main concern? The gossip of your neighbours?" I asked myself this the way I might have addressed an advanced student in my teaching days. Of course our neighbours' good opinion is important to us but surely not to the exclusion of our own needs, desires and consciences. Ripples of fear lapped at me but I fought them back. Laying aside the social expectations, the extra workload, and Ewan's dictates, the work of milling was not unpleasant. I cast my mind back searching for the best memories of my difficult days in the mill. Yes, as Ewan proclaimed, the mill's design streamlined production and required little in the way of heavy labour. I liked the clattering rhythm, the warm aroma, the orderly management of the accounts, the sense of competence that came with running such a large and vital piece of machinery. Ewan had faith in my ability. It was so often impossible to know what he felt but this fact, surely, was unassailable. He would not see his mill in anyone else's hands. I had seen the mill conceived of and raised. We had worked side by side there. Shouldn't it be so—that he trusted his wife above all others?

In the end I knew I could not outright defy Ewan's dictate. Just as well to agree as to be forced. The longer I sat alone in the gloom the more my conclusion felt like a decision, and the surer I became with my decision. Ewan did not return to the house. Eventually I climbed the stairs and crawled into bed.

THE FOLLOWING MORNING I FOUND EWAN SITTING AT HIS PLACE AT the kitchen table. I placed a steaming bowl of oatmeal before him. The normalcy of this small act pointed us back towards familiar territory.

"You are my wife. A miller's wife," Ewan said.

It was not an order, not a question. I heard a note of vulnerability, of relief in his voice. There was no contrition in the tone but perhaps an explanation offered in lieu of apology. There was an offer of restoration.

"You must listen to what I say, Ewan. You must take into account how I feel. It's the nature of marriage. I'm not a servant."

"You can manage a mill. It will be an easy thing for you."

"Yes," I said. "But send for that boy. He can help with the farmers."

Ewan nodded.

SUNDAY MORNING AS DAWN BROKE EWAN SADDLED UP HIS HORSE. Before he left he returned to the kitchen and stood before me as though he had something to say but could not recall what it might be.

I spoke into the silence. "Be careful on the roads," I said. "Safe journey."

"Be sure your grist is clean and dry before it sees the eye of the stone. Thumb your grind to keep it fine."

I stood at the window and watched him go. A gulp of abandonment then a surge of excitement, then uncertainty. It being Sunday I had only my necessary chores: feeding and milking, setting my feet on well-worn paths. By the time I sat down to a full pot of tea and a slice of ginger cake I was nearly giddy. There was freedom to be had in Ewan's absence. My little library, I realized with surprise, I had all but abandoned. It was impossible to open a novel in Ewan's presence, even on Sunday, without feeling his disapproval. He did not prevent me from attending church, from Sunday visiting, from reading stories or poetry. This I needed to reinforce to myself. Yet I could do none of these things without having him raise an eyebrow and pass a comment about the silliness, vanity and gossip central to all these "womanish" pastimes. I could not draw him into a discussion, conversation or even an exchange of opinions on the subject. He disdained discussion. In fact, he disdained my company. Newlywed notions of us strolling, arm in arm, by the brook of a Sunday, sharing intimacies and building confidence in ourselves and our union I had long since buried. Monday morning would bring its own worries; Sunday I would claim for my own. I cut myself a second piece of cake and set off for the Yorkshire moors with the Brontës. The afternoon I would pass with Abby who was just regaining her feet after the arrival of her sixth child, little Jacob.

Early Monday morning I met young Angus MacCarron at the mill door with a brisk good morning. He was big for his fifteen years and a lout, as advertised. I immediately directed him to help me pull the desk out from the wall like a schoolteacher's. Ewan simply figured in his head and stood over his book to note his numbers in pencil; I intended to sit and write entries in ink beside full names flowing across the page. I hoped this nod to my past profession would bolster my sense of authority and with it my confidence and perhaps the farmers' respect. The mill had grown stout with new weight, with responsibility.

"Where's the miller?" young Angus asked.

"Mr. MacLaughlin will be away for a short while. I will be here in his stead for the duration."

"What?"

"I beg your pardon."

"Who's getting' the millin' done?"

"You will address me as Mrs. MacLaughlin or ma'am. I will be in charge of the milling. You will be attending to the kiln and to other duties as instructed."

The brat guffawed in disbelief.

"Angus MacCarron, if there are jokes you will share them with me so I can laugh too. If not, we shall both attend to our respective duties. Is this clear?"

"Eh?"

"The correct answer to the question is 'Yes, Mrs. MacLaughlin' or 'Yes, ma'am.' If you hold an alternate opinion, which you have every right to do, you may return home now to explain to your father why you will not be bringing fifty cents home tonight. Do you understand?"

I watched the lad synthesize this information. He was a boy of harsh breeding. I imagined him bullied at home and sassy when out of harm's way. But loutishness aside, he was not stupid and I watched as his inclination to mock this startling arrangement gave way to practical considerations.

"Yes, ma'am."

"Good. Lay the kiln fire then. We are certain to have a grist or two of oats in today." I struggled a moment with my conscience but honour is a poor match for necessity. I needed the boy's allegiance. I called to him as he turned towards the stairs. "Mr. MacLaughlin says you are well known to be a good worker, smart and attentive. He promised me I'd have no trouble with young Angus."

The boy stopped and regarded this news with surprise. Could it be true that he had established a good reputation for himself? Suspicion and pride wrestled for supremacy on his features. I smiled slightly, nodded a tight affirmation, calling to the boy's naïve hopes for himself, coaxing him forward like a fawn peering out from the cover of the underbrush. Yes, it's true (I tried to tell him with my eyes), you are held in high regard. You must rise to expectations.

"You and I shall make a happy team, don't you think?" I puffed up my voice with what I hoped was both kindliness and authority.

"Yes, ma'am." He beamed and scampered down the stairs to his post.

I tied one of Ewan's clean aprons over my coat and smoothed it down trying to settle my racing heart. That was the boy. Men are not so easy to fool. Already in the distance I could hear the clop of hooves.

Tom Joudrey turned away, indignant. "Who'll be in charge of the stones next time I come? The cows, I suppose. Or the chickens." And he hauled his load back home despite my entreaties.

Willy Ban arrived next with oats for meal and corn to crack for fodder.

"Ewan will be gone a short while," I said, "a few days, a brief trip. He has a commission, is attending to a mill that is not operating properly, his expertise is needed, he has been called away, no other millwright would do."

Willy looked dubious. "I'll come back another day."

"No, leave your grist here. Angus will help you with it. I'll see it gets ground. Ewan will not be gone long." They unloaded the grain, Willy perhaps choosing to believe Ewan would grind the grist when he returned.

By the time the next wagons arrived we were busy with oats in the kiln and had the vertical fodder stone grinding away. With each new customer I had to explain Ewan's absence but as the morning unfolded, as each man saw that someone before him had handed over his grain, the farmers became increasingly willing to chance the new "miller." They were reluctant to abandon the outing of a trip to the grist mill; a lazy day was too rare to be so easily aborted. And like a dreadful accident, it was hard not to watch the exhibition, I suppose. A woman taking orders was one thing, but this was a different kettle of fish altogether.

All went well until my stomach began to whisper that dinnertime was approaching. Only then did I realize I had neglected to consider dinner for myself and the lad. Of course there was no one to carry a hot dinner down to me in a pan swathed in towels. Had it been only myself I would have gladly soldiered on, but I would not have the boy reporting that he had been starved at work, that the miller's wife was too lazy to feed him. There would be scandal enough without that. So I stopped the stones, called to Angus to let the kiln alone and the two of us marched together up the hill past waiting farmers, my face flaming. Of course the kitchen stove was cold, the lunch a hurried affair of fried eggs and cheese and Saturday's old biscuits with jam and hastily boiled tea. Dishes were left greasy on the table, farmers impatient in the laneway. Nonetheless the remainder of the day moved along well without incident.

At the end of the day I directed Angus to stop in at the Cunningham farm on his way home. "Ask Mrs. Cunningham for two dinners to be delivered to the mill each day for the remainder of the week. Tell her they are for you and the miller." I did not favour my odds. No doubt she would have heard the news. On the one hand Delilah Cunningham was always eager to feel a coin in her palm, but she was perhaps even fonder of grasping a superior moral position. I imagined her on her step, arms folded tight across her weasel bosom and glaring down her nose at Angus.

"Is the missus ill then?"

"She's hearty enough I'd say."

"Good. I'm happy to hear it. It'll be no bother to her then to attend to the miller herself. I've enough to do feeding my own without cooking for the road."

However the exchange transpired the result was the same. Not even the prospect of cold cash could lure Mrs. Cunningham into countenancing such bizarre behaviour. I learned to prepare a stew and bake my biscuits before bed and carry the pot down to the mill with me in the morning. I could simmer the stew over the kiln fire. The biscuits, of course, were never quite fresh but I could warm them in a towel in the kiln. There was no pie, but the boy did not complain. He likely knew no better fare at home, for which I was grateful. My beautifully polished kettle I sacrificed to the open flame of the kiln fire where it blackened like a miner's boot. I also learned that by the end of the day I did not have the strength to churn my butter so I woke earlier to do this chore before dawn. On Wednesday evening when I climbed the hill I found a loaf of Abby's fresh bread wrapped in a cloth on the table. Tears of gratitude welled in my eyes. I must scold Abby for this. Abby, with a brand new baby and all her brood, had no time to be making extra work for herself. I fretted over my washing. Monday had come and gone and, of course, I had had no opportunity to see to it. I wondered if Saturday evening might serve. I could hang it on the line before midnight and it could dry on Sunday while I slept. But a line full of wash flapping on the Sabbath? Perhaps it was the exhaustion combined with the kindness of the fresh bread, but I sank into a chair and sobbed.

On the first Sunday after Ewan's departure I rested. One week gone and another yet to endure. For the first time in my life I returned to bed after feeding the animals and I slept, deep and hard, past noon. A child could run this mill, Ewan said. This is true enough supposing the child understands how the wheel transfers its power from shaft to pulley to gear every step of the train from the millrace to the stone nuts and the stones themselves, and supposing the child learns each sound and can follow each as it is laid on top of the previous one. Supposing the child can follow the song of the damsel from two or three stones at once and can smell the heat of a stone running too close and keep the buhrstone fed while following the progress of the oat shelling stone. Supposing the child can maintain his composure in the face of the grumbles and sniggers of men and supposing the child has a mother to fetch him a hot meal at dinnertime and keep the house cozy and clean and tend to his clothes and his household, then, of course, a child can run the mill.

By my second week enough of a routine had emerged to keep me steadied. Through a combination of liberal praise and veiled threats I managed to keep young Angus useful and just this side of surly. The mill itself offered an odd sort of refuge. There were moments when the work wrapped itself around me and absorbed me completely, carrying me away from my troubles.

On the second Sunday after Ewan's departure I waited, unsure. Despite the Sabbath I set bread and baked it, revelling in this commonest of domestic tasks. It felt simple and comforting and nothing like work. Surely this was necessary work for what would Ewan think to return to a home with no bread in the pantry? And when else was I to find the time for such a chore? Nonetheless guilt buzzed about my head like a mosquito. What was baking bread if not regular women's work? What did the Sabbath prohibit if not our regular labours? The sun rose and brightened, filled the sky, then leaned again towards the earth and set. I lit the lamps. Just as I made up my mind that he would not be coming and that I must mill another week, the dog barked. I ran to the door with a lamp as Ewan swung down from his saddle, his silhouette ghostly in the dark. Relief flooded me with a shocking intensity that weakened my knees. I leaned back letting the solid wall of the house hold me, the lamp quivering in my hands.

"Ewan."

"Aye." My husband's voice in the dark.

He did not halt his progress but led Billy into the stable where I knew he would be unburdening the poor beast and doling out its reward after the long journey. I pulled the soup up to the fire and warmed a loaf. Presently I heard his bustling outside the door and he entered clutching his pack. Such a magnificent thing to see him there, shuffling out of his heavy coat, hanging his fur cap on its peg, tucking his boots in behind the stove. I backed away afraid to approach lest the truth of his body be altered.

He sat at his place at the table, leaned back in his chair, stretched out his legs in front of him, hooked his hands behind his head and began to speak. I served him soup with the fresh bread and butter and cheese and a pot of raspberry jam, then sat across from him in amazement at my near-gregarious husband. He spoke a full ten minutes about the Curry Point mill. He complained of the owner's slovenly workmanship, how he was afraid the man would not follow his instructions precisely, leaving the mill no more than a limping, problem-riddled heap—a duster. He would leave the man to his instructions for now but he would have to go back to inspect the work and see what further could be done. The ratios had been all wrong—no wonder the thing couldn't grind chalk—but the man could not understand anything put before him with a pencil. Ewan said he repaired the wheel, built a new spur, re-jigged and moved one of the stones, left intricate instructions for improvement of the dam.

I frowned. He must have worked day and night to accomplish so much. Finally he looked over his bowl at me. "Your milling went well, I suppose?"

"I'm glad to see you home. I had an awful armload trying to manage your work and mine as well."

Ewan looked surprised. "But young MacCarron came?"

"Yes. But he doesn't bake bread or roast a dinner or scrub clothes or churn butter."

"But your milling went well?"

"Yes."

"Ah. It's our labour commends us to the Lord." He fell silent then, and as far as I could tell, was happy.

CHAPTER NINE

THE MORNING AFTER EWAN'S RETURN HE SET HIS DESK BACK against the wall of the mill where he liked it and sent the ink and nib back up the hill. He commented not one way or the other on my running of the business. Our lives reverted instantly to our old routines, so the entire experience shrank to little more than an unlikely adventure, an anomaly, an accident of life. In the evenings of the following week, when all his custom had been ground, Ewan would work through the problems of the Curry Point mill. Even though he knew the miller would take the quickest, simplest and most economical solution to his problems (and why wouldn't he, the poor man?) Ewan continued to sketch and figure and tap his pencil for long hours. Although my experience was limited and Ewan's answers to my questions laconic as always, even I could see that Ewan's plans vastly outstripped the practical proposal. Having completed what was required he was now designing castles in the air. Deep in thought he regained that transported, utterly absorbed look I had seen on his face when he was designing and building his own mill. I envied him this. While I should have been pleased to see him so engaged with his work, in truth it deepened my sense of loneliness. Ewan was stark company at the best of times so it was not the loss of companionship

I missed. I am ashamed to say that misery loves company. I longed to be so preoccupied, so drawn in. I longed for a greater meaning to my endless cycle of chores.

Cold closed in as we headed further down through December. Listlessness tugged at me. I had missed my cycle when Ewan was gone but how could I not? Working like a man. My days were peppered with bouts of felling morose and ill. As Christmastime approached I brought an armful of evergreen boughs into the house and urged myself towards some small effort for the season though I knew from experience that Ewan would work as usual on Christmas Day. I visited Nettle for the few supplies I would need to make the Christmas pudding which would elicit no comment.

At a single sharp bark from her dog, she stuck her head out the door of her shack and beckoned me in with a jerk of her chin making her look for all the world like the witch in Hansel and Gretel. Ah, I thought, I will make a gingerbread house for Abby's children.

"A bag of hard candy and a bag of gumdrops, Nettle," I said, and remembered to leave an extra tip for Nettle herself in honour of the season. Not that she appeared any merrier than usual. But who was I to talk?

Making the wreath, the pudding and the gingerbread provided a distraction and a bit of variety if nothing else.

On Christmas morning I woke to a soft snowfall. Ewan had already left for the mill as usual. I pulled on my coat and boots and stepped out into the fresh, white hush and turned my face to the sky. Giant flakes drifted down all around me. Somewhat buoyed in spite of myself, I was thankful I had made my small efforts. I set to my chores, then packed up my gingerbread creation and headed up to Browns' where I knew there would be Christmas cheer in abundance.

Indeed the family enveloped me the moment I entered. The children clamoured to show me the treasures Santa Claus had left them.

"Look, Mrs. MacLaughlin—an orange and a stick of candy! And the whole of it's for me!"

"See mine, Mrs. MacLaughlin?"

"What have you got in your package, Mrs. MacLaughlin?" young Peter asked.

"I've brought a surprise. Shall we set it out here on the table where everyone can have a look?"

The children crowded around as I unveiled the little house with its candy-shingled roof and walls and its gumdropped laneway. I had made six gingerbread figures—one for each child—cavorting in the egg-white icing snow.

"Look at the windows!" cried Harriet. "They're like real glass, but candy!"

"Look at the peppermints!"

"This gingerbread boy is me! See, Mama, he's got a snowball!"

When I looked up Abby was staring at me with the most bewildered look on her face. She smiled then, of course, and gushed about the house, but I had caught her out. I felt my social self peel away, outwardly listening to the children's questions and exclamations but underneath an awkward ache tugged me away from them.

Later, with the children sent outside to play, Abby turned to me. She cupped my chin with her hand and peered intently into my face. "Penelope, I believe you have that glow. Am I right? When did you have your last…?"

Answering her whispered questions, I pressed my palms to my womb. Yes. I had been so foolish with fussing over my troubles that I had missed the very gifts set before me.

"Yes," Abby nodded. "There is a glow, I'm sure of it."

I walked slowly and carefully down to the mill feeling more certain with each step. I found him by the fodder stone.

"Ewan," I whispered, setting my hand on his shoulder, "I think we may be blessed. A child."

Ewan cocked his head, stared at my abdomen. "Ah, your extra labour when I was gone. This is your reward."

I caught a merry laugh as it bubbled up, caught it just in time and contained it in a smile. Had he been a different sort of man I would have teased him that a man's absence from his wife is seldom rewarded in this way. Instead I leaned over and kissed his cheek.

I SANG AT MY WORK AND PRAYED AND WORKED AND SANG SOME MORE. I felt so strong, so certain. On Sundays I visited with Abby revelling in her little ones as proof of how it would be, splashing optimism everywhere, painting the world with certainty. Abby gave me little dresses as patterns for the wee gowns I stitched and decorated. Mrs. Cunningham deduced or heard the news of my condition. When I met her on the road on my way back from Nettle's she shot a doubtful frown over my body and advised that after this long time I shouldn't get my hopes up.

On a winter day like so many of the days that linked dramatic weather—a seasonal day wrapped in batting, an everyday day—I was hauling water to the barn, breaking the ice on the pails and topping them up with fresh water from the well. The barn was cozy with the warm redolence of animal breath and I took my time with the beasts, stroking Billy's nose and Pride's too when she nuzzled over, jealous, patting the flanks of the cows. I had a bred heifer that would freshen in the spring and each day I ran my hands over her and down her hind legs, across her udder, preparing her with my smell and touch, feeding a handful of molasses oats with my ministrations. I carried armloads of hay out to the loafing shed where the sheep greeted my benevolence with bleats of praise. I had just given the horses their winter rations from the oat bag when I felt it. A nudge, a shift. If it had been a sound it would have been a rustle. Involuntarily I looked down at the front of my coat the way one might turn towards a tap on the shoulder. Beneath my palm, beneath a layer of stretched skin and a shallow dome of flesh, a human child had moved. No longer me, now a person in its own right, a baby swaddled by my body, of me but not me. My child, Ewan's child, whose arms and legs were guided by its own separate little heart and mind. Such a flowering of pure love enveloped me I could barely breathe. "Again, my dear one," I whispered, coaxing, now clutching my womb with both hands. I waited, my heart as broad and steadfast as the great gentle horses beside me. It came again—a flutter this time. I wept with wonder of it. The quickening.

From that day forward I never sat or stood or moved without thought of the baby I carried beneath my heart. I carried the babe through the cold of February, the ice of March, the inconstancy of April, the dawn of spring and into the fullness of summer. When the water ran low Ewan returned to Curry Point for a fortnight. I hardly noticed his absence. I carried my bundle as it grew and kicked, speaking to me as I spoke to it.

OUR BABY DAUGHTER CAME WITH THE SUMMER DAISIES, WITH ALL the hope and joy that happy flower brings. Ewan smiled and held the child, his disappointment at her sex soothed by her vibrant health. I felt our lives were beginning again, that everything up to this point had been a long meandering opening chapter; necessary detail perhaps, but now the story would begin.

"Our next will be a boy," I promised.

"Aye," he said.

THE YEARS OF DAISY'S INFANCY WERE THE HAPPIEST OF OUR LIVES. Although Ewan worked long and hard he stayed closer to home for a couple of years. He travelled to work on other mills but he seldom stayed away for more than a fortnight and he only left when his own mill was shut in the coldest days of winter or the hottest days of summer's low water. On Sunday afternoons I took the opportunity to nestle the baby into Ewan's lap. I sat by him in case she fussed. He was frightened, I could see, by the strange warmth that blossomed between them. But it attracted him too, like the campfire of strangers. His heart inched forward with such caution.

"It's fine, Ewan. You won't hurt her. Look at her eyes," I said, setting my hand ever so lightly on his shoulder. He brushed her cheek, his thumb rough with stone but sensitive to the finest powder. "See how she loves her Papa?"

Nothing could repress my spirits. I set Daisy up in her own little manger in the barn while I milked my cows and tended to the calves and hens and fed the pigs. She dozed in the shade while I weeded my garden. Ewan had built a cradle that I kept in the kitchen as I churned and cleaned and baked and made my cheese. I told her stories and sang her songs. She cooed and kicked and laughed away the gloom. Of course Abby made a great fuss over her. We stole what time we could from our work to watch the little ones play. I know she indulged me, listening to my fascinated observations and boasts as though she had not seen all of this six times already with her own.

Sundays were newly made for me. I delighted now in the outing to the little Presbyterian church. Before Daisy I had attended sporadically, always feeling removed from other women, always feeling a mild censure, or pity, or curiosity at least. My days of work in the mill seemed far off now; I had stories of my own to trade—funny things the baby did or said. All manner of prosaic details seemed worthy of comment. On Sundays my skirts fairly twirled as I moved through my few chores. I sang softly as I dressed our baby girl in her finery. I had dyed a patch of leftover bolting silk the softest yellow and stitched a wee pinafore with smocking in shades of blue and mustard for her. I put on my Sunday dress with the double row of buttons down the front. Ewan took his bible down from the shelf. My delight seemed only to confirm his opinions about church as a parade of gossip and new hats. But in my joy his disdain could no longer touch me.

"Come to church with us, Ewan. You could drive the cart while I tend to the baby. It would help pass the day for you at least."

"Humpf."

"You're not really reading that bible."

"In all labour there is profit: but the talk of the lips tendeth only to penury."

"Oh, for heaven's sake." I turned my back on my husband quickly to hide my smile. I tied the ribbons of Daisy's little bonnet under her chin and blew on her cheeks to light up her smile. "Now we're pretty," I whispered, rubbing my nose against my daughter's in fun and planting a kiss on the little cheek.

"Come, my sweet. Wave bye-bye to Papa." I set off with my daughter in my arms for a couple of hours of rest and social chat surrounded by others with similar joys and hopes, troubles and woes.

Before I knew it Daisy was toddling. She outgrew her cradle and Ewan built a little bed for her nursery. In the evening whenever Ewan made it up from the mill for his supper before I had put her down to sleep she would watch him with her big blue eyes. One evening she forsook her rag dolly, hauled herself to her feet and made her way towards him, clinging to chairs to steady herself, finally reaching out to grab the great trunks of his legs just as he stood from taking off his boots. Ewan stared down at her, stumped.

"Pick her up, Ewan," I prompted. "She wants to visit with you."

He reached down and lifted her into his arms where she laughed like a summer brook and patted his face. For this she earned one of Ewan's rare and hesitant smiles. For Daisy there was nothing odd in her father's social awkwardness. She never expected conversation from him any more than she did from the lambs or the calves. Her delight was in handing him his dinner from the basket I carried to him and, on days when he came in for his supper, carrying his boots to the mat behind the stove to warm.

Ewan worked, as always, from first to last light and more when he could. The envy I had once felt for his passion had been turned on its head. I saw that it is one thing to build a mill and another entirely to spend your life watching it turn, turn and turn. Not that Ewan was envious of my joy. I knew he did not experience joy the way most others do and so he could not envy it. In all truthfulness I don't think he could recognize it. He was suspicious even of happiness. But in the place of happiness I believe he could experience a kind of rightness or balance, a sense of enhanced satisfaction perhaps. I had seen him transported when absorbed in his mechanics. Of course he never shirked his work as a miller. On the contrary he seemed to do battle with work, to conquer it, wrestle it into submission and beg for more. But Ewan was an engineer by vocation. When men sought his expertise and he could spend a night, a day, a week, solving a puzzle of power and motion he was like a thirst-starved man landing at an oasis. No, I lie. And what is the point of a story if the truth is swept behind the stove or covered with a mat? It was the look of a drunkard who had been denied drink and suddenly was presented with a fresh jug. The challenge of the puzzle was an intoxicant. I am embarrassed to admit it, but as I said, what is the point of whitewashing? It was my own happiness, our Daisy, that allowed a generosity of spirit to seep back into me. My misery had made Ewan's gloominess seem like his proper punishment. Now, in my delight, I wanted to spread my joy. I had hit upon a wonderful plan and was waiting for a chance to plant the idea in Ewan's mind.

Daisy and I returned from church one Sunday to find Ewan at the table with figures and equations spread across the paper before him and his nose in his *Miller's Guide*, his bible tossed aside. He shut the book in haste as we came in and he stood to leave but I set my hand on his shoulder.

"Ewan," I said, laughing, "Why shut your books? Why not use your day of leisure to study and figure if that's your pleasure?" He looked at me as I began helping Daisy with her buttons, half expecting a lecture on the Lord's Day, but he said nothing. This and my high Sunday mood emboldened me. This might be the moment.

"You have such a fine mind, my dear. Imagine a life built around the work you love. Suppose you were to make an engineer of yourself? So much of your skill is lost in simply running the mill. There are factories everywhere with steam engines and all manner of mechanical innovations. The country is growing and you're a young man yet. You would have twenty-five years or more to work yet, after your education. Anyone can see how you revel in invention, how apt you are—such a talent."

He stared at me in horror, as though he had caught me in the act of setting fire to the haymow. "We could live frugally while you study. And you have brothers who could help you. Surely they would help us along—you helped them, after all."

"Forsake ye not the law of your father!" He spoke with a cold, steely certainty, but if I were silenced by hard looks and harsh tones I would never say anything.

"What law, Ewan? You've honoured your father's trade. You did your mother's bidding. You helped establish your younger brothers. You have done all a dutiful son could do. Your talents are yours to make the most of now. You know the parable of the talents…"

"So now you are ashamed to be the wife of a miller! You are ashamed to dip your hands in the labour of the Lord, ashamed of the dirt on your hands and the soles of your boots, and on *my* hands and the soles of *my* boots. Now I have a wife who wants to parade through the streets of the city showing off fashions and raising spoiled skinny brats who pass their days reading poetry and playing cards, who disdain the labours of the body. 'In the sweat of thy face shalt thou eat bread, till thou return unto the ground,' sayeth the Lord."

"Ewan, for heaven's sake. You deliberately misunderstand me."

"You imagine your sons growing up soft and womanish without ever knowing the *shame* of sweat or calloused hands—never knowing the *shame* of their father's work!"

"Stop, Ewan, you know that's not true. I was only saying there's no reason you should be held back by a wife and a baby or two. We could manage. The farm and the mill both produce an income. You could do the work you love. You could follow your true vocation."

"My vocation is as a miller. As my father's was. As my sons' will be."

"Tell me this then. If God wanted you to be a miller all your life why did He give you the mind of an engineer?"

"The first three boys go to the mill! If God had wanted me for an engineer He would not have sent me to be the third-born son. He sent me to be a miller and He will send me sons who will be millers."

"Are you sure you haven't confused God's Law with your mother's law?"

He was on his feet now, enraged. And I knew I had gone too far. Daisy clung to my skirts, whimpering in fear.

"Three sons," he said, leaving the words frozen in the air. Then he was gone and our Sunday lay in ruins. He would remain angry for days, perhaps weeks now. And I was to be left with this time for contrition and regret, or so my husband would suppose. He would turn directly to God to support his notions, leaving me disarmed. I heard him at his appeals before bed and set out to meet him on the same battleground.

"Holy Father, make me worthy of Thy service. Take the labour of my hands and bless us as we labour in Your glory. Lord, forgive my wife her temptations and evil thoughts. Make her diligent; heal her of her sloth and her pride and make her deserving of Your blessings. Oh Lord, send me a son to carry on Your holy work according to Thy will. For Thine is the Kingdom, the power and the glory, for ever and ever. Amen."

"Our Father who art in heaven. Thank you for this wonderful day, our home, our hearth, our health. I thank You for our wonderful little daughter and ask You to guide my hand and my heart in the raising of her. I pray you open my husband's heart and his mind to the possibilities of Your wondrous world, to help him raise his eyes above the labours of his trade and see the miracles of Your creation. Send him patience and wisdom. Above all I ask for the blessing of another child."

"Holy Father, accept the labour of my hands as I work in Your service. Forgive the indulgences of my wife. Forgive her her trespasses, keep her hands from idleness, and make her worthy of the blessing of a son. Make her humble and obedient to Thy will. Take my labour as an offering of contrition for her headstrong notions. Bless me with a son…"

"Oh Lord, please give my husband the wisdom to moderate his excesses, to see the beauty and diversity in Your divine plan…"

And so it went. But duelling vespers was a game I could not win. My prayers had not the slightest impact on Ewan except to highlight further my shortcomings. Ultimately it was me who suffered from the nightly barrage of imagined sins, unfair criticism and worst of all the insidious repetition that my behaviour was to blame for my empty womb. Like water on stone, as they say, wearing away, drip, drip, drip.

Then Ewan received a letter from a miller in King's Cove craving his expertise. The man had a wheel that needed replacing as the one he had had never been exactly fit. Also he wanted Ewan to devise a delivery system between the wheat stone and a new bolter and to diagnose a persistent problem with a bearing. Ewan stared at me with accusing eyes and declared that he would go and that I would manage the mill as I had before. A bit of work would do me good, he said. God had smiled on me the last time I had kept the mill. Only the laziest most miserly wife would object to such a small task as running a bit of grist through the stones.

I did object, however. What was I to do with Daisy? As it was she loved dashing about the brook and the pond and the dam, the mesmerizing lure of the waterwheel. During the summer she was always pulling at my arm for a chance to float her little stick boats, searching the bank for the best leaves for sails. Like her father she loved to build little levees and dams and divert trickles to make pools. Come winter she loved to run out on the ice, slipping and sliding. How was I to tend to Daisy and mill at the same time? Did he want his daughter left in the hands of that brutish Cunningham girl? "No Cunninghams," he said. "I was in a mill by her age. Set her to sweeping."

Ewan left the day after Christmas. It was several weeks before I received word from him via the post and Nettle's delivery. His job was extended, he said, and he would be another two weeks. I waited but instead of his return, another note arrived. He had received another commission from a carding mill a little farther along the shore and would look at it before he left the area.

Winter had well and truly settled in. The house breathed in the cold all night, sucked it in through the cracks in the wood, the skin of the window glass and held it silent as a lung. The windows, opaque with frost-painted finery, shimmered with cold. The cold called out to cold, gathered cold, folded cold over itself, growing layers, thick and still, of cold. In the morning ice lined the washbowls and the wood creaked. The clang of the stove lid, cast on cast, was the sound of cold, as lonely as an echo. The cold came in the darkness that pushed in at both ends of the day. But below the frozen surface, beneath the frozen soil, through the fissures in the rock and the land, always beneath our feet, water trickled through the land to the brooks, to the rivers, to the sea.

On the sixth of February I awoke as usual. From the brightness of the stars I could see it would be clear and fine when the sun rose. The snap of flame in the firebox thawed the air in a small sphere around the stove, struggled to push beyond. I always left Daisy in her bed, in the pocket of warmth of her own making, carried her clothes to the kitchen and set them above the stove to warm while I tended the beasts in the barn, feeding hay and hauling water that sloshed in icy taunts on my fingers and feet.

As usual that morning I called for Daisy when I returned. The kitchen, warmed and brightening with the earliest sunlight, always lifted my spirits. She ran from her little room, hopped up and down in front of the stove, her feet bundled inside her heavy socks, her woolen nightdress shedding its sleepy creases. She chattered as she dressed, her little arms and legs trying to keep pace with her mouth.

It was as if the words that flowed through her were dammed by the silence of sleep and the morning opening of the sluice sent them spilling in a rush over her. "The cow was in the kitchen in my dream but we were friends and we had bread and bacon. Sometimes people play with other little girls all day long. That's what I'll do when I go to school. I'll knit my own socks. I'm learning to knit now, aren't I? Tinker tailor soldier sailor. Tinker-tailor. Tinker-tailor…"

We ate our oatmeal with sugar and milk. I had had our tenacious little Shorthorn bred late and hoped she would carry us through the winter. Down at the mill I had finished with a large order of oatmeal and had several grists of wheat awaiting me. Daisy bundled her dolly against the cold and we strolled down to the mill, her little mittened hand in mine. Although I had no oats roasting I set a fire in the kiln fireplace for the little warmth it could throw. At least there was no danger of Daisy by the open water at this time of year and she could play by the hearth as I worked.

I was an hour at the ice, hacking away, freeing up the axle. At first it's nothing for the motion of the wheel to break the ice that forms at the bearings but as the cold thickens, the ice grabs at the waterwheel itself, slowing it even as the water tries to push it forward. At last, I roused the wheel. Inside I heard the spur wheel rumble in victory and was glad to retreat inside, out of the wind. I found Daisy playing hide and seek with her dolly by the oat bin on the meal floor. I engaged the flour bolt and the French stone. On the main floor I checked my stones, inspected the fresh flour, spreading it across my palm and holding it up to the light of the window. Satisfied, I retired to the chair by the desk. I sank, exhausted but pleased that I would, with today's work and tomorrow's, complete the order of wheat flour I had committed for sale. I closed my eyes, listening to the buhrstone's growl. I remember the peace of this moment, the soft drowsiness that settled over me like a quilt. Had I known this moment was to be my last moment of true peace I would not have let sleep steal it from me.

The rhythm of the mill jumped a beat, stuck, tugged, jolted. It was the mill that woke me, I know, because I was already on my feet as the scream hit my ear.

Her arm was caught, swallowed to the shoulder in the bevel gear.

My daughter being consumed before my eyes. The blood was terrifying. The gears strained to meet each other, clawed towards each other, the mill strove, pushed on by the spur, the wheel, by the river. I do not remember running to her or throwing the clutch, although I know I did. I remember grabbing her, snatching her. In one moment she was helpless in the teeth of the beast, in the next I held my bleeding and mangled daughter in my arms.

I wrapped the arm, hanging like a red mitten from a string, in close to her body. I bound her with my apron, wrapped her in my coat. I ran up the hill with her in my arms, the blood soaking us both. But how could I leave her to fetch the doctor? I flung the saddle onto Billy and clinging to Daisy, galloped to Cunninghams'. We laid her out by the stove and young William was sent to fetch the doctor. My beautiful daughter soaked layer after layer of rags with crimson.

We did the best we could to staunch the bleeding while we waited that impossible forever for the doctor. But he came at last. Of course he could not save her arm. But perhaps he might save her life. Once he had done all he could for her he bowed to my pleading and carried us home in his buggy. I sent him upstairs to fetch down Daisy's own little bed which I set up by the stove in the kitchen. She slept and woke and slept again. Abby came and went, how many times a day? I remember her touch and her voice in my ear. I watched and prayed and plied Daisy with sips of broth and rum. I stroked her hair. She slept. I sat on the floor with my head resting on her mattress where I could touch her always.

Mrs. Cunningham clattered the kettle when she boiled root tea. She scraped the chairs across the floor, stomped back and forth from the shed to the wood box, woke Daisy with her thumping and clanging. I had asked her leave us be but she assured me she could not shirk her Christian duty and I had no strength to fight.

Sometimes I found tears on my cheeks. Once, Mrs. Cunningham caught me wiping them away. "There's no point crying now. You've got the damage done—raising a girl in a mill. It's unnatural."

Where had Abby come from? I often lost track of when she came and when she left. What I remember is how she rose like fiery spirit, like a gryphon, a dragon, on powerful silent wings and collected Mrs.

Cunningham, her coat and boots and muffler all in a single swoop, and dumped them outside together in a heap on the snow bank beyond the door. I remember her standing guarding the door, holding the poker. I remember watching her and feeling the weight of that poker as if it were in my own hand. Abby stayed while I slept.

Daisy woke and tried to speak. Her eyes sought the corners of the room, trying to knit facts together.

"Mama's here. There was an accident but now you're going to get better." That spark of life filled me with hope—more than that, a desperate certainty. Then a fever overtook her and no amount of ice or snow would douse it. My Daisy died. She was lowered into a winter grave and lies in the churchyard.

The bloodstains on the gear teeth, the brown patch on the mill floor where her body was torn in two, were so much smaller than I could have imagined. The colour soaked through the wood, faded, an indelible stain of so very little consequence.

I uncapped the bottle of India ink and dipped my quaking pen into the same inkwell that Ewan had used for his initial drawings of his mill eight years ago. The thread of ink staining loops and dips across the paper seemed impossibly distant. How could so little represent so much?

To my husband, Ewan MacLaughlin—

CHAPTER TEN

PENELOPE

Lying in bed and forcing breath in and out of my body seemed more work than I could manage. Yet I could not let the animals starve or leave the milking cow to suffer. From my little stool I leaned into the Shorthorn every morning and buried my face in her flank. Then I tossed the milk onto the snow where it melted a shadow into the pristine surface. What would Ewan think of that—too lazy to even skim the cream? But where was Ewan? Not here. I no longer expected him to come. I did not expect anything. Abby came by as often as she could, easing and cajoling, comforting and prodding. I could see she was beside herself that Ewan had not returned, had not sent a letter even, but I did not have the strength to reach out to anger. Abby sent Harriet down with her schoolbooks to do her lessons at my table. "For company," she said. Abby always sent a little soup or bread for me which prompted me, eventually, to at least clean up the milk pail and send the milk up the road where it could be of use.

Harriet would set a place at the table for me to eat no matter how I pleaded poor appetite.

"Momma always presses me to know are you up, how's your fire, what's in the wood box, have you et? It makes her cranky when you haven't done a thing and so joyful if I can say you had bowl of soup and swept the floor. Sometimes I've wanted to tell just a little fib and say oh yes you were at your mending or making a cheese or some such, but then I can't. I'd catch the dickens for sure if she found out it was a lie. And Momma always finds out. Here now, Mrs. MacLaughlin, just take this broom here and sweep a bit. Give a good start and I'll finish up for you if you can't manage it all."

Eventually it took less energy to concede than to resist. By and by the sight of the girl at her studies by the lamplight, chewing on her pencil, worked itself behind the web of grief that had grown over me. I managed to part the veil enough to feel the warmth of her young life. Enough to force my hands to clean the lamp chimneys, then to make up a few oatcakes for her to have over her books. I hefted my sadness onto my shoulders, fixed it to my bones, and began to walk with it. One afternoon Harriet begged me to come and look at the crocuses that had bloomed purple and white and yellow among the stones by the door. I had never seen them in such profusion, in such dogged brilliance. They leaned into each other ever so slightly, a crush of ladies all got up for a dance with their delicate dresses covering souls hardy as leather. When the next day I sent Harriet home with fresh pound cake, she fairly danced with anticipation of her mother's approbation. As though she, herself, had brought the change, which of course she had.

Early in April Ewan returned. He did not speak of Daisy's death. I told him where she was buried and he fixed his eyes on some imaginary point on the wall across the room and sat as though I had not said a word. I did not know I had been harbouring such rage. I lashed out with a vehemence I had never known before, demanding that he look at me, that he see his part in her destruction, the consequences of his foolish, stubborn notions.

"A woman in a mill! With you off minding other people's business. Never mind what people say, the shame of it, the load of heavy labour on a woman's body—look what your preposterous ideas have done! My place is in the kitchen keeping my children safe, not chasing them around rolling gears and flapping belts and whirring pulleys. That damnable mill chewed up my daughter and spit her out."

He let out a choking sound; perhaps he was crying. I could not see through my tears and my fury.

"In two pieces, Ewan MacLaughlin! We wrapped her arm and tucked it in beside the rest of her little body in her coffin. Did you know that? Sell the cursed mill if you won't stay home to run it. Leave me to my own business while you run your millwright affairs."

He stood utterly still. I recall how our helpless silence over-filled the room, pushed against the walls and the windowpanes.

"As you wish," he said, finally. His voice was reedy with emotion, hesitant. I barely recognized it, tinged with uncertainty. What had he said?

"Have it your own way next time." Was he was crying? "Do as you like. While you carry my child or care for my child you will not mill."

He stepped away then and the air riffled around me. I strained to hold the words, to make certain.

"Have you promised me this?"

"Yes."

He was gone then. The wonder of it blinked over my grief, interrupted my anguish for a moment. While you carry my child or care for my child ... Have it your own way. I did not forgive my husband. How could I do that when I could not forgive myself? Now that he had acknowledged some part of the blame, as much as Ewan ever could, my anger churned stupidly then lay still. I found my way to the kitchen table where I sank into a chair and rested my head in my hands and waited for grief to carry me back to familiar shores.

The following Sunday Ewan sat alone in the room off the kitchen with his bible. After several hours he bundled himself up against the sharp spring breeze and tramped off towards the woods. I remembered with such clarity how the kitchen had come alive with the aroma of the spruce gum he used to fetch home for Daisy on his Sunday tramps. When he returned he found me in the parlour where I often retreated on Sundays, huddled by the parlour stove. He looked so incongruous there, so ill at ease, I struggled to remember if I had ever seen him in this room before. Even now he could hardly be said to be inside the room. He stood, perfectly framed, in the doorway, neither in nor out. He was older now. I don't know if I had not noticed his aging or if it had come suddenly with the tragedy. He was such a solid man it was startling to see him small, to see him without his forearms out in front of him, his hands tight around some tool. Here with his arms hanging lonely by his sides, his eyes roaming without purpose, he was no bigger than an ordinary man—an inch or two shorter, a tad deeper in the chest, a shade leaner, that was all.

"The Lord is forgiving," he said. "There will be blessings yet."

I ruminated on the possibility that he meant to comfort me. I believe he meant to comfort himself. How comforting to imagine that he could to give me instruction—but what did he know about anything except murderous machines?

Nearly every night, Sabbath excepted, he planted his seed deep into me, thrusting with all his might. Even on nights when he worked through without sleep, he left the mill sometime near midnight to visit our bed. I would waken to his crouching between my legs, startle awake as he pushed himself into me. Despite my loneliness and grief my body prayed a physical chant for another child: a child a child a child to the rhythm of my husband labouring above me.

By harvest time I knew I would have another chance. I was pregnant again. I would not be bullied into overexertion this time and I would not humour any superstitions or cockeyed beliefs. This time I would brook no interference. Daisy would have a brother or sister to help keep her alive for me.

I held my growing child in my womb with exquisite care, like an egg on an outstretched palm. I knew the Landrys out by the foundry had a daughter who was simple but who could work well enough at rough chores if you were patient enough and stern enough and had five dollars a month for her parents. So Myrtle came to milk and churn and scrub, to heft and carry, while I stirred my curd or boiled a pudding or sat with knitting. With Myrtle's hands at my disposal I set three squares a day on the table but did little else. In the afternoons I rested, in the evenings I retired early, in the mornings I lay in bed a little while. Ewan frowned and fidgeted but held his tongue and worked as though he could hide my laziness from God with his own sweat. Many nights he napped in the mill and did not come to the house at all except for breakfast.

At six months I asked to see the doctor. Mrs. Cunningham was the closest we had to a midwife and I had no intention of bearing her pokings and proddings and listening to her bitter tales, at least until the last possible instant. The doctor placed a tube on my belly and listened, frowned and listened again moving the tube here and there over the hummock of my womb. Two heartbeats, he said. Twins. My belly had barely swollen enough for one child and I could see the doubt in the doctor's eyes that accompanied the evidence of the second. Bed rest, he said. I'll have a word with your husband. Honey, he claimed, was an excellent anti-toxin, and milk excellent to encourage fetal growth. And liver and dandelion tea. Avoid chills and draughts. Beef broth is an aid to the blood, with a teaspoon of this powder mixed in. Bed rest, he repeated.

When I first felt the pains I knew it was too early. Seven months by my count. I held on to my little ones with all my might. But my might was like that of an industrious ant—impressive considering the size of the body but of little account beyond the anthill. I could not stop a force of nature. The pain was wrong, the doctor's voice far away, too much blood soaked the sheets. The struggle seemed to go on without me then to call me back with a ferocity that left me exhausted. Mumbling filled the corners, grave voices. Often I did not know who was in the room with me and then Abby would have my hand in hers and I would feel her determination flow into me. I would see these babies into this world.

My first son was named Ewan Laughlin MacLaughlin. I called him Hughie. I called him Hughie for the six and a half blessèd hours he lived between my breasts warmed by my body and stove-heated towels. I stroked his tiny head with my thumb and poured a lifetime's love into the weak little vessel. Ewan built a casket so tiny it would not have held a man's boot.

My second son was Alexander Isaac. Young Alex, a warrior from his first laboured breath, fought off the angel's outstretched hand for three weeks and five days. I lived on the scent of him for twenty-six days, on his blue feather skin, the delicate pulse at his temple, the pretty oh of his lips. I held him every moment I could. I held him as he drew his last rattled breath, waited for the next, waited and waited, coaxed and massaged and pleaded. Even then, as the heat seeped out of him, I held him tight through the night. In the morning I surrendered the tiny corpse. Myrtle was sent home. Ewan slumped on the cot in the room off the kitchen and wept unceasingly for his dead sons.

To me, Ewan spat out words like mouldy meat. "Now that's what comes of rest and servants and lounging around and doctors and vanity and everything fit for a queen." Rage turned his face vermilion and his eyes dark as damnation. All his body rose up before me. Perhaps he raised his hand to me, perhaps I only felt it raised because of the violence of his anger. Even buffered by my sea of grief I cringed before him, stiffened for the blow, closed my eyes but nothing happened. I waited in vain as I had for the next breath of my son. When I looked up Ewan had stepped back in silent defeat, his eyes dead cold. I could only bury my face and weep.

Two years passed. Once more a seed was planted in my womb but it washed away before the promise could even take shape. Ewan's drive to work reached ludicrous proportions. Summer and winter he travelled wherever he was called, designing and building mills, refurbishing old dusters, integrating improvements in established mills. By now he was gone more than he was home. Stories trickled back. Wherever he worked he left behind seeds of a legend. I heard it said he worked without sleep. It was said he would work all week without pause, tumble into a coma at exactly midnight on Saturday and be roused by the cockcrow on Monday morning. To "work like the Gunn Brook miller" was to work as though possessed. Nonsensical stories accompanied the probable and the exaggerated. It was said that he tossed handfuls of bread onto the millpond to assuage the gods. It was said that he could do mathematics in his sleep—that he could doze off with a sheet of figures before him and wake with perfect calculations done. His gruff, laconic manner was offered as proof of his unworldly gifts.

I was milking five cows now and making butter and cheese for sale, tending to the pigs and horses and hens as well as my growing flock of sheep. I had fleeces to wash and card. I had my house to keep, of course, and my garden with all the provisions to put up for the winter. And when Ewan left I had the added burden of the mill to run. He no longer arranged for a boy to work with me, not Angus MacCarron or anyone else. But once Ewan was out of sight I had no compunction about inviting Abby's boys to help out, or more to the point, to keep me company for a few hours a day. Frankie was a young man now and Peter so close to manhood he could feel it in his fingertips. Abby had had her seventh child but with Harriet now finished school Abby's load was lightened. She often wandered down to the mill with a pot of warm dinner or she sent Harriet over to the house to churn my butter. On Sundays I would make the trek to the churchyard to visit with my three children who lay under the stone Ewan had carved for them.

Slowly but steadily I plodded on. Another blow waited for me however. In the spring of '86 Abby and Frank, finally fed up with fighting the stones for soil, accepted Frank's brother's entreaty to join him in the West. The brother had settled his family onto promising farmland outside Winnipeg. There was land, opportunity, prospects for their growing family, a better life. Anyone could see that while Abby was sorry to leave she could barely contain her excitement for the adventure. She was a woman made for adventure. I did my best to wish my dearest (and if I were to be honest, my only) friend well. Abby was soon lost to frenzied preparations. When I sat with her on Sunday afternoons we struggled as valiantly as parting lovers—I strove to enter her optimism and she struggled to curb her buoyancy. She felt the loss too; I know she did. I believed her when she said our parting was by far the highest price she would pay for leaving Gunn Brook. As I lay alone in bed at night, numbed, I would count off the advantages of the move for her and Frank and especially for her children. What kind of a friend could expect to be considered above a woman's children?

The day Abby left I closed the mill and ran up to the road to see the family off as they passed. Abby jumped down from the wagon and ran to me. We shared a final rocking embrace through our tears before she turned and hiked up her skirts to trot after the wagon. She and Frank were both laughing as he reached down to haul her aboard without interrupting their progress. I watched until the wagon, laden with kids and trunks and baskets and carpetbags, disappeared around the bend. Then I watched the empty road.

My life slipped into lonely routine. The mill seemed to catch me, pick me up and carry me around my daily cycle of chores with the same inextricable force it laboured under itself. I seldom ventured beyond the property now. I had no interest in sewing circles or frolics or teas. I spoke to few people and even then, only as necessary to carry out my business. When I required kerosene or molasses or some other trifle I visited Nettle and would be startled to hear my own voice in halting conversation, sluggish from disuse, my wits dull and my speech plodding. Whenever I managed to venture as far as the Coach Road I would carry on a little farther to visit the churchyard. I passed my Sundays in the privacy of my parlour in accordance with Ewan's council, but certainly not because of it. For all intents and purposes Ewan visited spring and fall to cut firewood, sow grain and harvest grist, and to plant his own seed inside me, but he did not, in any real sense, live here. I had been abandoned to the mill.

The waterwheel was my heartbeat. Every morning I climbed out over the wooden sluice, often slick with wet, and lifted the gate to send the water forward over the resting wheel, weighing down first one bucket, then the next and the next. The weight of the water inched the wheel forward, creaking, until it shrugged, shuddered and rolled to life. I stood there, astride the sluice, the water rushing beneath my skirts. As the wheel found its rhythm it nudged the sluice with each rotation, pulsing its life up the soles of my feet, through my body. Beside me a wall of water rolled over the dam so close that when I stretched out my arm the spray settled on my sleeve darkening patches of brown wool, the mist enveloping my hand. Here above the rocky riverbed, between the desperately treed slopes of the steep banks, my only connection to the world was the throb and rumble of this mill-beast that surrounded me. Oats were dried, shelled, ground, buckwheat cracked and separated, wheat crushed to flour and sifted. Like the cogs, I drew my power from the imperative of movement, passed on only and exactly what I had been given.

IN THE WINTER OF 1889-90 I HAD BEEN MARRIED FOR FOURTEEN years. I was forty-four years old, had conceived four lives, birthed three babes and had no living children. I had a husband to whom I was less than a servant (because a servant at least can be dismissed if she proves inadequate). It had been six years since I heard the laughter of a child of mine, five since I felt the warmth of one at my breast. When Ewan was home he worked like a galley slave under the lash. I worked like the wheel, no beginning and no end, and always felt the sluggard. I listened to my husband praying for God's forgiveness for my indolent ways, promising my reformation, praying I be made worthy. Often I tried to call up my dead children to keep me company but it was such an effort and they did not stay long. The house was too cold and too quiet. What child would not be frightened off by the loneliness of the place?

One season dragged its load to the doorstep of the next, year followed upon year. I had once told Daisy a story about sailors lost in the horse latitudes. She had laughed at the name, horse latitudes, then cried at the story. A vessel freighted with horses for the West Indies was becalmed. No wind, no current, not a ripple in sea or sky. Day after day the ship sat motionless as the crew watched their water barrels empty, one by one. The captain cut their rations in half, then in half again. One by one the animals in the hold perished from lack of water. Each day the sailors would hoist new horse carcasses up to the deck and drop them into the sea. Sailors peered overboard as sharks swarmed to the meat. In desperation one day a sailor, mad with hopelessness and thirst, jumped overboard with the carcasses and was lost in a shout of red. That night a parched young sailor prayed and fell asleep on his watch and dreamt of a wonderful bird—body as small as a sparrow but gold and royal blue with a scarlet tail as long as a man's arm. The bird flew over and discovered the unlucky ship and taking the towline in her beak pulled the ship out of the doldrums. The sailor awoke from the dream to the flap of a sail, saw the seas parting at the bow of the ship and felt her begin to move through the water. He shouted to his shipmates. Overhead he spied a flash of colour then nothing. Had he dreamed the bird into existence?

It was on the cusp of 1890 that I dreamed my lovely bird. That day the air was heavy with the omen of weather to come. Both cold and cloudy, the wind was icy enough to bind the waterwheel's axle to immobility within an hour. When the ice locked up the wheel it had to be chipped clear, then the heat from the wheel's motion would carry it a while until ice gradually crept in and built up again.

I was hacking away at the ice for the second time that morning when I looked up at the squeak of a boot sole on snow and there on the dam stood a man regarding me like a curiosity in a travelling show.

"Missus," he called down, as though the word were a statement, a question and an answer all at once. "Missus." He set down his pack, climbed down the slope and took the axe from my hand. "That's no job for a lady, surely. I'll set this loose in no time."

I stood for a moment, uncertain.

"Let me have a go at it."

I relinquished the axe but held my thanks until I saw results without disaster. He appeared handy enough with the tool so I left him to it and returned to the mill out of the wind. Soon afterwards the wheel huffed into action. When I finished engaging the French stone I found him standing in the doorway, his mittened hands shoved into his armpits, laughing. "All clear, missus!" His cheeks glowed chilly pink and his eyes sparkled with an enthusiasm that transformed his vaguely horsy face into a handsome one.

"Come in out of the cold, at least." The surliness of my voice surprised and shamed me. In it I heard echoes of Nettle's cold suspicion, her hard greetings. When he proffered his hand I took it and prodded a thin smile onto my face.

"Horace Lacey, at your service, ma'am."

"Thank you, Mr. Lacey," and there I stood, conversation exhausted.

"Tell me though, missus, how a lady such as yourself comes to be mistress of all of this?" He spread his arms as though intimating an estate of a thousand acres. And when I peered over to search his face for irony, for censure or doubt or mockery I found only curiosity. He took in my curt explanation, stood quietly, his fingers running along the edge of the oat bin, looking at me then away into the soft gloom of the mill. He had eyes of the most astonishing blue. A young man of perhaps thirty-five years.

"And you? How do you happen to be tramping across my dam just ahead of a winter squall?"

"I was through here a few months ago, just as the leaves began to turn. With the railroad survey crew."

I nodded. Yes, a gang of surveyors had travelled through in the fall with their gear, their camp, their scrawny and determined-looking little cook. I hadn't seen any of the surveyors themselves as they were as busy with their work as I was with mine, but the cook had come knocking at the kitchen door once with a pony cart and a purse full of coins. He had an awful stutter and it was all I could do not to reach out and try to shake the stalled words from his mouth. I had sold the man a lamb, a pail of fresh milk, ten pounds of barley and a sack of flour and he had gone away contented.

The survey gang renewed local talk of the railroad, enormous possibilities, false promises, money to be made or lost, and grumblings about Upper Canadian politicians. The likelihood of a camp of men breeding bottles of rum was a notion much whispered about, and no doubt explored, by many of the local men. Mrs. MacCarron swore the strangers had stolen her best carrots and onions from her garden and complained loud and long that they'd stripped her apple trees. I'd be more inclined to believe she took the opportunity to ship a bushel or two of produce through Nettle and pocket a dollar or two that her husband didn't know about.

"Why did the railway people send you back? In mid-winter?"

"They didn't. I came on my own. To see this land again. How can there be a country so vast? How can there be so much in the world below heaven?" He lifted his arm above his head to touch the hemlock beam above him. "Such trees," he said. "How can there be so many trees?"

How could I answer this peculiar talk? "I must check my grind," I said. "Go down and warm your hands by the fire."

A few minutes later he appeared at the top of the stairs. "Do you like the rumble of it?"

"I beg your pardon?"

"The rumble of the gears and all. It comes right up through the soles of your boots. I was trying to figure how a body would feel about it after a while, day in and day out. Does it say hello to you in the morning? Or is it like some complaining old fool always moaning and groaning from the daybed?" He leaned against the stairs then, like an old man leaning in for support and put on a blocky old voice that plodded forth in a sing-song imitation of the mill's rhythm. "Bring me the jam pot. I don't like this cup. The weather's too sunny. Now make my bed up."

It was such a thing to see a person carry on just for the pleasure of it. My face contorted into a smile, muscles roused from sleep and pressed into service after such dormancy. How long had it been since I had laughed?

"How does the rumbling feel?" he pressed.

"Well, I don't know, Mr. Lacey. I can't say I take a great deal of time pondering how I feel about rumblings." When I looked up again he remained waiting patiently, expectant.

"I suppose that however I feel on any day, well, it simply makes me feel more so."

"And what would it be that you feel today?"

"Heavens, Mr. Lacey." There was nothing of the coarseness in his tone that normally accompanied a personal question from a man hanging around the mill. There was nothing that suggested more than the interest he showed in all his surroundings.

"Cold. Cold is what I feel today."

"Well I'd best get that teakettle up to the fire then."

He had just poured out a cup of tea for me when the spur began to drag again then stopped. He scurried off with the axe to hack away.

The blizzard came upon us as blizzards often do. The promise of snow can sit for hours in the air, as it had since that morning, then all of a sudden the world is engulfed. The growl of the mill buffered the sound of the rising gale at first and down on the meal floor we remained snug and unaware. When the spur caught and slowed again Mr. Lacey picked up the axe once more. When he opened the door a gust swirled in with a lash of sleet behind it. Icy pellets stung our faces before he forced the door shut again against the wind.

"I'd say we are done with our grinding for today," I said, and doused the kiln fire. "Come, Mr. Lacey. You'll need proper shelter. The Cunninghams are just half a mile down the road and into the woods a short piece. They're not the epitome of hospitality, but grudging shelter is better than none in weather like this."

But even at the top of the hill it was clear we had left it too long. A gust whipped snow around us in a blanket and I could see nothing but white. The mill completely disappeared although it sat only a hundred feet behind. I turned and blinked into the whiteout, ice clinging to my eyelashes, turned again and brittle fear gripped me. Three steps and already unsure of my direction. Then a glimpse of the trees by the road on the left. Straight ahead. I would not have been able to find Cunningham's laneway myself in this. Drifts built up in waves across the road, snow inches deep and then suddenly a foot or more. "Walk in my footsteps, Mr. Lacey. You'll have to come with me." I knew the situation was untenable of course. A woman alone taking in a man for the night. But there was no remedy. My whole life was the same: untenable yet unavoidable. I bent into the wind and started up the hill. A swirl would rise up and obliterate everything but then the storm would inhale and for a moment, shapes appeared, enough to re-establish bearings. There was daylight yet. My confidence returned. I spotted the maple tree by the porch, then the laneway, then the house. Finally the doorstep. We stamped our feet and brushed off what snow we could before entering the cold kitchen.

"I'll build up this fire in a jiffy, Mr. Lacey. And scare up some supper. I'll just fetch a few potatoes. And there's meat in the shed." I had no fresh bread or cakes to offer. Without Ewan to feed I lived like an old prospector, often spooning porridge or soup from a tin plate.

"Let me see if I can't coax a spark or two," he said, and took the poker from my hand. I scrambled down to the cellar, rooting through bins collecting an armload of vegetables, balancing potatoes and carrots, dropping a turnip trying to pick up an onion. By the time I re-emerged Mr. Lacey had the fire crackling away and I could hear him in the shed splitting more kindling. The sound of it cheered me. Splitting kindling is a job I detest. This most domestic of the men's chores reminded me, more than any other, how much I lived alone.

I would fetch up some apples and take advantage of my company to bake a pie.

Outside the blizzard mounted in savagery but its howls only seemed to make the kitchen cozier and more cut off from the world, a calm island in the chaos. Once Mr. Lacey had produced a tottering stack of kindling he set out for the stable despite my protestations. I was leery about my little Shorthorn's willingness to accept him.

"Mrs. MacLaughlin, there is not a cow in all of Christendom that can resist my wiles. If I can't bring you a brimming pail I promise I will throw myself upon the storm in penance."

How startling to hear banter, to see playfulness in a grown man. He brought me home my children in the kindest, warmest way. As I worked with my hands in flour I felt them near me, held close in sweet domesticity. I could have spoken their names aloud except for my fear of breaking the spell. But my heart relayed the messages—lay the table, Daisy, and fetch us some fresh butter from the pantry. Then a little boy's voice, Momma's made a pie. As clear as though it had been spoken, Hughie to Alex, as they filled the wood box two sticks at a time, their little arms embracing the chore. They would be six years old now and dreaming of great strength. Perhaps I would have little trousers to mend that evening—I fingered the cotton of my apron—buttons on little blue trousers with a pocket for treasures. I sprinkled a pinch of cinnamon over the sweetened apples and folded pastry over the top. Baking in the oven next to the supper, the aromas blended, transporting me. Abby touched my shoulder. We laughed together, her children intermingled with mine, laughing too. There was the stamp of boots outside the door, the latch, a puff of chill consumed by the stove's heat. A frothy pail of milk and a warm voice.

"We're well acquainted now and friendly as fleas," he said about the cow. He pulled three brown eggs out of his coat pocket and winked as I stretched out my hands to receive them. They were warm still, thanks to the broody hen with the torn comb. "Everyone's snug as Jesus in the manger out there—winter's singing them to sleep."

His presence did not shatter my reverie, merely lapped over it. I set bread for the morning while the meat roasted. Mr. Lacey laid the table. Over dinner we spoke while the storm spun around us like a cocoon. I learned what little I know about Horace Lacey.

An Irishman. A Roman, but large-minded. The wonder he drew from the world around him was not the wonder of the new immigrant to an unfamiliar world but more that of a pilgrim on a journey. His survey crew had finished their work two months ago and he was happy enough to be keeping his own company for a while.

"I left the rest of them snug and drunk in a pub at the end of the route and I dare hazard a guess there may be a few of them there yet," he said. "I wanted to come back once more before I move on. It's one thing to see a country in her summer green but I wanted to see her teeth as well. So I've been on the tramp. Not a great show of ambition for a man, I suppose. But it's a wondrous thing—a body could go days without seeing another soul if he had mind to. With the quiet of it and the vastness I get to feeling like the great thinkers and the great poets, how they must have felt, you know, before they bloomed into all those lovely words. The painters too, like Michelangelo and them—it's a feeling like you just swallowed God—everything empty and full at the same time."

I set down my fork to listen to him.

"But I sound foolish. You'll be wondering what you've taken in."

"Not at all. Now tell me the truth, have you hidden a notebook or two and a fistful of pencils at the bottom of that pack of yours? Have you sequestered a poem or two there?"

A blush of red crept up his neck. "You're a woman of uncanny sensibility, Mrs. MacLaughlin." For a moment we both sat listening to the blizzard, the warmth of the fire and the comfort of a hearty supper subsuming us.

"Now tell me how a fine woman like you passes these long winter nights. I've a hunch you have a little library tucked away somewhere."

Now it was my turn to blush, not because he had hit accurately upon a past joy of mine but in embarrassment that I had deserted my old friends so completely over the years. Gradually Ewan's judgements had chipped away at my old self until even though I had the house to myself I had not taken full advantage of my freedom. Ewan's constraints had settled into my bones in ways I had not even noticed.

"A modest one."

"Perhaps we can compare our resources."

"Certainly. But first, won't you have a slice of apple pie with your tea?"

"Delighted, Mrs. MacLaughlin."

"Please, call me Penelope."

After supper he pulled several books from his rucksack and I tugged open the glass door of the parlour bookcase, the hinges sticky from lack of use. We sat together in the kitchen lamplight while he read to me from Blake and Wordsworth and young Canadian poets I had never heard of before—how would I have heard of them? He finally consented to share a few lines of his own "jottings," as he described them. He surprised me with the richness of his images, the depth of feeling he displayed for the land he walked over. To hear feelings expressed at all set me off kilter, made me a little light-headed, a stranger in my own house.

Later, we read, turnabout, from my copy of *Pride and Prejudice*. Mr. Lacey presented the most brilliant and thoroughly convincing Mr. Bennet. And when we came to Mr. Darcy, I laughed until I cried at his portrayal of the character. I, or Miss Lizzy rather, declared I would never have him, not for ten thousand pounds and soon we had left Miss Austen behind and had transfigured her characters to our own backwoods heroes. While my girlish titters often disintegrated into helpless laughter Mr. Lacey never broke stride. He arched his eyebrow at me and flipped the tails of his imaginary coat.

I did not unearth the character of Lizzy Bennet so much as Horace Lacey unearthed a Penelope faded with neglect and disappointments. He called her up with a slow, kind incanting of her name. How long had it been since I had last heard my name spoken, and spoken with such gentle kindness? His kindness was my undoing. When the warmth of his hand touched my cheek he opened a longing, as deep as the earth itself, to share tender breath with another human being. Suddenly I did not feel old and ugly and clumsy. I did not feel like myself at all, yet at the same time felt more profoundly myself than I ever had.

Nearly fifteen years married and there were secrets I did not know.

Beneath the skin that is old and ill-used and ugly, beneath the plain face and too-wide shoulders, beneath layers of failure and inadequacy, there is another skin that shimmers to the touch. It opens through a thousand mouths, hungry as babies. Breath and fingertips and the softness of lips dance there as lightly as the wing beats of butterflies. Beneath the secret skin is a cavern that grasps at love so greedily it pulls it in until it bursts like a freshet and overflows, wave after wave over everything.

The blizzard lasted the night and all the next day. The following morning the sun rose over calm fields of perfect white, spotless and sparkling. No one moved except to shovel dooryards and paths, find the woodpile and the well. Then late in the morning I spied the old fellow who had taken over Browns' old farm prodding his unlucky horse through the drifts, breaking a trail. The old bugger was always first out, looking for an excuse to poke his nose in, gather fresh news. Instantly I flew into a tizzy of grabbing and stashing all evidence of Horace. Suddenly practical as a thief, I thrust Horace's rucksack at him and ordered him upstairs in a flurry.

"You be Jane and I shall be Mrs. Rochester!" he called, laughing over his shoulder as he mounted the stairs two at a time.

Once the old fellow had passed on the road, mercifully bypassing my door in favour of juicier news prospects elsewhere, Horace returned, laughing and shaking his head. I was not laughing, however. He came to me and held me and kissed my neck, rocked me in his arms. Tomorrow morning the roads would be full of people restless for outdoor air and company and news.

He was heading west, he said, trading what was left of his surveying wages for a train ticket. He meant to see the Rocky Mountains and the ocean on the other side of them. He meant to see San Francisco.

"I hope to write a poem about a storm," he said. "No, the opposite. About a calm? About the worlds we carry inside."

For a foolish hour I swirled around ridiculous notions of escape, of tromping over frozen streams on Indian rackets, leaving the beasts to their fates in the barn, I suppose. Leaving the graves of my children. Leaving the Mrs. MacLaughlin I had become behind like a shed skin while some imaginary Penelope-girl wandered like a gypsy and camped in the snow. But of course I knew the truth. If I hadn't I wouldn't have flown into panic at the sight of a neighbour. I knew, of course, that although Horace had not said so, he had no intention of packing a wife on his back, certainly not someone else's, and not a woman ten years his senior who had been no beauty even as a girl. This I knew but tucked it away in case I ever needed a rational ray to shine on my situation.

I packed as many provisions as it was convenient for him to carry: cheese, sausage, butter, bread and tea. Perhaps there was a final kiss and a lingering embrace as in books. I do not recall. What I remember is that the world gleamed still and white and he was gone.

I prepared a prayer, a litany, an incantation to keep him with me, to keep him with the young woman he had coaxed from her dim neglected corner. I listed all he was to me. His wonder, his playfulness, his simple eloquence, his strength and company and helpfulness. His hands, his handsome solidity, the blue of his eyes. His speech—the poetry of it, his profligate tumble of words for no practical purpose but to see further, probe deeper, laugh. His gentle kindness. In the evening I conjured him in my bed, in the daytime in the mill, in the mornings at the table. Often I placed him just beyond the door, around the corner, busy at some small task, just about to join me. My children were not afraid to come out when he was there.

And I would keep more than this. I knew almost at once that I was carrying a child. I was not afraid. I felt only a warm hopeful happiness, the lingering pleasure of a dream after waking. I did not think of Ewan at all. The woman who carried this child seemed a different woman altogether, one who had never heard the name Ewan MacLaughlin.

CHAPTER ELEVEN

ALTHOUGH HE NEVER ABANDONED HOPE, EWAN HAD GIVEN up monitoring the machinery of my aging body. My sags and swells went unnoticed. He had been home two weeks in April when the baby quickened. As I bent over the oven door to pull out the biscuits for supper I puffed out a surprised "oh!" and stiffened upright, clutching my womb in that unmistakable posture, belly forward with hands protective around new life. Instantly self-aware, I felt heat rise in my cheeks, smoothed my apron and resumed my work. When I dared a glance at Ewan I found him staring. He looked away, looked back, opened his mouth to speak then closed it and cocked his head. All these weeks, these three months and more past, and I had prepared nothing to say. As incredible as it sounds, it's true. Had I imagined the moment would never come that I would stand in front of my husband with a bulging belly? Did I imagine the child would be born secretly into some imaginary chapter of some imaginary novel and live in the bookcase? In all my imaginings of Horace Lacey, I had failed to imagine at all. The Horace I had kept with me for the last months dissolved into the delusion I had created for him. I stood alone here, carrying a child who would never know his father. The Rockies? San Francisco? Then what—the jungles of Brazil? Or had I imagined he would appear in a puff of smoke at this very instant and carry me off?

"That child's too small. It can't live."

I said nothing, thinking what? That perhaps Ewan would tire of the question? Everything in his world was counted and measured and calculated: demonstrably true, mathematically provable.

"How many weeks have you been carrying the seed?" he asked.

I would give birth to a child born eleven months from his leaving and six from his return. I turned away eyes lowered, then gathered my courage and turned back to face him. "Fourteen weeks," I said.

His eyes widened and his head pushed back as though trying to expand the distance between us. Not a word exchanged for what might have been the six days of creation. In the interminable silence the wall I had constructed between what I knew in my heart and what I knew in my head crumbled. It dissolved into nothing and there I stood, a stranger to myself in the face of the naked truth. My guilt, the shame it would bring to us, to the house and business, the magnitude of my sin, I saw reflected in my husband's face.

"That child..." Ewan indicated my womb with a flicker of his eye. He could not even incline his head towards me.

I could hardly believe, any more than Ewan could, the implications of the situation. I owned nothing that did not come to me on the condition of my being Ewan's wife. Without Ewan I was nothing but a disgraced woman with a bastard child. Not even a foolish girl who could be redeemed in time and perhaps forgiven in a purse-lipped sort of way, but an ugly old woman, once a schoolteacher, once a mistress of a prosperous farm and business: cast out with no shelter for my child or myself. Nausea rose through me, drenching me.

Eventually Ewan found his tongue.

"I turn my back and you are cavorting with the Devil."

"No ... a man." I could hardly believe my own inane sputtering.

"You are my *wife*. Before God."

I could scarcely find breath to fill my lungs.

"Who?" he demanded. "A customer of mine? In my own mill? Everyone has been laughing at me. Men have been laughing behind my back for years. Everyone knows. Or are people guessing the father's name? Placing bets?"

"No."

"For years?"

"No. I swear. This was the only time. In all the years of loneliness. There was only this once."

"Loneliness." He staggered back a step as though I had called up Satan's name. "Loneliness…?" He shook with the fury of humiliation. We were both so unaccustomed even to ordinary conversation that this interchange was unbearable. I made my way a few tottering steps to a chair and sat, afraid I would collapse.

"So help me God if you don't tell me the absolute truth right now, if you deceive me a second time…" He stopped and struggled for breath. "I swear that if you lie to me now and the truth is revealed later, as it will be—make no mistake—I will set you and your bastard on the road. Do you understand?"

I understood. We were trading truth for truth.

"Who is this man?"

"He's not from here. He has come and gone. No one knows him. No one saw him."

"Do you think I'm a fool? How can a man appear from nowhere and disappear? How? How!"

"The railroad. The new Short Line will be passing just north of here … you know this … you remember they surveyed the line last fall."

"So help me God…"

"I didn't see the surveyors then—only the cook. You know this is true—you were here at harvest and you remember. You know I sold the cook that lamb. And flour. But one of the surveyors came back in the winter, just to see the land in the snow and ice. Just to look…" The story sounded ridiculous now. "He was caught in the big New Year's storm. You know there was a storm. It was such a huge storm. You would have seen it too, even in New Brunswick. He came through, helped me at the mill. Storm stayed—for the two days of the blizzard and a day to dig out."

Silence.

"He was kind," I said.

"And so you were kind to him."

"Forgive me."

"In the eyes of God … you…" He closed his eyes and rocked back on his heels. His hands kept opening and closing as though gasping for air, as through grasping for tools.

"Forgive me."

Again the silence of judgement. It stole the air from the room.

"This man. This man surveyed for the Short Line in the fall?"

"Yes."

"He has a name?"

"Yes." A man living pristine on a shelf beside Jane Austen, free from selfishness, malicious motives, fault, blame. I was not trying to protect him (he was not here after all), rather I wanted to protect the memory of my past self that he evoked. But there was no doubt that if I had to provide his name to save my child's future, I would.

"If I wrote to the master surveyor in Oxford, if I wrote to say this man left his watch behind and where could I find him to return it, could he point to the name in his ledger book? Or is this a fiction thrown at a lame-fool husband to cover the tracks of a neighbour or a neighbour's son or some message boy sent out from town? Or what? Some passing peddler? Some gypsy? Some bible salesman?"

"The name is in the ledger," I whispered.

"Are you taking him his child? Will I come home in the fall to find my mill abandoned to the mice?"

"No." Was he prepared to keep me then?

"Maybe he has a wife? Maybe other children besides this cuckoo's egg?"

"No." I acknowledged to myself, now, how little I knew of him, how even the surveyor story I had taken at face value. Even the name. "I don't know."

"So you think you will live here with his child? Under the roof I built? While people laugh at me? A September child?"

"No one will ever know. Say you were home for the new year—arrived just as the storm began. That will work well enough. Say nothing at all. No one will ever question you. People know how you travel,

Ewan. You've passed through here between jobs before. Half the time I don't know where you are—how could anyone else guess? I'll say you came in with the snow, left at sun-up after the storm cleared."

We both needed a moment to absorb this plan dropped on the floor between us, messy and pitiful, like a stillborn calf. It embarrassed me to see how naturally, how apparently effortlessly, I could craft such a deceit. This facility was evident enough to Ewan as well. Silently he stepped towards the door. But I couldn't have him leave without giving some sort of answer.

"I beg your forgiveness. You'll never have cause to doubt me again. I promise."

He turned in anger. "You promised that long ago in the presence of God. What became of that promise?"

I had so little to offer in exchange for mercy. "All of our children have been taken. Perhaps the child won't live to see the world."

"I will not have this man's name spoken. Ever. You will write it down and give it to me. I will read it and burn it. It is my surety against future treachery. Never forget that I can test your story at any time. Do this now."

Although my legs trembled they carried me to my desk in the parlour. I willed my hand steady enough to form the letters legibly. I felt like Judas but unsure of exactly who I was betraying. My fear swelled with my uncertainly. Was this a trap? I could not think beyond my instructions so I followed them. When I returned to the kitchen Ewan did exactly as he had promised. He read the name and fed the slip of paper to the fire, stood there with the lid to the firebox open and watched it burn. I waited for him to speak.

"I visited on the new year. I came overland from the south, stayed only a short time, only the two days of the big storm. Then I set off to the west."

"Yes."

Ewan did not raise his voice or a hand to me that day, but I had never laid axe to ice as bitter cold as the words he tossed at my feet. "If a different truth is ever known. If anyone ever sneers at me for a cuckold—ever—I will find a lawyer and get rid of you. Do you understand?"

"Yes."

"It is my right under the law."

"Yes, I understand."

"We'll see what comes of this in September. We shall see what the harvest brings." He turned on his heel and left.

Ewan could not have been better placed to turn me out and marry a young woman who could bear him a son. This truth tumbled over me endlessly. Whenever I scrambled to regain some semblance of normalcy or composure, some confidence in my position, this immutable fact washed over me again.

However, fretting or no fretting, life continued. I carried my butter, eggs and cheese to Nettle as usual and stood outside her door with my basket. I noted how her cabin had suffered the ravages of time. Rot advanced along the lowest boards of the shack. I could have kicked my foot through in a few places, I'm sure. Where a pane of glass had been broken she had covered the hole with a scrap of canvas. The door had to be jimmied and fought with and even so it left a crack big enough for a June bug to crawl through. The roof, a jumble of make-do, could not possibly have been tight. She bundled a hodgepodge of clothes onto her body like a tramp and more of the same around the cask of beer she kept brewing in the corner until the two of them were nearly indistinguishable in the gloom. It was clear the cask was not only to keep her custom brisk but to dull her own desperation. The beer on her breath mixed with the horrid odour of teeth as rotten as the boards. She took my basket and handed me the sugar and the tea I had ordered. She sought my gaze and held it long and hard, constricting my windpipe. Then her eyes drifted down my body, stalled on my womb and I felt myself colour. I made my exchange of goods, nearly grabbing my tea from her hand, and I fled.

Ewan did not set me out. He never again referred to the child's father. In fact, a sense of calm or perhaps resignation seemed to have settled over him. He seldom worked through the night anymore. He still worked away for the greater half of the year and when at home he still worked hard and long, but he retired after dark like his neighbours. He still knelt at his bedside every night and asked the Lord to forgive his wife. He asked for mercy. "And forgive us our trespasses," he prayed, "as we forgive those who trespass against us." With the exception of his prayers he never again alluded to the wayward conception.

My pregnancy progressed with relative ease. I did not lose my child to early pains or incompetence or inadequacy or indolence or overwork or sin or virtue. She was born on the last day of September 1890. I called her Charity. Ewan looked down at her with an even gaze as though he were judging a calf or foal, then looked back at me and asked when I would be out of bed and back to work.

Ewan seldom acknowledged her except when she would burst forth in some high-spirited excess in his presence. "Stop up that noise," he might say to me as though a kettle were whistling. What might have looked cold from the outside I understood at the time as charity, generosity even, and this was an overwhelming relief to me. I took great pains to keep her out of his way, to minimize her childish noise or any disruption she might cause. I set her chewing on honey or molasses bread when Ewan came in for his dinner. As she grew I scolded and bribed and cajoled her into restraining her energetic behaviour during those few hours of the day when Ewan occupied the house. Sit quiet now with the jam pot while Father has his breakfast. Off you go while Father has his supper. Off and take Dolly upstairs for a nap or I'll give her to the gypsies. Hush now and don't fidget and we'll visit the new kittens when Father goes back to work. He imposed strictures, yes. He did not want her running all over the countryside, he said. There was no need for us to be flouncing off to church, and of course Scotch River village remained out of bounds. But I had circumscribed my own movements so tightly in the past years this was hardly an imposition when she was so young.

Still, Charity was not an easy child to contain. She was a clever girl but high strung, adventurous but moody. She lived close to the surface as though her feelings were pushed up right under her skin and could at any moment bubble over. The yellow in a buttercup or a snowflake on her tongue brought tears to her eyes, a fallen robin's nest devastated her, and at the sight of a newborn calf she would run to hug its neck and bounce with joy, unable to let go.

On the day Ewan declared that Charity would not go to school I was more startled by the fact of his intervention than the content of it. "You are a teacher," he said, "so teach." It seemed small penance to have her barred from school. Not even a penance. I had never been farther than the barn without her and our separation would have wrenched us both. And anyway, the trek to the schoolhouse would have been onerous for a small girl so used to staying home. She'd never miss what she'd never known. I pried open my crate of schoolbooks, wiped off the volumes, felt the soft crack of their spines in my hands, a flutter of lightness in my heart.

OUR LIVES, CHARITY'S AND MINE, BREATHED IN AND OUT AROUND the seasons. The summer and winter were ours. With Ewan safely gone I took possession of our lives. True that in the winter I traded my worry over her disturbing Ewan to suffering the terrors of keeping her in that snarling mill. I often imagined Ewan repeating his promise to me, word by icy word—"as long as you carry or care for a child of mine..." I kept one eye and one ear on my grind, one eye and one ear always on my little girl. Charity despised the mill, afraid of its dark corners and looming shadows, terrified that she would be grabbed and yanked into the hungry teeth of the gears as she knew her long-ago sister had been. Certainly my stories had had the desired effect there. While I milled she would sit at the mill desk or draw up a stool to the kiln fire with her books and her dolly.

Quite without my notice my milling expertise had grown; I developed confidence in my judgement. I learned to manage multiple stones and the kiln with ease. I became practised at cooking at the kiln hearth and as Charity grew I had her to fetch and carry between the kitchen and the mill. She was always happy for the diversion of errands. All in all we managed the work tolerably well.

During the long winter evenings, once I'd shut down the mill, we spread our books out across the kitchen table and explored the world beyond. I squandered my egg and cheese and butter money on paints and inks and stacks of copybooks, enough to spoil a family of children. Storybooks filled the shelf in her room. She learned to read in a trice, it seemed, and before she turned ten her penmanship put shame to mine. She sang and danced and drew and could entertain us both for hours reciting poetry or presenting plays, wrapped in a shawl as Helen of Troy, then in battle dress as Brutus and Cassius both, then in frills as a spring daffodil. She conscripted her little dog into various roles, all of which required costumes and fawning. I wiped away tears of laughter as she carried on, which only encouraged her to greater heights of drama. She delighted in history and literature as long as she could learn about people or animals or living things. She would not attend to mathematics lessons and it was all I could do to foist basic arithmetic on her. Beyond stories about the natural world she would have nothing to do with the sciences.

"I do not care for parts of things," she declared in her romantic heroine voice. "Gears and rock and two thirds of a dozen—what of it!" And she would twirl away and pout. Her progress in sewing, food preservation and housekeeping left much to be desired.

In the summers I pushed the boundaries back farther, took more liberties. The days stretched and the sun warmed, the river ran shallow and the pond dropped. Water slowed until only a trickle found its way over the dam and the wheel rested. Free of the mill, we were turned out into the fresh green world like colts on a spring pasture. Often Charity and I would wander down the road hand in hand to attend church on a Sunday so she could meet other children. Although I curtailed her visiting, I did not outright forbid it. There were three or four farmhouses down on the Scotch River road where she struck up friendships with other girls. I never disobeyed Ewan's dictum against buying or selling in Scotch River but occasionally in the summer we visited the village for an outing and ate a picnic lunch by the water. I dreamed up all sorts of little adventures for us including long walks along the railway tracks, along the very path her secret father had helped survey. We ate strawberries, then raspberries and blueberries, then blackberries with thick fresh cream. I boiled jam and strained jellies. I pickled cucumbers and dried herbs and tomatoes. I filled my lovely new Mason jars with beans and peas and cherries and pears. I skimmed pound after pound of sweet cream from the abundant milk of summer pasture and churned it to butter. Once a week I heated curd and pressed a cheese. We were busy, yes, but the days stretched out in the sunshine. My daughter played and laughed and we lived free and happy. I indulged her with toys and clothes and attention. In light of what was to come I thank the fates I allowed her these joyous days of childhood.

ONE EARLY SPRING DAY BEFORE EWAN HAD RETURNED FROM HIS winter jobs, Charity and I visited Nettle to pick up and order supplies. Nettle hooked her crooked eye into me then let her gaze fall on Charity where rested it until I stepped between them to break the spell. Nettle tucked a newspaper into my basket with my order of calico, buttons and raisins.

"You're a clever reader lady, ain't ya? I come by this paper here you'll like—and only a penny. It'll start your fire once you're done. I saved it special."

Newspapers were not uncommon on Nettle's counter, short stacks of them heading up or down the road. Occasionally I would take a copy she was trying to peddle. I smiled the best I could, nodded, and handed over the extra penny she was after.

Later that evening with the mill closed and supper over and Charity busy with her books, I opened the newspaper for a peek at the wider world. On the back pages my eye was drawn to an obituary marked with the sooty smear of a thumbprint:

> *Feb. 23, 1899-Mr. Horace Lacey- DIED age 46 in San Francisco. Mr. Lacey, a native of Limerick, Ireland, spent many years in the Maritimes before embarking on a journey to the west. He met with a terrible accident when a team of horses bolted on the crowded streets of San Francisco.*

My hands shook as I read the notice. If some small storybook part of me had imagined ... imagined what? I couldn't say. If he had come from nowhere once perhaps he could materialize again? In another storm? For another chapter in the story—he plays with his daughter, makes love to her mother? I peered over the paper at Charity, her eyes lively with concentration over her book, her father's name in ink by my hand. The notice confirmed his name, at least, and a few details he had told me. I had not constructed him. He lived in this world and he died in this world. Like it or not, I had shared him with the world.

More real to me, I'm ashamed to admit, was the sinister implication of Nettle's leading me to the notice. She could not know? Of course she could not. And yet, could her selling me this very paper be a coincidence? The dirty smudge beside the note? Of course it was coincidence—she had peddled newspapers to me before. This time was no different. Who was Nettle to me anyway and what business was it of hers? I would not be cowed. "…if a different truth is ever known I will set you and your bastard on the road." My obvious course was to do nothing, say nothing, admit nothing. Guilt or innocence aside, I would simply act as though I had never seen the notice at all. Why would I have seen it? I ripped it out and tossed it in the fire. Instantly the guilty hole in the page grinned up at me. I balled up the page and tossed it in after the notice. Then the newspaper itself, with the missing page, taunted me and found the same fate.

Every year as spring approached Charity and I took up our guard. We moved the bulk of Charity's playthings upstairs to her room, took her drawings down from the walls, stashed away her dress-up scarves and ribbons. Her pen and ink and a single primer and copybook were tucked neatly out of sight on her shelf in the pantry and her doll sat politely atop them. With Ewan's return imminent I became aware of everything left out of place, every chore left incomplete, every imperfection. And I would resolve anew to inspire practicality in Charity.

One mid-April evening as the light thickened to murky, as Charity read aloud, performing some new adventure for me, as I prepared our supper, the dog sat up in his nest by the stove and cocked his head. We quieted and strained our ears into the silence around us. Charity ran to the parlour window where she could see across the yard and out to the road. "It's him!" The slap of hastily shut and stowed books, the clatter of hurried supper preparations signalled to both of us that one season had ended and another begun. I grabbed Charity's coat from the peg behind the stove. "Quick, quick," waving it at her like a matador. "Get your father's horse. And make sure it has oats and water and hay. And tie a blanket on it. Don't forget the blanket!" She ran out into the water-heavy snow of spring, her coat flapping. I watched them from the window, riveted, could not turn away: the girl runs towards the man in the laneway then slows suddenly, approaches with caution, holds out her hands to take the horse's reins while the man unties bundles from behind the saddle. The man hoists the burden to his shoulder and strides towards the house with the deliberate steps of one who has been too many hours in the saddle. The girl leads the horse into the stable.

The door to the entry banged then the kitchen door opened. Ewan pulled the door snug behind him, set his bundles on the bench by the door and removed his outdoor clothes. He was warmly and sensibly dressed as always. He was never a man who needed a wife to clothe him. Then he lowered himself onto his chair at the kitchen table. I had not considered this chair to be anyone's or anything in particular for the past four and a half months but as he sat down it became his chair again as it always had been.

"Ewan," I said. "I'll fetch your tea."

And so all our winters ended and our springs began. At first light the following morning Ewan strode down the hill towards the mill. In the house he carried himself as though he were a familiar guest. Yet in any legal way of thinking Charity and I lived on his forbearance. In the mill his foot fell heavy. He thrust open the door as though not a soul had trod there since he last closed it behind him four or five months ago. He simply took up his work as though he had left it yesterday. His first job was to dress the stones and so he strode directly to the French buhr. He pried the vat, the wooden housing that enclosed the stones, up with a lever and rolled it out of the way exposing the naked stones. He swung the wooden gallows into position above the stone and before I knew it the runner stone was lifted off its mate, both stones lying pattern-side up waiting for his chisels. Unaccountably, my heart lurched as Ewan manhandled his way through the mill. I had no claim on it. I certainly did not love it or want it. It was not my place. And yet something flinched inside me, a jolt as violent as it was mysterious, when he reclaimed his domain.

He spread his bills and picks and quill stick across the floor in preparation. When he looked up his eyes fell on me as though I had only that moment come into being.

"What?" he said.

If it was a question I had no answer. I bowed my head and darted down the stairs to gather up the kettle and tea and all the accoutrements of home that I had cluttered around the kiln hearth. When I emerged again he was hunched over his stone, intent, the bill in his hand tap-tapping with a strong, steady rhythm. He seemed a part of the stone. He would dress his stones one at a time progressing from runner stone to bed stone, from French buhr, to the granites, to the fodder stone, to the shelling stone, by daylight and then by lamplight. As he finished each one he set them back together, balancing the runner stone in perfect harmony with its mate. If a stone is inexpertly balanced, if it lies a hair off plumb, the stone wears unevenly, scraping away at the grooves with each rotation. The longer the trouble is left untended the worse it gets until finally the entire stone needs be ground flat and clear and new patterns etched into it. I had never seen evidence of such neglect of course, but Ewan had seen examples. He had been witness to this unconscionable moral blight at other men's mills.

When he finished dressing his stones he cut firewood until the frost was gone from the ground. He had fencing to mend then, and spring planting, and the first crop of hay to be made before he could leave again. And he milled through it all. He set himself to his tasks, burrowing through them with the determination of a weasel, stopping only to eat three times a day. Daily I sent Charity to the fields or the woods or the mill with his dinner. "Put a breeze behind you," I called after her constantly. "Don't be caught idling where your father can see you." When the last load of hay was forked into the mow Ewan left as suddenly as he arrived. And we exhaled.

THEN THE RIVER SWELLED WITH FALL RAIN, FILLED THE POND AND the thunder returned to the waterfall over the dam. Mowers and reapers and wagons were hitched to teams throughout the county calling Ewan home once more. Ewan harvested his crops and cut the firewood for the house and kiln. He ground the fall harvest day and night, rain or shine. By mid-November the first rush of grinding was complete and custom slowed to a steady, manageable flow. He dressed his stones for the winter season and then he was gone until spring when the cycle began again.

CHARITY GREW TO BE SUCH A HANDSOME GIRL, TALL AND SHAPELY with glossy hair that she brushed out into long tresses at night. One fall evening with Ewan freshly back from refurbishing a mill in Digby County, Charity wandered through the kitchen as I was trying to get Ewan's supper on the table.

"Set a cup of tea before your father! Do you want him wasting his good daylight while you lounge around like a groundhog on a warm rock?" My voice was sharp with the change of seasonal routine and it rattled her. She scurried to the teapot but then dropped his overfull mug, sent it crashing to the floor spewing hot tea in all directions and shards of mug with it. I stepped in to prevent any rising drama.

"Never mind. That old cup was worn thin and ready to crack. I'll tend to this. You fetch your father a fresh cup."

Ewan watched the little scene impassively but throughout his supper he continued to follow her with his eyes, watching her over his plate.

Before he returned to the mill he paused at the kitchen door. "How old is the girl?"

"Fourteen," I said.

"Aye, fourteen," he nodded.

CHAPTER TWELVE

In the summer of 1905 I received a letter from my husband. This had become so unusual I tried not to be alarmed. *Dear wife*, it read in Ewan's precise hand. *I have engaged an apprentice. He will be coming home with me. Set up a room for him. When I return home I intend to stay, attend to my mill, and teach my apprentice for as long as the Lord sees fit to spare me. Your husband, Ewan MacLaughlin.*

I stared at the letter. Ewan had always spurned the idea of an apprentice, turning away any fathers brave enough to approach him on behalf of their growing sons. Despite the twinges and aches that spoke to me on rainy mornings I had never considered that Ewan might feel his own advancing age. I would need a while to consider what his constant presence would mean for Charity. To cap her spirit and hold her to her chores for a few hours a day for half the year was trial enough. Maybe I should look for a position of some sort for her. In town, perhaps. But I couldn't imagine it; we had not been separated for more than a few hours at a stretch since her birth. Besides, she was too young, not yet fifteen.

As the days passed I found my thoughts no clearer. I told Charity precisely what Ewan had told me in the letter and said no more about it except that she would need to look smart and pay more attention to her work.

EWAN AND THE NEW APPRENTICE ARRIVED ON A DIMMING EVENING IN late August, weeks before I expected him. I had locked up the mill only half an hour earlier and had just built up a fire to warm the soup for supper. Ewan came into view first and swung down off his horse. Charity yelped and spun into a tizzy, whipping around the kitchen in a whirlwind, gathering up the flotsam of her varied dramatic lives. I watched, motionless, as a second horse dragged up the lane; a slender straw-haired figure perched like a nervous chipmunk on its back. Ewan stepped forward and took the reins of the second horse. The boy grasped the saddle horn, kicked his feet out of the stirrups, and shifted his weight until he began to slide off the saddle, his legs buckling when they hit solid ground so that he tottered backwards into his mount. The horse skittered and the boy caught himself and struggled to straighten.

"Run and get those horses. Your father will have had them spent miles ago. Hand me those ridiculous sashes. I'll put them in the fire where they ought to have gone years ago."

She gaped.

"And close your mouth. The horses will mistake it for the oat bin."

Laughlin Wainwright was the boy's name. From Saint John town. "Set your bag in there," I told him, indicating the room off the kitchen.

"He'll sleep upstairs," Ewan said.

Although the boy's table manners were rather rough and ready he washed well before sitting in to his supper and spoke passably well when addressed, but he was bone weary: too sore to sit and too tired to stand. His jaw had made some fleeting acquaintance with a razor, I guessed, and his chest had begun to broaden. Vestiges of boyhood innocence flitted across his face as he took in his new surroundings. There was no doubting he was a handsome lad, but something in the shape of his face made me want to turn away.

Charity, enthralled by the idea of a visitor, sat daintily as though in the court of the Queen and engaged in what she imagined to be pleasant conversation with a gentleman as though this were one of her games.

"That's a noble mount you have there, I couldn't help but notice the sheen on his coat. And such a beautiful roan. I do so love a roan."

"Mr. MacLaughlin got me that horse in Digby. His name's Teddy. We rode the whole way."

I struggled to stifle my amazement. "Get up and make the tea, Charity."

Once Ewan closed our bedroom door that night he stood stiff and still, his legs apart, arms crossed over his chest, staring at me until I felt self-conscious as I changed into my nightdress. "What does my wife think of my new apprentice?"

The question took me aback. When had he ever asked my opinion?

"I don't know what to think," I said. "After all this time, and with so many able local boys, you bring a lad from so far away. Is it true you bought him that horse for his own? His people ought to have provided the horse, surely, if they imagined he needed one."

"So you want to criticize the way I run my affairs?"

"You asked what I thought. I'm telling you."

His eyes glinted cold. A leer, the essence of an aborted smile perhaps, passed over his face like a shadow over the moon—there then gone. A shiver ran through me and I turned away to brush out my hair, but I could feel his eyes on me. For the first time in my memory Ewan climbed into bed and slept without kneeling to say his prayers.

When I awoke the next morning he was stretched out beside me, his hands behind his head, staring at the ceiling with a calm I had seldom seen grace his features.

"Best leave the boy to sleep this morning. You get the fire going."

IN THE FOLLOWING WEEKS WE CAME TO SEE WHAT YOUNG LAUGHLIN Wainwright was made of. His mother ran a boarding house in Saint John, he said. His father had been grievously injured in an accident at the shipyard and had suffered a great deal before his death ten years ago, he told us over supper.

"There's no point in all this chatter," Ewan interrupted and stared the boy into silence. "There's no talk at the table here."

It was apparent that the boy was accustomed to entertaining company. Easy-going, with a wittingly disarming smile and an all-too-ready wink, he was handy with a story and sang in a honey-smooth tenor voice, which delighted Charity. Ewan had him tending the kiln fire, hauling bags of grist and flour, inspecting and adjusting belts. Ewan had bought a new stone and supposedly was teaching the boy the art of dressing it. We were a long way from seeing Laughlin's mettle there. In the evenings after supper Ewan seldom returned to work in the dark anymore. Any unfinished custom he simply left for the next day rather than light the lamps. Instead he hauled out his old drawings of the mill and spread them over the kitchen table. I had not clapped eyes on the drawings since the mill's construction and did not even know he had kept them. He called the boy to him. Laughlin sat at Ewan's elbow as Ewan pointed here and there at the drawings and spilled out a lifetime's knowledge. I peeked up from my mending and watched the boy feign attention. If Ewan had ever thought to stop his lectures and ask the boy a question or elicit a comment he might have discovered the boy's indifference. But Ewan would never think to do such a thing. Disinterest in the mill would never have occurred to him.

Charity, for the moment, was enthralled with her game of entertaining a "visitor" and the boy was equally taken with the idea of being one. She laughed without restraint whenever Laughlin offered some foolish antic or story. In no time at all she was singing the songs that Laughlin had brought. I grew uneasy at how comfortable he had made himself. He spoke to Charity about the mill as though he were a master miller already and claimed there was very little to it, at least for one as apt as himself. I found my tone with him grew curt and then stern. He answered me with an attitude barely this side of saucy.

One night after supper when it was too dark to work, Ewan sent the boy down to the mill. "Fetch my chisels and my bill." Then minutes later to Charity, "Run after him and tell him not the bill but the whetstone. Bring only the chisels and the whetstone." Then he seemed to forget about both of them, focus his gaze on the angles formed by the corners of the room and wander off in his mind. Meanwhile Charity and the boy were gone long enough to chisel a millstone from a cliff face but Ewan had no comment to make on that.

The boy had not been with us six weeks when he found a supply of rum who knows where and stumbled in grinning and stinking and leaving his horse untended in the yard. Ewan's face blackened. He opened his mouth to speak but then did not but rather pushed the boy towards the stairs and then, as it seemed to be necessary, up the stairs. He returned after a short while and resumed his seat.

"Tend that boy's horse," he said to Charity without looking at her. In response to no comment from anyone, he said, "There is nothing wrong with that boy but youthfulness."

ONE NIGHT WHEN I HAD PRESSED MY CHEESE AND MARCHED CHARITY off to the parlour with her lessons, away from distracting eyes, Ewan began lecturing over his drawings. The boy sat by him in his posture of engrossment. I began mixing my bread and was trying to distract myself by calculating the price I could expect to get for my fall cheeses. Perhaps Ewan's voice had faltered; I don't know what pricked up my ears.

"The ratio of head stone to power train is running to the crucial down fall…" I swung around to stare. Spouting gibberish. There were no other words for it. Never in my life had I known Ewan to use false information, never mind nonsense. A joke? Not Ewan. A trap? No, he was far too direct a man. I lifted my head, stared at him. Ewan was an old man! The truth of it hit me all at once. His hair had thinned to wisps and his scalp showed through, papery and vulnerable. His shirt hung loosely off his shoulders as his skin hung off his cheekbones. He favoured his left arm as though his right had been weakened or injured. I watched his eyebrow dip in momentary confusion like he had wandered off and just this instant found himself back in familiar surroundings. Then he shut his mouth as though his chin were hinged. So extraordinary was the movement I wondered if I had heard the jaw clapping shut. The boy looked up at him and nodded as though instead of a jumble of meaningless words Ewan had just answered the very question he had been puzzling over. Of course, the boy had never listened to a word in the first place so how could he tell gobbledygook from elementary hydraulics? Ewan rolled up his drawings with too much intent. "That is sufficient for tonight," he said.

A STRANGE AND PERVASIVE FEAR CREPT OVER ME. Charity flitted past before the butter was churned in the morning. She pulled a shawl around her shoulders leaving her coat on the peg by the door and declared, "What little rest I find for my poor wretched heart I find upon the moors."

The moors indeed! I drew my daughter away, pinched her arm until she squealed. "You are in danger of becoming too familiar with an apprentice boy. Too familiar!" The sound of my voice slapping such orders in front of her astounded me as much as it did her. "I forbid it!"

I felt her defying me, and when I corrected her, felt her smirk behind my back, more and more in league with the boy whom I now hated. I warned her well and often to mind herself. I called out the danger but she would not hear me. Such is the way with the young. They see what is in front of their eyes at any moment. To them everything is what it seems; the world is an easy place to know.

Then suddenly she did not smile. One morning she dawdled by the door with the milk pail in her hand. Not that this in itself was unusual but when I looked up her eyes were ringed in darkness and she had pulled her coat in tight around her. She had angered me already that morning and impatient, I barked at her, "What, I suppose the cows bite now, do they? Move along for heaven's sake!"

The boy came down the stairs soon afterwards and set off to tend the horses.

BY NOVEMBER IT WAS CLEAR THAT CHARITY WAS CARRYING A CHILD. No doubt there had been some game, some fantasy that started the play. The young are easy to fool—so easy they can't help but fool themselves. That boy had nothing to lose and all to gain and once he grasped the trophy he knew he had grasped everything. She had lost all she had.

My head and heart tumbled over each other like two cats in a fight. But when I clutched Ewan's arm and tugged him into the privacy of the woodshed to tell him the news he smiled a slow languorous smile that had been years in preparation. The muscles around his eyes and forehead relaxed and his face brightened to such a degree I could hardly recognize him, as though all his cares had been lifted. I could not understand him and shook his forearms with vehemence, repeating myself, afraid the shock had addled his brain.

"Yes," he said. "They will marry now. They will live here and the boy will have the mill, and his sons after him."

"But your mill? To a prentice boy who is nobody and a daughter who is not…"

"Yes. And who would question it—my mill handed to my own daughter's husband? Would you dare question it?" He turned his head towards the window, smiling.

Dumbfounded, I gaped at him unable to know what I must know. Why had he brought home this unremarkable boy, pandered to him, blinded himself to his faults and handed his entire legacy over to him? Finally, the scales fell from my eyes. I felt like Eve in the garden finding herself face to face with the serpent. Lining the words up to speak them was like hefting cut stones onto a foundation wall—each word so heavy, so dense, it left me breathless with exertion.

"That boy. That Laughlin. MacLaughlin. Of course. That MacLaughlin is your son."

He met my eyes and held the gaze for a moment. He did not turn away in shame but in pride. I felt like a slow and stupid child. I shrunk in shame until outrage stepped up to rescue me.

"Your son was already born! That spring you returned and found me carrying a child. I threw myself and my unborn child on your mercy. I listened to your pompous talk and begged your forgiveness while you had just returned from the birth of your own bastard son! You had seen him, held him, named him, saw him suckling at the breast of some hapless woman!"

He paid me no heed.

"The day my Charity was born you knew what use to make of her. Of course you suffered her under your roof! You had already written her fate. You fattened her like a hog for slaughter!"

He cleared his throat. "The Lord works in mysterious ways."

"The Lord…!"

Granddaughter. I would have killed him right there if I had had a weapon at hand. Then what would have become of you? The story would have gone untold, ended there with a wild old woman hanged for murder. Perhaps you would never have been born. But I was left to carry my fury as best I could. What else could I do? I could not even pray. Perhaps it is God that grows the grain; I leave this to you to ponder. But it is man who determines which kernels will be planted as seed and which will be hauled to the mill for grist.

CHAPTER THIRTEEN

EWAN

ALL EWAN'S CHILDREN WERE DEAD. First the death of young Daisy when he was working in King's Cove. That job was a beautiful puzzle, complicated by twin shafts and a head of water just barely adequate to power them. The site had not been well chosen in the first place but the constraints of geography sharpened the challenge. He extended the flume and built up the dam, redesigned the power train and added a labour-saving cup elevator. He had just begun fitting a new shaft the day the letter arrived. They had all been called up to dinner and Ewan was stewing over the order due from the smith. He remembered drawing a knife full of butter across his potatoes—six gudgeons, hackle screws, bridging box. When the miller's wife set the envelope with his name on it by his plate he assumed there must be some bother with the order. Ewan's forehead creased. Was the world populated only by idiots? The order was perfectly straightforward. Would he have to go himself and fashion the ironwork? Ewan cut several bites of beef. He piled a bit of potato on each forkful before eating it, already impatient to be back at work. He licked his knife and slid it under the envelope flap. The letter was edged in black and written in a woman's hand. A death at the foundry interfered with them filling his bill? *To my husband,*

Ewan MacLaughlin—. Husband. The letter was addressed in error. Someone else's husband. No, it had his name on it. What was *his* wife doing at the foundry in King's Cove? Ever so slowly Ewan's mind climbed out of his project, gathered one by one abandoned truths about the world beyond this job. The woman's hand was his wife's, attending to business at his Gunn Brook mill. Why was she bothering him? His wife should be able to mind affairs without disturbing his work here. *To my husband, Ewan MacLaughlin*—. He reread the note several times until the information sifted from the paper to settle on his heart. The wee girl. The bevel gear. Angels. He set down his fork and refolded the letter, flattening the crease with his thumbnail. He folded it in half again and then once more before he pushed his plate away, stood and crossed to the stove where he dropped the tiny bundle into the flame. All eyes followed his steady, even strides towards the door. Missus jumped to her feet at the bang of the screen door. She dashed to the firebox, jabbing frantically with the poker for the knot of paper, trying to retrieve it, but it disintegrated into feathery wisps at a touch. At the mill, Ewan took up his task just as he had left it before dinner. For three days and two nights he worked without pause and without a word of explanation. He would not stop to eat or sleep although he took a mug of tea or drank from a dipper of water when it was handed to him. He worked until exhaustion collided with the Sabbath whereupon he slept from Saturday midnight through to first light on Monday morning. The child was dead and buried. For four more weeks he worked like a madman, afraid to loosen his grip on his tools. When the job was complete what could he do but to pack up and head for home?

 As Ewan followed the road up along the Gunn Brook he met no one. His mill sat closed up and silent. No one met Ewan in the yard. The kitchen sat warm and still. The little broom he had made for her propped in the corner by the pantry, her little boots by the door. He did not know what to do. He did not know what was true. God had set a formula, devised an equation, designed a theorem that he could not crack. This was the worst of all, to be left mired in ignorance, immobilized by doubt. And so, in frustration and uncertainty and impatience, Ewan had forsaken his post. He had promised his wife all she wanted. He granted her leisure and luxury that was not his prerogative to give. He had been punished for this with two infant sons conceived, born, died, buried.

Fifty-three years old with no heir to his trade and saddled with a lazy, useless, barren wife. This could not be the Will of God. The terror that he had been thrust outside the Divine Plan plagued him. At first he could not pray. But neither could he turn from God. During the enforced idleness of Sundays he read the story of Moses. He tried to remember how, when he had been banished from his father's mill, God had led him out of Breton Crag, across the water to the land of milk and honey. Merton's millstone on the riverbank had been a sign and a promise. He read the story of Jacob and Rachel. He had worked for seven years in servitude to Merton before God laid his due before him—diligence rewarded, and indolence and drunkenness punished. He had been without a wife and God had looked down and set one before him. But she must be worthy of the gifts given. He read the story of Job. He read the story of Abraham and Sarah. He read the promises made to men. When he could stand no more he calculated the angle of the sun, estimated the volume of the maple tree by the millpond, recited the laws of hydraulics, calculated ratios of velocities and power. And still the Lord's Day pressed down on him. There was never such longing as Ewan's hunger for Monday and the cool, sweet respite of work.

Since the loss of his sons there was nowhere Ewan would not go to work. He travelled to Tignish, Yarmouth, Bathurst, Harrington Harbour, Orono, Pittsfield, Flat Bay, Stephenville. Up any one of the hundreds of rivers that drained the expanse of the great northeast. It was a lonely river indeed that had not met with the industry of a man willing to set a dam and pluck the free-running power. His reputation preceded him. "Ewan MacLaughlin. He can power a factory from a rain barrel." Some of his jobs were nothing more than sticks and stones—the simplest constructions for the most basic of mills—and some were renovations or refits of ill-considered old dusters or log-hackers—making the best of a bad lot—but occasionally, after he had travelled for days, slaved and sweat, after he had suffered fools and slack-jaws and sinners, he would find himself up some stony river and wrapped in a project that drew him through the eye of the needle. When all he knew and all he had done transported him above an elusive problem and set him free in the land of absolutes. Matter must follow where the laws of the Clockmaker dictated. There amidst the dictums of gravity and propulsion Ewan could, if all factors converged, float a moment with God. Solutions were set before him. These moments were sweet and rare but occurred often enough to reassure him that despite the failures of his wife, he had not been forsaken. Ewan would yet be favoured.

In the year 1888 he came into a commission to build a series of mills: carding, tanning, grist, and a bakery. Never mind the new steam mill by the railroad tracks, the Canaan Falls mills up the St. John River would reassert the benefits of waterpower. This was precisely the sort of project where God might speak through him. And so it was that Ewan was prepared to recognize the sign that God sent him when he finished off his summer duties at home and set off south, over the hill toward the Bay of Fundy where he crossed to New Brunswick and rode his weary horse into the courtyard of a handy Saint John inn. He did not see the sign at first. The little boys had been in the courtyard when he rode in—the oldest lad hauling water to a washtub although he was barely tall enough to lift the pail off the ground, his younger brother dashing out across the lane eliciting curses from the hostler whose cart missed him by inches, another toddling after a long-suffering mutt with a feathery tail and yet another by a pile of kindling flailing a stick in his little fist and delighting in its contact with anything. As he crossed the courtyard Ewan's eyes were directed to the young woman who appeared out the back door of the inn. Instantly all the little boys abandoned their pursuits and flocked to her. With the slanting sun illuminating her golden hair and youthful skin, the Madonna stood transfigured in a tight circle of sons. Above her head she held a loaf. The boys lifted their arms to her, their faces radiant with love and gratitude. Sons, sons and more sons. She began to break the loaf apart with her fingers, handing out the staff of life to the eager, uplifted hands. Like God raining manna down upon Moses and His children. Like Jesus with the loaves and fishes. Ewan stood, riveted, his skin tingling, breathless and light-headed. All around the air hummed with a kind of ecstasy that surrounded and buoyed him. He felt a stirring in his loins.

Am I who hath withheld from thee the fruit of the womb? Behold my handmaid. Go in unto her that I may have children by her. He watched her feed her children and as the light leaked from the courtyard, watched her gather her sons as sheep into the fold. She and the little ones disappeared into one of the ramshackle cottages that backed onto the inn's yard. Through his supper, his tea, through his ablutions before bed, the image of the Madonna and all her infant sons clung to him. When sleep finally swallowed him, his dreams rose up vivid and shocking with open moors and distant trumpets and light that floated up from the ground like mist. There she stands accepting his presence without acknowledging it, her four sons become eight, then legions around her. She strokes the hair of one, a sandy-haired lad, caressing him, kissing his cheek. She draws her hand across his young chest. Ewan understands this boy is his son as well as hers. She looks straight at Ewan then and sends the boy wordlessly to him.

Other dreams follow, bulging with breasts and buttocks and soft young flesh.

In the morning, with the sun already well above the horizon, Ewan found his sheets splotched with dampness. For once he did not rush to the siren of daylight. He rose slowly, lingered over breakfast and drank a pot of tea sitting on the courtyard bench by the inn's back door. The Madonna of his dreams was a washerwoman. He watched her arrive with one parcel of linens and carry off another. Her countenance fixed, serious but lit from within. Pious, he thought. She passed so close by the bench Ewan could have reached out and caught her apron. He watched her come and go, with her hips and breasts and hands, her pretty waist and errant hairs that ringed her cap in a halo.

He made enquiries in the stable. A rough-looking character staring down a shovel turned to Ewan, happy with the excuse to extend his lounging.

"That's Lizzy Wainwright," the coarse fellow said. "Her man took the quick way down off a scaffold at the shipyard couple o' months back. Tough bugger—it never killed 'im. Might've been best if it had." The coarse fellow tried to look wise and sympathetic but managed neither. "There's somethin' broke in there inside him—sure as a dog shits. I seen him the odd time hobbling over the yard. Them's the good days though. More likely he's lying useless on the bed howling for rum or a go at the laudanum. No better than a babe."

Ewan asked if Mrs. Wainwright was a woman of good character. "I s'pose," the stableman said, then added a remark about her physical abundance that Ewan found distasteful. He glowered at the groom who snickered and picked up his shovel.

After the accident there had been a pittance from the shipyard. And the yard workers had taken up a collection as was usual in such circumstances. There was concern and sympathy and all the rest, but these attentions necessarily wane over time. Sure, a couple of his old mates came by with a tot of rum from time to time, but new concerns replaced the old. Charity ran thin. Lizzy Wainwright with her little cottage backing onto the courtyard of the inn went to work scrubbing linens, her hands red and raw from lye. Once her clotheslines were filled she crossed the courtyard to scrub pots or floors or windows or anything else that brought a penny or a loaf for her four little boys or a dram for her suffering shell of a husband.

Ewan approached her washtub and introduced himself. He half expected her to be waiting for him, to know his mission, to have been prepared for his arrival through a dream or a vision of her own. But she was not. He laid out his proposition as clearly as his India ink plans of millrace and spur wheel. A becomes B which moves to C. She could not have failed to understand his intent. Even so, she stood dumb for a moment or two.

Then she slapped his face. She grabbed the poker by the fire and pointed it at his chest. Her eyes wild, she leaned an inch or two towards him so he could hear her fiercely muted hissing. "You take your filthy mouth and go on! I'm an honest workingwoman. What are you doing speaking to me like that and with my little ones all around me? Have you no shame? I ought to report you to the magistrate!"

Ewan stood his ground. "Speak to God," he said with quiet earnestness. "God has sent me to you."

She gaped at the man standing there, sober as a moose, calling on God and talking filthy in the same breath.

"I'll be back this way in the fall," he said.

"You'll be *on* your way, mister!"

"I'll leave you to your work and your considering. You'll have forty days then forty more." He bowed slightly, turned and headed back to the stable. Shortly afterwards she saw him ride out the lane.

Men—always after one thing. For all her outrage, he wasn't the first to come to her. It took no time at all for men to spot the vulnerable and to start circling for the kill. The first proposition, not three weeks after the accident, had sent her fleeing to the outhouse to sob out her indignation. The second time she swung a cast iron pan and had the bastard scurrying like the rat he was. Since then she had passed many a saucy-tongued lecher in the yard or the halls of the inn. Men were cowards, always preying on the weak and quivering in the face of anyone stronger than them. Why don't they fight the shipyard bosses? Why not take on the bastards who treat them like animals? No. They hide from the brave union men who ask them to do their duty and make the bosses pay for the men they ruin. The cowards turn on helpless women instead. Well, she had her youngsters to think of. She called out to her oldest son to run after his brother and keep him away from the well.

SUMMER PASSED AND FALL HOVERED. By summer's end it was all too clear that Lizzy could not keep four youngsters fed and one man drunk on a washerwoman's pittance. Already she had put the boys to bed whimpering from hunger, and this amid the plenty of the harvest and with the sun warming the world. This before the hearth began begging for fuel and bare feet started howling to be shod and before the inn's brisk summer traffic gave way to winter's few stalwarts. She knew now that she would lose her children. One way or another they would be taken from her: by cold or hunger or charity. Her husband would never work again. She did not mean to be cruel in her heart or her thoughts but the knowledge that her husband's death would release her to find a fit provider for her boys revisted her shockingly often. But her husband's death was not imminent. He suffered and he would go on suffering, perhaps for years. He cried out whenever she chose bread for the boys over the rum that dulled his pain. She turned herself around and around, inside out and upside down trying to figure out how to avoid the inevitable. She could not lose her sons. Yet who knew better than her how little pity graced the world. Soon there would be no solutions she would not consider.

Lizzy Wainwright found herself increasingly drawn into an unlikely fantasy. Imagine if she could scrape up the money to rent a little house where she could rent out a couple of rooms. Suppose she could put two or three shipbuilders or dockyard workers in each room. The board could feed them all and buy the coal and she could keep her boys and nurse her husband. There were other women, widows mostly, who did this—she could name off half a dozen she had heard of in this town. But those women were not so poor. They had been left proper homes and she had only a cobbled-together cottage. Between the youngsters' howling and her husband's wailing for rum there wasn't a decent man in the province who would board in such a pitiful cupboard even if she did have the space of a bed to spare. And so she was tossed back into fear and terrible contemplations.

Ewan MacLaughlin, he had said. "My name is Ewan MacLaughlin." For all the drunken gropes and coarse remarks she received from louts and oafs she never had a man give his name. Or use hers. More and more often she found herself puzzling over the odd, clear-eyed man with the indecent proposal. "You have forty days then forty more." He was old but handsome in a dark, unusual way. He was odd, there was no doubt, but odd enough to be believed. He did not try to get around her, trap her, trick her, seduce her, insult her. He spoke to her almost like she was a man. Well, obviously not a *man* because of his intent, but as though she were as capable as a man. The insult was so intertwined with this confusing flattery that she could not lump him with the others and be done with it. And of course she could not speak about the incident to anyone.

Ewan MacLaughlin spent the rest of the summer at Canaan Falls, fifty miles upriver. A beautiful project. He would install a windmill for auxiliary power. He devised a system to pump water back up into a reservoir for use on low-water days. Grain ripened, water rose, autumn imperatives called him back to his duties at his own mill.

After eighty days he packed up, set out at first light and rode all the way back to the Saint John inn.

Lizzy Wainwright was annoyed with everyone on that day: her nerves as raw as her hands. What annoyed her most was that she must have, at some point, counted out the dates—forty plus forty. What annoyed her most was that she could not stop looking over her shoulder to the laneway, jumping at the sound of every hoof beat. She had enough problems without foolishness building nests in her head. She whipped her oldest boy for losing a cake of soap somewhere between the cottage and the washtub and tore a strip off the Irish girl in the inn's scullery for dropping the geranium by the back window and smashing the pot, although what was the inn's loss of a flowerpot to her? As the sun approached the horizon Lizzy twisted with a confusing mixture of relief and disappointment, dread and hope. After she wrestled all the boys into their bed she took herself outside to sit for a moment on her upturned washtub and gulp a few breaths of evening air. She leaned over to rub her poor tired legs. A tear of exhaustion rolled down her cheek and she swatted it away. A moment of rest always invited desperation to slink out from some black corner to find her. "Go away," she ordered it. She held her sagging head in her hands.

When she looked up, there he was. Even in the fading light she recognized the compact solidity of his outline, his clean, efficient movements. He emerged into the courtyard from the lane, dismounted, slung his saddlebags over his shoulder, handed his horse over to the groom and headed directly across the yard towards her washtub. Although she could not remember rising, she was on her feet as he approached. He took off his mud-spattered overcoat and handed it to her.

"Can you clean this?" he asked. "Bring it to my room." He turned and left her holding the coat.

LIZZY BRUSHED THE COAT AND BROUGHT IT UP TO THE MILLER'S ROOM.

"Have you considered my proposal?" he asked her.

Had she considered it? Of course not. Yet here she stood and when she opened her mouth her sentences had been neatly prepared. "I need a home for my children," she said. "I need a house where I can take in lodgers. Then I could keep us all, feed us all, with my own labour." She said this as a piece of information. She had not conceded anything.

"Yes." Ewan could see she was a hard-working woman, clever and forward-thinking and devoted to her family. Blessed with four sons while he had none. She understood his dilemma and he understood hers.

"The Lord has brought us together," Ewan said.

"I don't know about that." Bitterness tinged her words but her tone did not seem to touch the miller. He wanted to know about her husband. Did he remain a man? Would he believe a child born to her was his own?

A flash of anger lit her cheeks. He wanted to leer over salacious details, see her abased. There were occasions when she was required for certain services, certain manipulations, none of which were his business.

She met his eyes with defiance, but a defiance that fizzled and died for want of anything to defy. Ewan MacLaughlin might have been asking for hay for his horse for all the leering in his eye. She swallowed and could not find her voice. That she should find herself so deep in such business negotiations…

"He remains a man, like you say," she said.

And was it possible for her to remain distant from him when required, the miller wanted to know. "There can be no mistake, no mixing of the seed."

Once in a blue moon her husband would find that slender nether region of drunkenness separating disabling pain from disabling inebriation. In this state he was drunk enough that she could tell him what she needed him to hear in the morning. With all she had to manage these days, this was a simple matter.

"He'll believe it's his. There won't be no mistake." He will. Won't be. Had she agreed then?

"A son."

"'Less the child is a girl."

"No. If you conceive, I will have a son."

"Wanting a thing don't make it so. This I know for pure fact."

"I don't need a girl. I'll not pay for a girl."

"So if it's a girl, what do I get then?"

"If it's a girl, you get the girl."

Lizzy knew then that this strange man, for all his absurdity, was not deceiving her. She knew now that her decision was well and truly made and instantly it seemed as though she had set upon on this course of action months ago. If Ewan MacLaughlin were going to lie, this would be the place. Better for him to promise the moon, then simply disappear if the child were a girl. She would have no defence. How could she accuse him and chase after him with her husband alive and lying there in the bed?

"If I take the risk then I take the prize," she said. Not just a rented house by the shipyards with a couple of rooms to stack up half a dozen working men with their meagre pay, their laundry and bottomless appetites—day labourers working today and ruined tomorrow—but a proper inn with rooms for several respectable lodgers who paid up front for a month of decent board and a couple more rooms for travellers who might take supper and a pint in the snug with a cozy fire. There would need to be a stable for their horses. She would have an Irish girl or two for the scullery. She would have a man for the stable and for heavy work. Her boys would tend the hearths and run to the shops and tend the horses when they were not in school. And there would be a room off the kitchen for her husband. There would be money for doctors, and if they proved as useless as she supposed, then for rum or opium even. Double or nothing was just straight odds. This would be her only chance to make something of them all. "Triple or nothing," she said.

It took surprisingly little time to iron out the arrangement. He would plant the seed now and every time he passed through. She had a year to conceive. During this time she would receive a small stipend—enough, when combined with her washing and scrubbing, to keep her family from freezing or starving. When he saw the evidence of a child he would double the stipend. Upon the birth of his son she would receive a lump sum (enough to establish herself in the sort of inn she described) and a biannual payment for rearing the boy.

Should she give birth to a daughter—not a cent. If God did not smile on the arrangement then their business was done, secrecy necessarily assured by both parties.

They shook hands like any two men completing a deal. She took off her petticoat. He dropped his trousers and lifted her skirts. After all that had been stripped from her, tossed at her, required of her; after all her fears and suffering, with the welfare of her four sons hanging in the balance, this small thing was not nearly as bad as she had feared. The world had taken greater liberties with her than this.

She conceived readily. The miller was true to his word. When he could see the swelling of her belly he doubled the small stipend that kept them all alive on potatoes and turnips. For the following months she woke each morning with the knowledge that the child she carried would make or break them. She suffered terrible nightmares in which her boys were hauled off one at a time—as she searched for one, another disappeared until she awoke frantic to find her reality only slightly less precarious. She meted out the money slowly and spread it widely to avoid suspicion. They had milk one day and sausage the next. Then only potatoes. On Sundays when she managed an extra tot for her husband, enough to let him float above the pain, he boasted loud and long about the coming child. He had been a fine man once—tall and proud and strong. Now that she no longer set her boys to sleep whimpering with hunger, guilt tapped at her heart from time to time. But guilt simply offered a holiday from the vicious, insidious fear that twisted its talons into her guts every time her hand fell to her swelling womb.

The day the baby boy was born and placed in her arms Lizzy Wainwright laughed like an imbecile. The midwife was concerned about hysteria but her fears proved to be unfounded. Lizzy named the new baby boy Laughlin according to instruction and sent the pre-arranged message. *Dear Sir, We have recently received shipment of the merchandise you ordered...*

On his way back from his summer commission Ewan detoured around to Saint John town. He held the baby in his arms. He saw his own mother's brow in the little face, his brother Sander's chin, and Ewan smiled until his cheeks hurt. He felt the blessings of the Lord descend on him.

Mrs. Lizzy Wainwright moved her family uptown into a sturdy two-storey house with a servant's room in the attic and an inviting verandah that wrapped around the corner to catch the morning sun. It was not a grand house, but it was fine and roomy. To the quizzical she spoke vaguely of an inheritance from a wayfaring brother who had struck gold before meeting an untimely death. Lizzy set to work to fill her house with paying custom.

Mrs. Wainwright ran a tight ship. She kept one eye open for bargains, which she loved, and the other for freeloaders, which she could sniff out from a hundred paces. She kept her husband quietly numb over the six years it took him to wither completely and die. The five Wainwright boys grew strong and healthy. They ate meat every day and always had good shoes and sturdy clothes. They split firewood and filled coalscuttles and swept grates. They ran messages and brushed down horses and attended school right up through grade eight. The youngest one, the bright-eyed Laughlin, was always a little better dressed, guarded a bit more closely, assigned the lighter chores. He was the most likely to end up with a toy or trinket that caught his eye. But such was often the way with the youngest, surely. When the time came, he was sent up the street to the high school rather than following his brothers out to take up some dockside apprenticeship—cooper or carpenter. Twice a year Ewan MacLaughlin arrived in Saint John with a tight package of surreptitious cash. There was always a room available at the reputable boarding house with the inviting verandah. Always young Laughlin was sent to polish his boots, warm his woolens, bring him fruit.

"Play up to him," his mother instructed. "Be a good boy. Recite a lesson or a Bible verse. Show him that bootjack that you made. Sing out your fourteen times tables." The boy could always extract some small prize from Mr. MacLaughlin: candy or toy or coin.

"Of course he likes you best," his mother said. "You're so wonderful handsome and clever. Who else has got such brightness?" Young Laughlin took well to his favoured status and, like so many of the favoured, never questioned its validity or deservedness.

Then, on the boy's sixteenth birthday, the Devil stood at the door, demanding his due. The boy's parting would be complete and irrevocable. This Lizzy knew, although the boy did not. She packed his bags knowing that what he did not take she would sell or disperse or burn. She squashed her pain with stern reminders that she had raised five sons to manhood. She had done well. She told the boy that Mr. MacLaughlin had chosen him over hundreds to apprentice at one of the finest flour mills in the Maritimes. With his charms and talents he was sure to best every miller in the region. She baked a ginger cake and kept a smile on her face as she talked about the promise of his future. True to her part of the bargain she revealed no secrets, dropped no hints. At first light the next morning she handed him over to his new master, stood on the verandah and waved them off.

CHAPTER FOURTEEN

PENELOPE

CHARITY AND LAUGHLIN WERE TO BE MARRIED. I argued to put off the date, thinking perhaps if she lost the child ... or perhaps Nettle or (God forbid) Mrs. Cunningham knew of a potion. I could find Charity a position away from here. With Ewan back to mind the mill maybe I could take her to town. But of course I was only grasping at straws; it was useless. When Ewan had made his plan he had sealed off all possible avenues of escape. He sent for the local minister. I remember frost had killed the last of the asters so there were no fresh flowers for the wedding, but I had a few dried rose petals to fix in Charity's hair. I remember brushing and braiding her hair—brushing, braiding, pinning up her long, beautiful hair, soft as spring sunlight. Her perfect skin, almost luminescent with youth. She smiled. I remember this, in all my anguish, her face lit with the adventure of it all. A bride. Ewan would not wait for a bridal gown so she wore her Sunday dress with a hasty wrap I made over from a cotton-silk dress she had loved and outgrown. I remember the blue of it with the stylized birds in ivory and indigo. How the blue caught her eyes! I remember my pitiful attempt to spruce up the parlour—red rose hips, drying fall leaves tenacious with colour. The boy must have had a suit, I don't remember. I know the minister took a cup of tea before he left. Angel food cake.

The boy no longer stalked my daughter around the farm and mill; now he had her in his bed in his room across the hall. I watched my daughter learn the lessons women know.

But all was not lost. There was hope to be found amid the wreckage yet. I watched her belly swell and I watched her being drawn into the wonder of new life. I pulled out the trunk with Daisy and Charity's infant dresses. She held them and hugged them to her. "Momma," she said, "you must teach me to sew. I'll learn this time—I swear it."

Still a month shy of her sixteenth birthday her pains began. I did what I could to ease her suffering. After a day and a night of struggle and tears she finally produced the child. Mrs. Cunningham, in her perfunctory way, declared that despite all the hollering, no damage had been done and Charity would recover her strength in due time. The child was exquisite. I nestled into the bed and held Charity as she held the new babe, the three of us entwined in bliss.

EWAN HAD HIS SON. And his son had his mill. And now his son had a son. Ewan rode to town to register the birth. In a moment of alleged befuddlement he registered the supposed Laughlin Ewan Wainwright as "Ewan Wainwright MacLaughlin." "Don't bother about that," he said to the boy when he returned home with the botched paperwork. "It's MacLaughlin's Mill anyway. It's better like this." He unscrewed the cap of a rum flask and drank deeply from it then pressed the cool curve of the bottle into the boy's hand.

This was the first and only time I ever saw Ewan MacLaughlin drunk. It was the last time I ever saw him whole. Whatever he had been holding at bay he ceased to battle. Satan's greed knows no bounds. Once he had Ewan's soul he came for his mind and his body, biting off great mouthfuls at a time. Ewan's right hand stiffened and his right foot turned leaden to the point that he could only step and drag across a room. He sat in his chair often drifting off then startling awake to thump on his chest as though rousting his dozing heart. He took to cackling at nothing, a most unpleasant sound, especially for a man who had laughed so seldom in his life. He would call out,

"Triple-or-nothing! A sporting girl!" and tumble into a fit of braying. One day I found him hopelessly tangled in harness by the horses' stalls, running oats through his fingers as though he had no idea what the strange substance was. That was the last excursion he made. The next morning I found him immobilized in bed, his right side dead to him, his left side weak and flailing. Before I had time to consider how I would manage to care for this remnant, Lucifer finished his task.

I hated Ewan MacLaughlin. That I had once betrayed him physically was too little satisfaction. This was the only grief I felt as they lowered his coffin into the grave. After the burial I gathered up my clothes and my effects and moved downstairs to the little room off the kitchen. I wanted Charity to have the pretty nursery off the master bedroom. Also, I admit, I wanted the boy to see all he had to manage. Of course my son-in-law saw only the grandeur of the biggest room with the bright windows, their views of the barnyard and the road beyond the lawn. He saw the wardrobe where he hung his new suit. And he saw the bed where he enjoyed my daughter.

With the reading of the will it came as no surprise that Ewan had left his mill and land and tools and outbuildings all to Laughlin. I was left the use of the house for as long as I lived, but the house itself was Laughlin's.

As for Charity, I feared for her. She seldom smiled. She spent most of her time stretched out on the parlour sofa with the baby beside her. She was made a woman too soon. She held her fingers out for her baby boy to clamp his tiny fists around and she patted his chubby belly. She held his legs and clapped his perfect little feet together, she blew her breath across his scalp to ruffle the gossamer down that swirled on his precious head, but when she sang to him the song came out in a half hum always strained through her teeth. I plied her with meat broth and milk that she consumed without argument or appetite but she could not make adequate milk for the babe. We would need to keep my dark-faced Jersey milking through the winter whatever the cost.

With Ewan safely out of the way Mrs. Cunningham felt free to pop up at her leisure to dispense teas and tonics and the gloomy advice that was her currency.

"That girl always had too much spirit. No wonder she's gone sulky.

Hard work is what the girl needs. She's awful young, but ready or not, this one had no choice on marrying—plain enough."

I took her tonics and turned her out. Charity's girlhood friends had been few enough what with all Ewan's dictates but still there were half a dozen she had shared girlhood enthusiasms with. After the sudden marriage and swelling belly it was clear that some girls had been forbidden to visit by their mothers. They did not want their cautionary tales softened by the inescapable goodness of my daughter. A few girls came around once or twice and admired the baby, but Charity had lost the bubbly energy that had made her such engaging company. And anyway, they no longer inhabited the same world. Charity had crossed a river. The minister's daughter came by with a knitted bonnet for the baby and pail of self-righteousness. Later I heard of the salacious stories she had spread about my daughter, for her own amusement and popularity I suppose.

Whatever I felt about Ewan, there was no doubt that we had depended on his seasonal labour. He had always seen to our physical needs. Now Ewan's and Charity's labour was lost to me and in its place I had only one swaggering ignorant town boy. With the fall harvest in full swing I returned to work in the mill. The boy boasted of the crops he had standing in his fields and he brought handfuls of the golden seed heads to parade in front of the local farmers, but despite my urgings he would neither reap the fields nor hire out the work. Up at the house Charity could not manage the churning or the heavy water buckets for the washing. Even the bread was often beyond her—more than once she wandered off to rest leaving the dough half kneaded on the table for the flies. Wagons lined up by the mill. I felt old and fragile and unable to fend off mounting despair. One gloomy afternoon at the close of October I sank to the floor beneath the spur wheel, collapsed on my haunches, buried my face in my hands and let the rumble encompass me. I believe I may have been sobbing when Laughlin found me there. He twisted with embarrassment but I was beyond caring.

"Oh. You've lost your husband. I'm sorry for your grief. I, I..."

I looked up at him in amazement. His imbecilic features fired my desperation into rage. I felt my skin turn scaly, the tears on my cheeks turn to quicksilver. I rose to face him; all my pent-up indignation, resentment and frustration erupted.

"You are too much a boy and not enough a man! You have a wife and a son and a household to provide for. While the harvest piles up all around us you have a year's living to earn. And there you stand, as gay and easy as a girl at a fair. Do you know the cows that feed your babe need to eat in the winter? This is why you have a team of horses with broad backs and deep chests. Do you know how many cords of wood you need to chop to heat the house and how many cords you need to fire the kiln? And do you know that in the spring you must plant those fields of yours? You have to plant turnips and oats and wheat and make enough hay to keep these beasts from one year's harvest to another and enough for next year's seed besides. And enough to replace the oats you ruin in the kiln through your incompetence, and don't forget you need enough for your family to eat through the winter. What you harvest for milling is as close to free money as a man can expect in this world. That is why Ewan made and farmed those extra fields of oats you spend your time boasting about. You stand there as helpless as your little one, waiting for someone to praise the sparkle in your eye, the sunshine in your singing, your handsome face. I know who you are better than you know yourself. I have no desire to stand around while we all starve to death watching you comb your hair. We are living right now on last year's work. Where do you think we will be next year at this time with you dividing your time between the daybed and the preening glass?

"You listen to me Laughlin Wainwright, Laughlin MacLaughlin, Laughlin Layabout, you harness those horses and get those crops off the field and prepare that land for spring. And when you smash your reaper from hitching it the wrong way to and driving it like a sulky, hie yourself over to the neighbours and prostrate yourself before the men, place yourself at their mercy. They are good and generous people and the men will help you for the sake of your poor dependants. They will help you out of pity for your youth and your ignorant incompetence, not because of your jovial company. From *pity*! Do you hear me? So hold your tongue for once and pay attention to what they tell you and perhaps there is an inkling of a chance that you will learn enough about farming to keep us from starving at least. God help us all."

He shifted weight from one foot to the other, focused his nervous gaze on a mouse running along the wall. So obviously was he weighing his options I almost heard the click of the scale weights sliding between his ears. I rallied what strength I had in order to scrub the worst of my anger from my voice. "You are young to have the trappings of a man, I know. But what's done is done. You're not the first young fellow who's had to learn a trade in a hurry. Start now and do your best. We'll help you as much as we can."

I stalked up the stairs to check the grind, leaving him there. The following morning he disappeared after breakfast and did not appear at the mill. When Charity wandered down at dinnertime she reported that he had gone to fetch a neighbour lad and together they had harnessed the horses to the reaper and driven them out to the field.

I did my best to forge a civil peace with my son-in-law. I could not bring myself to act the mother to Laughlin but I at least resolved to encourage and reward his progress and to make his failures as awkward as possible for him. I did my best to remember he was also a pawn in Ewan's games with fate. Laughlin seemed to be able to manage the least possible amount of work. If I could manage a fair acknowledgement for what he had done rather than grumble over what he hadn't, he might share his native gregariousness, which heartened Charity a little and brightened our home. There were evenings when work had not been too taxing and all had gone well, when the baby was sleeping and there had been a jam and custard pie for supper, when Laughlin would stretch his socked feet towards the fire, tilt back his head and croon out his ballads or take down the squeezebox that he had acquired on one of his adventures. On nights like this he could coax a spark into Charity's dull eyes. Her smiles were tentative, but if we could make Laughlin's life easy enough he rewarded her with moments of attention that I'm sure she took for love. For all the boy knew of love perhaps he took it for that too.

Before the snow flew that winter, Charity was with child again. So less than a year after baby Ewan was born, Charity gave birth to their second son, Samuel. Then twenty months later came Alexander, namesake to my own poor little boy who had lived and died a quarter of a century ago. Her occasional sparkle was doused. What energy she could muster was consumed by the drudgery of washing and scrubbing and feeding and changing. She could not be convinced to take an outing of any sort. She seldom left the house and never left the property.

EVEN AFTER YEARS IN THE TRADE, LAUGHLIN COULD NO MORE RUN a grist mill than he could fly between treetops. In the morning he tended to the horses then stretched himself out on the daybed and waited for his breakfast. As soon as I finished my morning chores I descended the hill to the mill, leaving the house and children in Charity's wobbly care. Laughlin followed within minutes. He hailed his customers with hearty greetings, believing they saw a miller before them rather than a foolish man-boy. When I finished with an order Laughlin made a great show of hoisting the flour up from the meal floor through the trap door as though none of the farmers had ever witnessed the magic of a rope and a windlass before in their lives, as though none of this had existed before he arrived at MacLaughlin's Mill. He loved it when the farmers brought wheat for the French buhrstone. Then he would tug the tin slip-sheet out of its crack at the base of the vat to check the grind. Although he could scarcely tell bran from bone meal, he leaned against the doorpost in the daylight pinching flour between his thumb and forefinger and letting it trickle onto the step, setting a little on his tongue and cocking his head slightly in deep consideration, as though the flour was whispering a message only he could hear. Then he would smile and nod and toss the slip-sheet aside onto the step or the ground where I would find it later, inevitably trod upon by some shod hoof or some hobnailed boot. I dared not even leave him to tend the oats in the kiln. He would toss three or four great junks of wood onto the fire then trot off to gossip while the entire batch blackened and burnt.

He hollered out to the farmers as they arrived, calling each by name as though all season he had been waiting especially for them. "Now, Henry Bailey," he would say, "now, Willis Bigney, now, Alec Sutherland, what have we got here, what have you brought me? Let's take a look at this, gentlemen." The farmers had smirked at first but bit by bit they began to loosen. The grist-mill outing had always been a vaguely furtive affair while Ewan or I was in charge. The men gossiped and laughed and leaned on their wagons but always with the wariness of schoolboys conscious that the teacher lurked just behind the wall. Their wives insisted on our meal and flour. Had they not, the men would have driven farther down the brook to Thompson's where the product was inferior (horse feed with twigs, in Ewan's words) but the atmosphere was festive. I had no interest in maintaining Ewan's standards of decorum in this new world; I only hoped to preserve the standards of grind on which our business depended. I hid in the bowels of the mill, kept myself out of sight as much as possible, kept my footsteps light and my eyes lowered. In my absence the farmers gradually followed the boy's invitation to slacken the reins. There was song, a harmonica, a flask, and less and less attempt to hide it between swallows. It grew easier to forget there was a lady present at all. Soon the farmers had the best of both worlds: a carefree holiday away from the farm and the product their wives demanded.

Laughlin and I circled each other like a couple of cocks sizing up the competition. I could simply walk out of the mill and leave it to him. I could retire to my room, claim the parlour and set up a fine little apartment for myself. I could pass my days helping my daughter, attending to my grandchildren, raising the little boys I had never been able to have myself. I could tend to my garden in the summer and my knitting and sewing in the winter, stitch together little shirts and trousers, take the boys on strolls to the woods, read to them the fairy stories from Charity's childhood books. This was always there between Laughlin and I and we would each dance up to the possibility, shove at it, jab at it like bare-knuckle pugilists and bounce back. Repeatedly we stood eye to eye on the meal floor or by the stones, this threat consuming the space all around us. He could banish me from his mill and do as he pleased without my meddling, my orders and criticism. I could turn and walk away. Neither of us, finally, could accept the consequences. Laughlin lived proud and easy on my labour and he knew it. He was not a stupid young man—not by a long chalk. And I could not leave Charity and the boys to suffer from his indolence and incompetence. And so we danced, each seeking the very limits to the tolerance of the other.

Time marched on. No matter the depth or breadth of our problems, no matter the wounds that lay open and the scars that glowed in the dark, the three little boys brought a sunshine that could not be dimmed. Little hands clapped and little feet padded. Bit by bit we forged a home, imperfect as it was. On heavy weather days or days when custom was thin, on lovely Sunday afternoons, at unexpected times on busy days, the boys brought moments of sudden merriment that left a hopeful confidence in their wake. Little Ewan, who could never manage his name and seemed as adverse to the moniker as I was, made Charity laugh by mangling Ewan to Yoo-hoo. He was so delighted by these new syllables that he sang them out all morning, sticking the nickname to himself for life. Samuel, trying to haul himself onto his pudgy little feet gripped the side of a pail full of cold well water, tipped it over on himself and yelped with such an innocent, startled look on his sweet face that a stone would have laughed. Baby Alec loved to place one thing inside another. As soon as he could crawl we began finding a missing spoon in the wood box, an odd sock in a teacup, a biscuit in the geranium pot. One morning Laughlin howled and pulled his dripping foot from the toe of his rubber boot where Alec had stowed a precious egg. For days we laughed whenever we thought about it and afterwards were diligent about inspecting our own boots before putting them on. There were times when I would lose myself in the glowing moments of this young family. The children built up love in us all. Laughlin and Charity moved through the disappointments of youth and met on the other side occasionally, tentatively, forging what they could from what they had.

CHAPTER FIFTEEN

THROUGHOUT MY THIRTY-ONE YEARS OF MARRIAGE I HAD CONducted my business affairs through Nettle and I continued to do so even after Ewan died. I had grown so accustomed to the bars of my cage that I no longer saw them—until Nettle's death shook me free. Her body was found slumped over the hitching post in her dooryard like a final message to the farmers, carters and drivers who had made up her living. Rumours ripped up and down the road. Murder even, for heaven's sake. Strangulation or poison. But she died from a body and soul worn through and worn out with work, age and loneliness. She died from the burden of other people's secrets, of living a cautionary tale, of flouting the rules. A woman alone—how do you think she lives? I admit to relief. She took with her that fear that she could, impossibly, have known. That she held the power to tell.

I continued to produce oatmeal for Mr. Corrigan, as I did for many merchants in the northern half of the province, but after Nettle's passing I shipped the barrels of oatmeal and flour from the train station in Scotch River. I was startled anew to find Scotch River so close, to find the foremost Scotch River merchant, Hector MacKinnon, so accommodating. Gradually I came to know the nature of the slight that had set Ewan so adamantly against the village all those years ago. I knew the story about Merton and how within a month of his naming Ewan as his heir, Merton had fallen, drunk, into the brook and drowned. I don't know how widespread suspicion of Ewan had been. Hector MacKinnon's father, then a newly established Scotch River merchant, had been unable to hold his tongue. Essentially he had called Ewan a murderer to his face. All of this seemed impossibly ancient to me, like tales of clan rivalries at the battle of Culloden. I set up an account for the mill at MacKinnon's. Then I set up another for myself.

Unlike Ewan, Laughlin certainly held no prejudice against Scotch River. Laughlin might saddle his horse in the middle of the day, if there were no interesting customers at the mill, and light out for the village. He might return home with a silk tie or bauble-encrusted walking stick. Or, most ludicrously, a pair of spats! I am convinced that Hector MacKinnon bought stock especially for Laughlin—who else would squander hard-earned money on such ridiculous fripperies? More than once when Charity went to buy household necessities she found the account drained. I made it clear to Hector that my new account was to be kept separate from the mill's. Any money Charity had a hand in earning we hid under my name, as well as occasional small bits of mill business that could be slipped by without entry into the books. A husband might have legal claim to his wife's account but certainly not her mother's. Laughlin kept a close eye on the mill accounts. In this area, like no other, he proved his intelligence and potential for diligence.

With his sons Laughlin was unpredictable. If a fine mood were on him, he might break into a jig or a hornpipe, showing the boys the steps and praising their progress. He would sing long ballads, inviting them to fill in lines for him. He might bring a handful of peppermints home from Scotch River and delight the boys with games of "which hand" or he might present them with some simple illusion. "I've got a few tricks up my sleeve," he might say and wink. Then apparently cut a piece of twine in half and magically restore it to its original length, or pick a certain playing card out of a pack or make a penny disappear. The boys would cheer and plead to know his secrets but he knew better than to break the allure of mystery.

But if he had suffered a setback of any sort during the day, or if he had overheard a snide comment on his abilities as a miller or farmer, or if his mood was off for any reason, he would turn on the boys as easy prey. I witnessed him offering Samuel a toffee candy, then from the little outstretched hand made the candy disappear. An instant later it re-appeared between Laughlin's grinning teeth. "Poppa, it was mine!" the boy cried, but Laughlin laughed a short, sharp bark and walked away leaving the child in tears.

One day when a farmer allowed Laughlin to grind the fodder for his stock but held back his flour for me to grind, Laughlin pouted the rest of the day and that evening he kicked at Alec's half-filled water bucket and goaded the boy. "Did it take you all that time just to bring in that much water? When do you start hauling water for the baths? Wednesday?" Alec, already sensitive about his slight stature, blushed in embarrassment. I beckoned the lad, leaned over to him and kissed his little cheek. I told him he was a wonderfully strong water boy and getting stronger every day and that he should never mind his father. The two of us locked eyes over the boy's head. Laughlin bent his features into a saucy sneer and deliberately tipped over his newly filled mug, spilling tea across the table and onto the floor. Then he stood up and walked out, stepping carefully into the puddle and leaving wet boot prints in his wake.

One evening when I had Yoo-hoo washing up the supper dishes, Laughlin, restless and bored, snuck up on the boy and draped a dishtowel over his head like a wig. "How's the little scullery maid getting along with her scrubbing?" Yoo-hoo was not easily cowed. He was bold in the way an oldest brother ought to be, I suppose: brave at the best of times, brazen at worst. Yoo-hoo snatched the towel away. "At least I do work! Not like you. You're not even a proper miller—everybody knows!" Instantly furious, Laughlin grabbed the boy and dragged him off to the shed to take the horse reins to him. While it tortured me to hear the boy cry out, I did not interfere. I simply allowed Laughlin the rope he needed to hang himself.

Charity fared much the same as the boys. For years she struggled through a dullness brought on by childbirth. Just as she began to break through the dim miasma brought on by one baby, she produced another. But as little Alec grew and left diapers behind, as no new baby arrived to take his place, as the older two set off to school, little by little Charity began to lift her head and sniff the air. I caught snippets of the girl who had disappeared under the weight of early womanhood. She could latch onto Laughlin's merry moods and pull herself up. She could forgive him. This, more than anything, set me smouldering. When she built up a bit of energy he wanted it spent on his behalf. She often did chores that ought to have been his, implied to me that he had done them when he had not. He remained happy to let me earn the money he spent so carelessly.

But what right did I have to criticize after all my own errors, my own stupid acquiescence? Getting by, getting along, keeping the peace, swallowing hope, lopping off desire and need and tossing them in the firebox, replacing them with musty straw. What right did I have to stand between my daughter and what happiness she could wrest from her husband? If Laughlin set his desires above everyone else's did this make him worse than most? That he found himself able to play the puppeteer to a family of marionettes, did this make him more of a devil than most of the men in the district? Yet I loved more than anything to grab those strings and twist them in knots. Only I could deal with him, eye to eye, as an equal.

"We'll sell up and go to the city," he said to Charity one evening when he had come back from Scotch River in a high mood, the smell of beer hovering around him like a cloud of mosquitos. "I could make some real money there. Not like in this backwater. A man can really stretch out in the city."

The only thing Laughlin ever stretched out on was the daybed. Before he could draw Charity into his pipe dreams and ridiculous fantasies that pasted over the inevitability of his drinking away and wasting the entire worth of the mill and the farm, I spoke up. "I have legal right to this house. Who buys a mill without a house? Especially in this day and age of Western wheat and steam power? You'd get nothing for it."

He fixed me with a glare which I returned undiminished.

"Oh, Mother," Charity said. "You and your precious mill!"

Now, Granddaughter. Rachel. Your time has finally arrived. Your patience will be rewarded. Your mother conceived you, her last child and only daughter. Born with relative ease, greeted by smiles. I sat with your mother and held you to my face, your delicate breath on my cheek. You were my little Daisy, my Charity again, fresh and new, unmarked by treacherous twists and turns. I felt my own mother and my grandmother with me and your mother and you. We were all one—old and young, girl and mother and grandmother, weeping with grief and joy, weeping with hope.

Laughlin's next move surprised me only in that I had boxed his behaviour into a contained pocket in our lives and I did not expect any significant contribution from him. Early one evening he came home from Scotch River where he had spent the afternoon playing cards in the hotel. At first I disregarded his chatter. Talk of war—there had been too much of this lately. The bloody Hun. I simply tried to turn a deaf ear to news of international machinations. But Laughlin grew serious. It was the absence of bluster that attracted my attention, the lowering of his voice rather than its customary escalation. He played his audience well. Duty. Democracy. The defence of small nations. He intended to enlist.

While I wasn't taken in by his speech about duty (I saw every day his approach to duty), I think he had fooled himself into believing it. I looked over at Charity and found her gaping at him. I could hardly take in the words he spoke but his movements stayed with me. Like an actor on a stage he stood and propped one foot up on the seat of his chair, leaning forward, resting his forearms on his thigh. The serious pitch of his eyebrows I remember, and his sudden handsomeness. Then he left his chair and set his hands on Yoo-hoo's shoulders in a manner meant to impress gravity on a child. He crossed the floor and stood behind Charity's chair. He kissed the top of her head as she sat with their new baby girl fussing in her arms. Everyone appeared to be on stage or to have walked out of the pages of a novel, playing at a story that was not their own. He slipped the ribbon off Charity's hair and ran his hands through her tresses. Charity started to cry and everything seemed false and unfamiliar. The boys remained motionless in their spots. For a flash I was back in the winter of the blizzard when I played *Pride and Prejudice* with Charity's father. Then Samuel, sensitive to the emotional import of the moment if not the exact cause of it, joined his mother in tears. Yoo-hoo stepped towards his father and said with a note of admiration in his voice, "You're going to be a soldier, Poppa?" As if on cue, baby Rachel shrieked like a banshee and shook her tiny perfect fists.

I WAS SEVENTY YEARS OLD WHEN LAUGHLIN SET OFF TO ENLIST. I was an old woman. I could no longer heft a sack to my shoulder and often I found myself hearkening back to the nostalgic days of my youthful strength. I was no longer a great horse of a girl and now I longed for what was lost. Nevertheless, after Laughlin left, life opened up, almost magically it seemed, like a lush valley before us. It was a trick of memory, I'm sure, but it seemed that within a week of Laughlin's departure the baby stopped fussing, the neighbours became friendlier, the bread smelled sweeter, the kitchen windows let in more light.

I moved out of the tiny room off the kitchen and back upstairs. Charity claimed she could not sleep alone and so we went back to sharing the large bed in the master bedroom as we so often had in the years of Ewan's protracted absences when she was a girl. I hired a young man from over by the Crossing to help me in the mill. Wesley Heighton paid attention. He fetched and toted and ran here and there to ensure I never had to strain myself. He never burnt a grist of oats or barley and he learned more about milling in eight weeks than my son-in-law had in eight years. Of course I had to pay him for his labour, but there was no more money-wasting, no more trying to guess and juggle and outwit.

Laughlin sailed for the battlefields of Europe. Now that Ewan was dead and not just away, now that Laughlin was off fighting for King and Country and not just lazy, neighbours edged forward to offer help to our temporarily fatherless family. John Sutherland collected our milk and carted it to the Scotch River cheese factory along with his own. He delivered our whey back to us in the same way. Harry Cunningham butchered our pigs. When the men were finished with their own hay crops they came for a frolic to put ours in the barn, which cost us nothing but the feast at the end of the day. The Gratto boys spent three days cutting and yarding firewood for the house. (The Gratto boys were a wonder to feed, the three of them going through five pies at a single meal.) One neighbour lad or another would be sent over to block up the stove wood and split it. Yoo-hoo would dance in frustration as he tried to master the bucksaw, as his little eight-year-old arms tried to match the strength of bigger boys who smirked and shook their heads, delighted to be admired for their manly strength and prowess.

 I traded the quick but erratic horse Laughlin had recently bought himself for a sturdy little Morgan named Kelpie. Every week Charity and I and the children would harness Kelpie to the wagon for the ride to Scotch River. With the new co-operative dairy and cheese factory that had been established there was no more need to be standing over a pot of curd or pounding away at the churn. The first day I bought cheese from the factory I slunk away imaging the eyes of the village on me, the village tongues wagging—"too lazy to make her own cheese!" But this was ludicrous. I saw half a dozen other farmers there hauling home their whey in cans, each with a great chunk of cheese sticking out of their pocket. Indeed, why have a cheese factory if not to make cheese? Our family joined other families beneath the wide oak tree in the factory yard exchanging news and sharing bags of fresh salted curds. The boys ran up and down the main street of the village with sticks of penny candy every Saturday afternoon. They gawked at Hector MacKinnon's new motorcar and ran their hands over it. Like other boys, they played at guns and soldiers, learned their sums and letters, and attended to their chores.

 On school days Charity packed the lunch basket for the boys in the morning. I herded them through chores and washing up. Then the three boys and I set off together. It must have rained and snowed and there must have been days of bitter wind and biting cold. There must have been days when Yoo-hoo was recalcitrant and when Alec's perfectionism tried my patience, when the cow stepped in the milk pail and Samuel was consumed by tears of frustration. There must have been lessons forgotten and battles of will and bootlaces untied but I remember it all as a single golden day: Yoo-hoo toting the lunch basket with one hand and swinging a stick with the other, out in front like a band major, Samuel skipping along beside me and chattering away, in charge of the little satchel containing their slates and lesson books. Little Alec with his hand in mine, always with some question, "What's that bird called, Nana?"

Young Wesley would have the mill up and running early in the morning entirely without my direction or intervention; we could hear its rumble from the top of the hill. We descended the hill to the mill together, then the boys skittered off, over the dam and up the opposite bank towards the schoolhouse. Always they turned and waved to me calling out their goodbyes. I stood and watched them until they disappeared over the rise, my heart as light as a summer cloud.

Of course not everything was perfect. However much the neighbours pitched in to help with the household, generosity never carried over to the business. Neighbours who helped expected their grinding done for free; they expected gifts of oatmeal and sacks of bran for their horses and pigs. They expected to smoke their hams and bacons and fish in the kiln but when they brought kiln firewood it was meant as payment for a debt, not a contribution. They expected credit to be extended at their convenience. They often bought the new fine prairie flour now available at MacKinnon's and brought their fodder to me for the less profitable work. The oatmeal business remained strong, but it was, by far, our most labour-intensive product and industry advances in production and distribution kept the price low. Meanwhile I paid top dollar for help in the grain fields in the spring and fall. Labour was in short supply and the thresher gave no bargains to the miller—man or woman. The boys worked like navvies in the spring, picking stones and shovelling manure, hoeing turnips and beets for the cows in the summer, stooking, piling straw and stowing grain in the fall.

One fall a new schoolteacher arrived at the Gunn Brook School. Maggie Everett was younger than Charity by several years and certainly younger in experience, but they warmed to each other immediately. Maggie hailed from out by Crooked Harbour. She had never been inside a mill and she expressed an interest in seeing it.

"You must come!" Charity said. "Come home with the boys after school tomorrow and we'll have supper."

Charity, with baby Rachel in her arms, met them at the mill and did her best to keep Miss Everett from the ravages of too much attention. Yoo-hoo pulled at her to come see the gears, Samuel tugged her out to the walkway over the dam. I was busy shelling oats but peeped out the window at the entourage clustered on the dam—Charity and the baby and the boys and the new teacher. With the mill running I couldn't hear their conversation but I saw Charity lean back with her palm to her forehead in melodramatic fashion then watched both women dissolve in laughter. In that moment I glimpsed my young Charity with her scarves and ribbons and *Romeo and Juliet* in her girlhood kitchen performances.

Maggie, being from way out by the shore beyond Scotch River, knew and cared nothing for the now-ancient gossip surrounding Charity's early marriage. She cared little for gossip at all. In Maggie's eyes Charity was accomplished and wise and educated. Charity's penchant for books, literature and drama captivated Maggie, whose aptitude well exceeded her education. It warmed my heart to see Charity looked up to, her talents recognized for what they were. In fact it was Maggie I credit primarily for re-energizing Charity's interest in the outside world. The two young women began to devise the concerts and the Christmas pageants and the recitations at the schoolhouse. With Charity's enthusiasm and superior knowledge and Maggie's organizational ability they soon had the Gunn Brook Schoolhouse the buzzing hub of the area.

Maggie always stopped in at the mill on her way to the house to say hello and to "investigate the work," as she would say. She always brought a laugh and left a smile. One busy day, when Wesley and I had several grists of oats backed up, Wesley halted in mid step on his way to a hopper. He set down his load and turned towards the door. I thought perhaps there was something wrong or I had not heard a customer arrive but when I looked over I saw Maggie waving to us as she passed the door. Wesley moved towards her even as she continued up the hill, stood and watched her until she was out of sight. Of course! I had almost certainly missed earlier signs of this. At five o'clock Wesley and I shut down the mill and we headed up to the house together for supper as Wesley intended to stay into the evening to finish the day's second batch of oatmeal. The kitchen was teeming with excitement. It seemed Maggie had unveiled her idea of presenting a scene from *The Mill on the Floss*. Charity was to prepare the script. There were to be costumes and a set and playbills drawn up by the schoolchildren. All through supper they proposed and counter proposed which scenes would be best, who should have what role and who should wear what, and how the stage would be organized, and what music could be used to the best effect.

"I-I-I c-could make you a w-waterwheel," Wesley managed to spit out in the middle of a discussion about stage design. "F-for the stage."

Maggie turned to him and rested her eyes on his face as though for the first time. "Thanks, Wesley. That's just what we need."

"There should be a dog in the play!" Yoo-hoo cried. "And we can train Kip to do the part. He could be the loyal companion, couldn't he, Mother? There's always got to be a loyal companion—like a comrade in arms."

Samuel jumped up from the table, threw his arms around Kip, and needed to be guided back to his place at supper. Wesley's cheeks had taken on just the slightest hint of pink but the rims of his ears shone scarlet. I found myself smiling, ambushed by this evidence of us as a happy family. Even supper was delicious. Charity's soup-making had improved several increments over the past months. I had failed to take notice before this, but it was true. Also she had baked a custard to go with the cherry preserves. And this time she had managed to beat the eggs adequately and had remembered to take it from the oven before it shrivelled to rubber.

WESLEY AND I WERE PROGRESSING WELL THROUGH THE HARVEST. Of course there were days when Wesley had to attend to his land, to the little farm he was struggling to build on his own. On these days I had to manage the mill alone, but when he was there Wesley was such an apt hand that I could wander my way through half the morning before I appeared at the mill door. Sometimes I would see the boys over the dam and off to school then return to the house to warm my bones by the stove and boil up the kettle.

One morning I puttered by the stove baking up hot biscuits and arrived at the mill mid-morning with tea and a basket of treats to warm the young man.

"Good morning, Wesley."

He answered with a nod and a grin. He checked the oats then sat down to his tea. After contemplating the steam from his cup he eyed me tentatively, "D-do you think Maggie Everett w-would go to the dance with me?"

"Now, Wesley, I don't know why she wouldn't."

"I th-think Marty Battist is going to ask her. Th-that's what I th-think."

"Maybe you should get there first, Wesley. It would be an awful thing for Maggie if she had to wait so long for you to ask that she finally had no choice but to go with Marty."

"Marty is real h-handsome. I'd s-say she'd want to go with him."

"Handsome is as handsome does. Which in Marty Battist's case is precious little, from what I hear. What is Mr. Battist doing to better himself? Has he got himself a bit of land and a trade and a sense of direction? Look at you now, a hard worker with fifty acres all your own and a good horse and lots of promise. You've hardly a taste of jam on that biscuit, Wesley. Don't be shy, for heaven's sake." Wesley looked doubtful of the praise but he helped himself to another spoonful of jam.

"I-I'll finish up S-s-sutherland's oatmeal today," he said. "Th-then I can get Ma-MacKinnon's order done."

"Good. We'll haul it to Scotch River on Saturday if the weather is fine."

Wesley sipped his tea quietly. Eventually he ventured out again. "Another thing too is that M-M-Marty d-doesn't stut-t-t..." He ears blushed bright red and he stopped speaking.

"Doesn't what?"

"You know."

"No, what?"

"St-st-stut-stutter."

I took my time gathering up our tea mugs and sweeping the biscuit crumbs into the dustpan. "I have secret for you, Wesley, if you want to take the word of an old woman. There's just one thing you need to get straight in your mind. What's so great about Maggie Everett? Why would you care about her? Why would you want to work all day just to keep her happy? Why, Wesley?"

The question shocked him. He was unsure if I were insulting the girl he adored. "Sh-she's…"

"Don't tell me, tell her. If you can tell Maggie what makes her special and different so that no other girl will ever do, she won't even hear you stutter. Don't go trying to flatter her now, that won't fool her. She knows what sets her apart. She's just got to know that you know too. If you can do that, you could have green horns growing out of your head and she wouldn't care."

Wesley played so furiously with the button on his shirt I was afraid he might pull it off. Fussing like that, he looked not much older than Yoo-hoo and I had to stifle my impulse to lean over and ruffle his hair and kiss his cheek. He had no idea how insignificant his perceived shortcomings were. I left him to his troubles, went off to check the trout I had set to smoke in the kiln.

Charity watched the slow, delicate layering of Wesley's love affair with Maggie. I watched her slip into Maggie's experience and out again, each time altering her own recollections, bending her own past to suit herself. I saw her reshaping the sparse moments of attention she had enjoyed from Laughlin into a lingering romance, and dismissing months and years of indifference. I saw her bend the songs Laughlin had sung for his own amusement into serenades to her, his jolly jigs into elegant waltzes, his groping into embraces. It frightened me to see how easily this was accomplished. Of course I knew these slippery slopes well enough. Hadn't my own life been shaped by tugs and slides into ridiculous fantasy? Charity was living proof, my constant reminder, my Pearl. My victory. Who more likely than Charity to have fantasy in her blood?

Of course I had never known the girlish drama and excitement of suitors and courting, but I had, without even noticing, imagined extended scenarios for Charity. I had assumed that she would be the object of much jostling for position. She was such a pretty girl, so bright and imaginative and for all appearances from a diligent family with both a farm and a trade. She ought to have had a stream of young men at her door. They ought to have fought for a chance to sit in the parlour with her. I ought to have been the one vigilant about decorum, alert to suitors who imagined the mill and the farm would devolve to the victor. Instead Charity had spent what ought to have been her courting years in a fog of melancholia and a howl of babies. How could I deny her the fun of vicarious courtship?

Maggie had many suitors. Farm boys buzzed around looking for a chance to take the schoolteacher to a dance. I heard about them all. Marty Battist certainly, but also Tom MacCarron, Alvin Joudrey, Willie DeYoung. Being from the shore she was a new face and slightly exotic with her high cheekbones and large eyes. She was neither pretty nor plain; rather her face was open and expressive and so she became what she felt. Happiness lit her face to radiance. In confusion she appeared to dissemble and I imagine that in sorrow she would twist pity from a cliff face.

"Alvin has the loveliest eyelashes," Charity might report. On days when work exhausted me, her musing and mooning only reminded me of my failures and left me impatient.

"And when a man is paid by the eyelash won't he be well set then?"

"Willie is as strong as can be and can twirl a full flour barrel above his head with only one arm."

"Yes, strong as an ox and nearly half as smart."

But most of the time I was amused by Charity's animation with her speculations and judgments. Most of the time her perceptions reflected her new maturity. She noted which suitors demonstrated care, concern, diligence, ambition. She noted how they treated their horses, how they spoke to their neighbours. I loved to watch her holding each of Maggie's beaus up to the light, examining the idea of them, testing their strength. Perhaps I was as guilty as Charity, seeing her enjoying the excitements that ought to have been hers. Certainly I was not the disinterested bystander I ought to have been. I wanted to see Wesley in the forefront of the race. Harnessed to his stutter, Wesley's eyes would glow at Maggie's lightning quips and I would sometimes spy him smiling to himself days later. I had no doubt he was reliving moments of her quick wit. He admired her devotion to those around her, her kindness, and her careful consideration that would mature to wisdom over the years.

My grown daughter and I eased into a gentle friendship. In the evenings with chores all done and the children in bed, Charity and I would sit together in the kitchen with our sewing or mending or knitting. We forged a new intimacy, one between women—mother and daughter of course, but two adults, two mothers. Charity had always been a blessing to me but now I felt a certain comradeship of equals I had not held for another person since Abby had left for the West thirty years ago. There were evenings I shared with her my fears about the future of the mill. I worried about the business that would be left for the boys. The modern steam-powered roller mills ground more cheaply and efficiently. How much longer would there be a place for small water mills? Charity's distaste for the mill moderated with her maturity to the point where we could mull over the boys' best interests together. We shared stories of the children, explored their respective characters, talents and shortcomings, their delights and their fears. We pondered educational possibilities. For the first time in my life I could share the joy of a child's future with another person. I wondered if this communion was what heaven would feel like.

One Sunday evening Charity and I sat knitting after a pleasant day with the children. She had been to the dance at the hall the evening before and was now luxuriating over all the news and developments.

"Alvin peeked around the corner at Maggie and who could help but laugh at the dear fellow. The wink! But Tom took her hand. Oh my. What a look he gave her! I thought she must have felt it down through her bones. We were all in a swoon, even those with no right to be!" She laughed the most enchanted, buoyant little laugh.

The night hung soft around us, the lamplight delicate. My beautiful daughter and I together in happy comfort with the children nestled safe upstairs. Charity's father's face came to me as it had not in years. Perhaps it was the angle of the lamplight, perhaps the tenderness that enveloped me. I almost told her. I almost said I knew how deeply a look could pierce the heart. I almost said I had once fallen under a spell. I remembered his hand on my waist and his mouth on my neck, the blizzard raging beyond the walls. My skin warmed at the memory of his hands. I nearly said, "There was a man once..." I opened my mouth, the whisper soft in my throat, my eyes on my lap.

Charity crooned on. "Tom is as handsome as the devil himself when he gets that look. He's not so much fun of course, but with his…" Little Rachel woke at that moment and began to howl from her nursery above us, piercing our bubble. Charity sighed, set her yarn and needles aside, and rose to go to her.

Instantly I became angry at how close I had come to betraying my own secret. "Tom MacCarron is a dangerous man and Maggie should show him the road right now! I don't like the way he stands over her. None of those MacCarrons have any respect for their women."

"Oh, Mother," she laughed, "you don't like anyone who's not your precious Wesley." Her voice trailed after her like a satin ribbon as she disappeared up the stairs.

THE WAR IN EUROPE DRAGGED ON. We heard stories of the trenches and the gas. There was no shortage of news from the front, no shortage of reports about our bravery and success and about the devilment of the Huns. Yet despite our reported prowess, there was no victory. The boys followed the development of the British airplanes. Even young Alec could explain to me the relative advantages of the Bristol Fighter over the Strutter. Three or four times a year we would get a short letter from Laughlin. The notes said little and were virtually identical—thanks for the socks, we're beating back the Hun, there's not as many luxuries in the trenches as a man might want. The boys folded up the letters and carried them around in their pockets as trophies. I wondered what they remembered of their flesh-and-blood father. The father they carried in their pockets grew to mythic proportions. The boys grew into their chores. They could saddle or harness the horses, make deliveries, stack hay, catch and smoke a salmon or a string of trout. The older two could even manage the bucksaw and the splitting axe and needed less and less help with the wood.

One summer day after the boys had hoed their rows and brought me home a gallon of raspberries from the bushes along the north rill, I sent them off to play. Soon I heard them arguing beneath the big maple at the front of the house. The windows were opened to the breeze and their voices floated in as I tended to my jam. The recriminations were for Yoo-hoo, who had, in an effort to impress his brothers with his strength, tossed their toy plane so high it had landed on the roof of the house. Samuel wanted to solicit my help to get it down but Yoo-hoo was dead set against this plan.

"You were smart enough to get it up there, you should be smart enough to get it down." He mimicked my supposed response so accurately I had to stifle my laughter to avoid betraying my eavesdropping. Yoo-hoo began firing rocks at it, hoping to dislodge it, I suppose, but his two brothers clamoured to stop him, afraid he would do more damage. Another round of arguments ensued but they moved away from the window, their talk grew indistinct, and I turned my attention back to my own business. By and by I became aware of the silence. I slipped outside and around to the front corner of the house. It was all I could do not to cry out. They were stacked up like circus acrobats, their backs to me, and any distraction at this point would have sent the tower crashing to the ground. Yoo-hoo stood at the far corner of the porch with Samuel on his shoulders. Perched on Samuel's shoulders was little Alec. I held my breath, my heart in my throat as, holding onto his brother's up-stretched hands for support, Alec wobbled to his feet, reached up, and leapt onto the porch roof. In a second he had scrabbled up to the dormer where the airplane had landed and sent it soaring to the lawn below. Yoo-hoo called for him to hurry, that Samuel was heavy. For a moment Alec ducked out of my line of vision. The next thing I saw was his feet on his brother's shoulders. The tower of three lowered itself to the ground in a controlled collapse like a telescope. Once safe, they rolled around on the grass laughing as I flattened myself against the wall and tried to slow my heart. While I dithered over whether or not to show myself, whether or not I should condemn their behaviour, they were up and off to the stream with their fishing rods.

In my final years of life I would often recall that day. It gave me hope when I needed to believe that they would grow to stand on each other's shoulders, hold each other up, and snatch their futures from the world together.

THE YEAR 1917 BEGAN TO DRAW TO A CLOSE. One morning I felt an odd jarring in the mill floorboards. Flour dust puffed off the panes of the window by my elbow. Charity said the jolt rattled the dishes on the shelves in the kitchen. Wesley felt it too and said it startled the horses in their stalls. It sent little ripples through the ink in the inkwells at the schoolhouse, the boys said. Everyone looked up from what they were doing; we all cocked our heads and waited. When nothing more happened we returned to our business. The news was not long coming—a munitions ship had exploded in Halifax Harbour. The war blew a hole in Halifax so big the entire civilized world turned and gaped. Nearly two thousand souls killed and ten thousand more wounded. No one could talk of anything else. Those who went into the city to help came back shaking their heads. "You can't imagine it. You have to see it. Everything's flat. Beyond comprehension." So close. The war was suddenly more than anyone had bargained for.

The explosion jarred me out of my complacent state in relation to my son-in-law. Over the years I had rubbed him into an indistinct blur which I stored somewhere in the basement of my mind. His absence had allowed me to imagine—no, imagine is not the word—I was aware of the possibility that Laughlin might not return but this possibility I accepted as a set of logistical circumstances. We were managing so well. In the event of his passing, the mill and the farm would belong to Charity, and I often amused myself with the infinite possibilities of life, of education for the children, for instance, if this or that asset were sold or kept or divided. I did not amuse myself with the possibility of Laughlin's return. Believe me, I did not wish him dead. I simply did not keep him in my mind as a real, whole human being. The explosion made him real for me again and reminded me that this war would end, eventually, one way or another.

Several months later we received a letter in unfamiliar handwriting from overseas. It was from a nurse in an army hospital in England. Private Laughlin Wainwright was safe, she claimed. He had lost two and a half fingers and his right eye in a blast. There had been some damage to his face and right shoulder; however none of these injuries would prevent him from leading a full and meaningful life. Although he was no longer fit for service, near full recovery was expected outside these unfortunate losses. Private Wainwright hoped to write on his own very soon, she claimed, as soon as he could manage a pen.

Charity frowned then brightened, then frowned again, uncertain of what to make of this news. The boys were more than ready for a father to guide them into manhood. She would have a husband again. But why had Laughlin not attempted a few words with his left hand? Why had he not at least dictated a few lines?

Charity wrote to him, but received no reply. There was nothing to do but wait. Spring came, and then summer. Maggie had thinned her party of suitors down to two. Tom MacCarron lost patience and demanded she marry him. Apparently there had been a visit one night, a confrontation, a scream and a chase, and undisclosed injuries to Mr. MacCarron. Shortly afterwards Maggie and Wesley were married under a brilliant October sky. Charity clucked through the arrangements like a mother hen. One would have thought it were her own wedding. But it was Wesley and Maggie who went off to settle down on Wesley's little farm by the Crossing.

After the wedding Charity took the nurse's letter down from the shelf once more and turned it over in her hands.

CHAPTER SIXTEEN

THERE HAD BEEN NO SNOW YET BUT WINTER HOVERED OVER us, grinning down at fall's unfinished chores. Newly married, Wesley had his hands full building a new room onto his house over by the Crossing so I was working alone in the mill. Charity had taken little Rachel across the brook and up to Gratto's to drop off a sack of oatmeal. When they returned I shut down the mill and we all set off up to the house for dinnertime. A man sat on a rock beside the road, on the rise between the mill and the house. I had seen someone there earlier, noted it unusual to see a traveller all the way up here but decided to mind my own business. Yet there he sat an hour later. He lifted his head to watch us approach. An odd-looking fellow, dishevelled and rough with a closed-over eye; he looked as though he had slept sideways on his features and had not bothered to smooth them back into place. He needed a shave. He looked away in such a brusque manner as we approached that my greeting died on my lips. Only after we were about fifteen paces past him did he speak.

"Charity," he said, crisp as the air.

She whirled around and he sat looking straight across the road presenting us the left side of his face in perfect profile.

"Laughlin?" The question in her voice arose from incredulity, not doubt. She let go of her daughter's hand and stepped back along the road towards him, slowly as though fighting some great headwind. She halted just beyond arm's reach.

"Where is your uniform?"

It was an odd greeting but she had not written a script for a homecoming like this. Where was the brave soldier she had built in her imagination?

"Traded it for this lovely suit of clothes. Let some other poor bastard see if he can wring some luck out of the King's rags." He turned his blind side to her, bent over to retrieve his rucksack and struggled to his feet.

"Laughlin, you're home. You're safe. Why didn't you answer my letters? We heard nothing after the letter from that nurse. I didn't know…" She touched his unblemished cheek and then the ragged one, cupping his face. "You're back," she said.

He made no effort to either embrace her or to shake her off. "What's left of me."

"Laughlin. We had no idea … This is our daughter, Rachel. Your father is home, my dear. Home from the Great War."

He nodded and took a couple of steps towards the girl. His limp was noticeable but not pronounced. He pulled a sort of glove, a knitted bandage, off his right hand and waved it in Rachel's face, showing off the stumps that had been his pinky and its neighbouring finger. "The alligators took these."

Rachel recoiled in horror, scrabbled into the folds of my clothes, swimming into my body. I lifted her up and held her close for comfort.

Here is war, I thought, and could think no further.

"Come up to the house, Laughlin."

Ours was a house for women and children—I saw this as we stepped in. There was a scattered airiness about it. The last of the asters and cosmos had gone with the frost but the window sills were festooned with bouquets of beautiful coloured leaves and clutches of bearded barley. There were pieces of a new school shirt for Yoo-hoo, half stitched, piled on the rocker. Alec often fetched home some wonder or other from his travels: a perfect pinecone, a wren's nest, a fleck of fools' gold. These trophies were displayed in all their glory.

Samuel brought his mother fresh sprigs of evergreens which she loved to hang in the windows to sweeten the air. Yoo-hoo's latest whittling project, which he claimed was a pistol, had been abandoned on the bench by the door. There were pictures the boys had painted on rainy Sunday afternoons and the few toys they had made for themselves and their sister. The tin soldiers and the bright red truck, store-bought from MacKinnon's, were inexpertly stowed in the vicinity of our little kitchen toy box. Always an item or two of child's clothing hung off the back of a chair and, despite our best efforts, an errant mitten or sock or scarf. No peg was set aside for a man's coat, no place for great galumphing boots, no scatter of tools, no tobacco bowl, no special chair set off with its kingdom of don't-touch-its.

Laughlin carried his head at an odd angle, his chin tucked in slightly towards his left shoulder setting the scarred side of his face forward and his blind eye out to meet the world. I wondered if his carriage was the result of injury to some muscle or tendon. When he turned I caught a glimpse of the answer. A film of fear simmered beneath the dullness of his good eye. The emptiness frightened me, then chided me for my hesitant and sparse welcome. For the first time in my life I wanted to reach out and soothe him.

"Let me take your coat, Laughlin. Welcome home. Dinner won't be long. I'm sure you could do with a square meal."

All that time convalescing, waiting, travelling and he never sent word. He sat at the table, his good side tight to the wall leaving Charity his wounds. Charity sat by him stroking his arm. When he answered no questions, she filled in the space. "The boys are at school. The mill is in fine order. Scotch River has a creamery now. And a cheese factory. But you came in on the train, surely? So you saw them. You're home," she kept saying. And, "Wait until you see the boys."

He ate with slow deliberation as though ranking each mouthful. I couldn't understand what had kept him away for so long.

"Have you been to see your mother?" The softness in my voice may have caught him off guard because he answered directly.

"I set up a stone for her."

"Oh, I'm sorry." That was that. Ewan and his concubine both gone now. I called to Rachel to come and help me and left the two of them alone. Upstairs held no more trace of him than the rest of the house. I had slept in his bed and pooled his wife's body heat with my own. My clothes and effects filled his wardrobe and covered his dressing table. I gathered my things, paused at the doorway to Rachel's room with my arms loaded. I considered nesting in with my granddaughter then changed my mind and carried my things back downstairs to the little room off the kitchen.

When the boys arrived home from school that afternoon, Laughlin blinked in amazement at the size of them. They had been tykes when he left. Now at twelve and eleven the older two stood with their backs to their childhoods. At nearly five feet Samuel was taller than his older brother by an inch but Yoo-hoo was broader across the shoulders and already carried the promise of his future burliness. Even little Alec, at nine and still far too small for his own liking, was bigger than Yoo-hoo had been when Laughlin left.

Not only at the initial reunion but every time he saw the boys he blinked in surprise. He never asked a question about any of his children. Although, to be fair, he rarely had a moment to get a word in edgewise with all the competition to fill him in on every little detail of life.

News of Laughlin's return spread rapidly. Our family regained the stature that comes to a complete family with a man at the helm. The boys no longer suffered the shame of dependence on neighbour men. I watched the boys struggle to reconcile this fragile and distant being with the heroic soldier of their construction, watched them balance the advantage of a flesh-and-blood father with the imperfections of reality. Charity was not so far removed from the boys' experience. She had spent so many of her young married years locked in melancholy; perhaps she had little more real memory of him than the children did. I watched her approach then back off then approach again from a different angle. She spoke about him this way and that, trying to fit this enigmatic presence into our lives like she was trying on a wardrobe full of outfits.

"The boys are overjoyed. My goodness, Mother, if Laughlin thought he'd slip back home unnoticed they certainly put paid to that idea. They've been spreading the news like feathers in a windstorm.

They're so proud of him. And he can hardly believe how big they've grown. Imagine suddenly being father to all that flesh and bone! No wonder he's a little stunned by it all. Who wouldn't be?" And when he came into the house she would be at his side, doting and solicitous.

The next day she might complain, "He's just a shadow. Then all of a sudden he fills the room, larger than life. He's everywhere. Then he's gone again." There were days when she was hyper-vigilant, and inched away from him when she spoke to him.

Then, "It's terrible what he's been through, Mother. We just can't imagine. He jumps out of bed in the middle of the night. He flattens himself against the wall. He looks like he's screaming but no sound comes out. Thank God he has his family at last."

Laughlin offered nothing about his fighting days. "Mud," he said. "And rats." The boys pestered him until he confided in each of them separately a story of how he lost his eye and his fingers. Each story was riveting, dramatic, heroic. Each boy glowed with pride at the daring of his father and at being the chosen son to receive this confidence. Of course no boy could keep such a prize to himself and very soon each discovered both his brothers had also received a story. Each tale was so completely different that each negated the truth of the other two. The boys attacked each other with a physical viciousness I had never seen in them before, each defending the desperate belief that his own version was the one true story—that he alone had been exempted from the betrayal of their father's lies. I noted how expertly Laughlin played out his game. He may have been carrying horrors we could not imagine, but his wits had not been dulled and he loved a good game as much as he ever had.

Old carousing chums and customers Laughlin had entertained in the past came by the mill to gawk and to discover, I suppose, when the fun would resume, when the singing and dancing and stories would start. But I am being unnecessarily harsh. Many came to welcome him home and to see his rumoured injuries out of concern as well as out of prurient interest. He remembered their names, shook hands that were presented to him. Those brave enough to speak of his injuries tried to dismiss them.

"You won't miss those two fingers at all except when you're

counting your money." "You're still more handsome with one good side than most of us are with two."

He remembered well enough where he had found his rum in the past and he renewed strategic acquaintances. Unlike his pre-war days he did not seek out sprees and balls and dances, he simply sought the liquor. The first time he wandered off and returned home drunk and clutching a jug, Charity put up a fuss. He looked at her through narrowed eyes, tipped over a chair, and left the house. Later that morning I discovered him in the barn, crouched by the corner. The damaged half of his face was lit by sunlight streaming in the window, which may have magnified my impression of his maniacal expression. He was laughing a slow, joyless laugh that wrenched his mouth into a sneer. His one eye glowed hollow as he jabbed at something with a stick—something I could not see. When he turned he held my gaze as though daring me to admonish him. Then, without a word, he got up, tossed his stick into the corner and brushed past me into the house. I heard a muted scrabble in the straw and when I approached I saw that he had impaled a rat with the manure fork with such force that the tines were stuck into the floorboards. The wretched thing had not been killed but simply skewered by a tine and pinned to the floor, twisting in wild desperation. It swung its body as best it could to face me, vicious with fear, its hindquarters mangled and bloody. Beside it lay the stick, one end dark and damp with blood where Laughlin had stabbed at it. At my feet lay fresh shavings where he had crouched coldly and patiently sharpening the stick into a bayonet. The deliberate, calculated nature of the torture chilled me through to my soul. I ran for one of Ewan's mallets to dispatch the suffering creature.

The image of that wretched rat set me trembling every time I thought of it. Nevertheless I tried to put it behind me. We're not the only family with soft patches to manoeuvre around, I told myself. "There's no yolks without eggshells," I remembered my own mother saying. If we had our times of treading on shells, well, we would just have to make the best of it. Laughlin split some wood. He fixed the fence. He visited the mill and hoisted a few sacks of grain.

He would wait until Charity had her arms full, in the midst

of some chore or other and then demand a slice of bread and jam or a wedge of cheese. He watched her closely as she left her work to do his bidding then took no more than a nibble of his prize and left the rest on the plate. When I finally objected she pulled at my sleeve with whispered desperation. "Mother, please, I beg you. He was only making a little joke." She developed a rash and I made up a calamine paste for her. It would soothe her for a little while and then the rash would flare up again. Her face grew haggard and her eyes took on a haunted look. Her old melancholy stalked her.

Spring came. Laughlin got a couple of fields planted with more or less the same stumbling, just-good-enough performance he had before the war. In June school ended and I sent the boys to help him with the haying. While Laughlin's inattention around horses and machinery made me anxious, I was glad of some male company for the boys. Despite his faults I worried about the dearth of men in the boys' lives. How would they manage the push and shove of the world beyond the kitchen when all they knew were women's voices and the golden rule? When I looked out to the north field I was encouraged to see Laughlin pitching hay onto the wagon and Yoo-hoo building the load. Charity was not encouraged, nor could she be convinced of the value of male company. But she would not elaborate on her feelings.

Her spirits lightened only when Laughlin grabbed a handful of the milling money and rode off. On these evenings Rachel would climb onto my lap and Charity would gather her sons around her and smile a sad smile and weave stories. "When you three brothers are old enough to go…" All her stories began with these words. "When you three brothers are old enough to go, there are harvest trains that carry men and boys, boys just like you, so far out west the sun sets in their laps. There is work in the fields for the harvest and then all the West opens for adventures for three boys together…

"When you three brothers are old enough you can take a schooner to Boston or Montreal where there are jobs of every sort, one for each of you. There are tall buildings and electric lights and streets full of horses and carts and motorcars and stores with oranges and chocolate in the windows at every time of the year. And there are three of you so you will never be lonely and you can watch out for each other."

The seeds fell on fertile ground with Yoo-hoo. "We could be cowboys," he offered.

"Oh yes! Wouldn't that be handsome?" Charity kept her boys enraptured with tales of their possible futures far away.

"Perhaps they won't all want to leave," I interjected one night as a story began. "Perhaps there is a miller in the lot and he'll want to stay and learn the trade."

"No! There are three and three will go. As soon as they are able." Her ferocity stunned me. I was sorry I had spoken.

ONE BUSY HARVEST EVENING YOO-HOO AND I WERE KEPT LATE AT THE mill finishing up an order of oatmeal. By the time we climbed the hill to the house we were both tired and hungry. Yoo-hoo had gone ahead of me into the kitchen. I heard him kick off his boots and complain to his mother, "Not a drop of soup even!" There were mumbled sentences about bread and butter then Samuel was sent to the pantry for cheese. I recognized Laughlin's voice in the background. I don't know exactly what transpired but just as I approached the doorway I heard Yoo-hoo turn a saucy tongue on his father. Laughlin appeared impervious but rose from his place on the daybed and shuffled across the kitchen floor in his sock feet as if to fetch a piece of pie from the pantry. He turned abruptly and grabbed Yoo-hoo by the hair, tugging his head back, exposing his throat. Yoo-hoo's eyes bulged in surprise and fear.

"You think you're more of a man than your father? Maybe we'll see who's the boss here. Ask your mother. Ask her if she thinks it's a good idea for the big shot to be sassing his father." He shoved the boy across the room towards Charity. "I'll ask her too."

I slipped into view, ready to intercede if needed. Charity, white as wax, reached out to her son, but when she took a step her legs simply melted under her and she sank to the floor in a puddle. I cried out and ran to gather her up, shocked to find she weighed little more than a child. I sent Samuel off for the salts, called Alec to bring water, Yoo-hoo to fetch a chair. What happened to Laughlin I don't recall, I remember only the dullness in Charity's eyes when she regained consciousness and her body quivering as she leaned on me as we struggled up the stairs to her bed. I remember the sallow clamminess of her skin as I tucked her in and the way she rolled away from me, tightening herself into a ball. I lit a lamp against the advancing gloom and sat with her while she slept. I noted her skin rash had flared up again. There was no glossing over the ravages of nervous exhaustion. Bed rest, I thought, but did not have the energy to think further. Laughlin's clothes were splashed around the room—socks, handkerchiefs and a dirty shirt. Simply tidying, I gathered them up and dropped them outside the room, headed for the laundry, but as I stared at the pile, fear for my daughter overwhelmed me. Perhaps I knew more than I had been prepared to admit to myself. I spent the night beside her and in the morning I sent Yoo-hoo down over the Coach Road to call for the doctor.

I was in the kitchen boiling the kettle when they returned. Laughlin was sprawled on the daybed. Immediately it was apparent that the doctor and Laughlin had met before. They looked at each other like two dogs colliding at a food bowl, hackles raised.

"Doctor," Laughlin said. It was more a taunt than a greeting.

"Private Wainwright."

"I suppose my wife will have a fine holiday now—doctor's orders? We'll see, eh?"

"Could I prevail upon your hospitality to see my horse gets some water?"

Laughlin gave a short, humourless laugh but pulled on his boots nonetheless and made himself scarce.

I led the doctor upstairs to Charity's room where he examined her carefully. When he was done he packed up his instruments and sat on the hardback chair by the east window that looked out across the barnyard. He watched Laughlin leaning against the side of the barn, smoking a cigarette. He sat a long time in silence, sighed deeply before he began to speak.

"She's exhausted. Melancholia. Bed rest, of course. But I suppose you knew that before you called me. Doctor's orders aren't what they used to be. People do what they like nowadays it seems.

"That's an awful rash she's got," he continued. "I image you've heard there's scarlet fever in the village. The Langilles lost a young fellow just last week. I just ordered the hair cut off D'arcy Cameron's girl—it saps the strength, you know. Scarlet fever is very contagious. A terrible thing. Fever and rash."

The doctor spoke to the windowpane. I struggled to take in the words *scarlet fever*.

"But she has no fever," I said. Her skin was cold, if anything.

He continued to sit in silence until I wondered if he had heard my objection at all. Before I could repeat myself he turned and looked directly into my eyes. "She needs rest. She cannot be disturbed. We don't want her bothered. Not at all. We don't want anyone barging in thinking he can have his way."

I revisited each of his statements. I took apart the whole of his message, hearing each sentence as separately as he had delivered them. He hadn't actually claimed Charity had scarlet fever.

"Yes," I said, "I heard there have been several cases of scarlet fever. It is contagious. Charity cannot be disturbed."

"That is correct. I believe we understand each other. There is no need to quarantine the house, just this room. I assume you can tend to her?"

"Yes."

"These cases…" He stared at Charity's frail body huddled under a mountain of quilts. "These cases can be difficult. But perhaps you know this?" He sighed again as he handed me a bottle of pink pills. He bent his head towards me, his voice low and kind. "Talk to her about her children. Have her take in a bit of sunshine if you can get her out when he's not around. I will stop in from time to time, shall I?"

"Thank you, Doctor."

"We met in France, Private Wainwright and I. But perhaps he didn't mention it."

"No."

"No, I suppose not." The doctor shrugged himself into his jacket and fastened his bag shut. "There are some awful feisty girls come out of a war. Well, terrible things go on. Terrible." He held out his two smallest fingers on his right hand, brushed his right eye with his palm, glanced at me and looked away.

Laughlin's injuries?

"I'll let myself out. I'll just remind him how contagious scarlet fever is."

I remember listening to his feet on the stairs, straining to hear the kitchen door close behind him. Now it was my turn to stand by the window and watch the deception in the yard below. The two men spoke briefly, the doctor nodding towards the house then shaking his head. I watched until the doctor climbed into his buggy and clicked his horse off down the laneway to the road.

I COAXED HER WITH BROTH, WITH WARM HONEYED MILK. I slept in the little bed in the nursery like a sentry guarding her door. I spoke to her about the children as prescribed. I described, reminisced, speculated, always trying to draw her in. They're better off without me, is all that she could say. I hushed her foolishness. I spent as much time as I could muster at her bedside, brought tea and messages from the children. When the boys were at school and Laughlin off gallivanting somewhere, I might steal the opportunity to slip Rachel into the room to curl up with her mother. A little five-year-old girl sworn to silence on her mother's life. Mostly Charity lay quiet although often I found her cheeks wet with tears. Some days I could coax her out of bed to walk around the room at least or to stand a while in the fall daylight at the window. Then one day I found her at the window on her own, standing, leaning a little on the back of the chair for support.

"Send the boys away from Laughlin as soon as they are able. Don't let them stay. Don't let them near him. Don't let them know him."

"You are up, my dear! How wonderful. Isn't the sun bright today?"

"Promise me. When I die…"

"Hush. Don't be foolish. Look at you—up and around!"

"No, listen to me, Mother. Promise me. Get them away."

"No one is dying, for heaven's sake! You're only having a little rest. To regain your strength, as you know."

Charity said nothing more but she ate most of the oatmeal and cream that I brought her. She spent more time by the window over the next two days. Although she still seldom spoke, I saw a spark of determination in her eyes, a smile, and I burst forth in optimism.

"Is the doctor coming tomorrow morning?" she asked.

"Yes. He'll be pleased to see you up. Let's bundle you up and get you out onto the verandah today for some real sun."

Then that night, after I'd settled her in and extinguished the lamp her voice drew me back. "Don't leave the boys to Laughlin. When I die."

"That's ludicrous, Charity. You're not dying!"

"I must tell you so that you know. So that you will promise me. So that you will never break your promise."

"Shhh."

"Mother, listen." She drew the quilts tight around her and spoke into the darkened stillness. "You know their father has a silver tongue. The Devil's tongue—wicked artful speech. He sets them there, with his words, paints them into the room. As he lowers himself onto me at night. 'Perhaps I should fetch them? It would be an education for them to see what their mother is good for,' he says. Their own father! He conjures them with his words until I can almost see their eyes round with innocence, my three beautiful boys shivering in their nightshirts, lined up by the bed. And not enough to paint them there, watching. He tells me he will have this one do this and that one, that. 'Little Alec wants his Momma's titty? Reach up in there for Poppa's prize.' The words he puts in their mouths, such filthy hatefulness that I can't bear to look at their innocent faces in the daylight. If I knew it was all wretched feckless cruelty maybe I could stand it. But he is capable. I know that. Sometimes he wants money or to be sure his beer is brewed or his chores done for him. Or he wants me to … please him. Sometimes he teases me just for his amusement. 'Yoo-hoo might enjoy an evening show. Shall I fetch him?' And then wink as though it were some silly game. The boys are getting bigger now, and they challenge him … He will use me to destroy them. Don't leave the boys to Laughlin, Mother. They must never know. They must never have to think of that part of him is hidden in them. And Rachel—keep Rachel with you always. Every moment. By your side. Always."

I could hardly take in her words. There is no such barbarity. There is no such depravity. She spoke through the haze of her melancholy, she was delirious, she would remember none of this when she recovered. But even as I groped at straws I knew that Charity had spoken the truth. How could she, how could anyone, concoct such a story? She would never have revealed such degradation except to save her children.

"Promise me."

I could not speak.

"Promise me."

"You're not dying."

"Promise me."

I struggled to keep my voice from trembling. "Yes."

She turned her head, shrunk deeper into her pillow. I lay beside her on the bed and listened to the blood pumping through my body. Sometime in the night exhaustion claimed me and I slept.

CHAPTER SEVENTEEN

RACHEL

RACHEL WOKE IN THE NIGHT FROM SOME BUMP IN HER DREAM. The wind was kickin' up a fuss. That's what Yoo-hoo always said and she repeated it aloud to hear her own voice in the dark. Moonlight brought out the white and yellow in her quilt. She'd never noticed it before, not quite like this, the way the light colours seemed to have their own secret lamps inside. I bet the moon is big to make so much light, she thought. She pulled back her covers and tiptoed across the floor to the window. A penny of cold formed at the tip of her nose where it touched the glass. The air was cold, but not freezin'-yer-pants-to-yer-backside cold. Her brothers always made her laugh with that one though Nana didn't like it. "Backside," she said and giggled. There was the moon and it *was* big—not the whole round open mouth of moon, but nearly. Moonlight caught the undersides of poplar leaves and made them glisten like sprinkled salt. Then the moon caught something else: a flutter of white in the yard below. Her mother's white nightdress! There then gone, it had skipped off, hand in hand with the wind. She craned her neck to see it again but the angle of the house blocked her view. It was her mother out there in the wind. Surely it was. Mama was not sick anymore. Mama had got out of bed like Nana wanted and now everything would be better, like it had been before.

Rachel wanted her mother intensely at that moment. She knew that she should not run outside at night but Mama would be happy to see her. Mama would be so happy she would forget about it being nighttime and she would bend down and fold Rachel into her arms. Now that she wasn't sick anymore she would lift her up into her arms and they would cuddle like bears.

Rachel slipped out into the hall and then, leaning into the wall, descended the stairs one step at a time, in the darkness of the stairwell. She scooted across the familiar painted boards of the kitchen floor, through the entry and out into the October wind. The wind whipped her nightdress out in front of her.

The moon lit one shallow layer of everything. Her mother was not here in the dooryard, not in front of her, not to either side. She did not know which way to go. Her eyes watered in the cold. She called out but the wind grabbed her words and ran off with them. She ran across to the barn but the barn door was too big and heavy to open and it was so dark and lonely here her mother could not possibly be inside. Should she go back to the house? No, she'd seen her mother and wanted her mother. She turned back towards the road. Her bare feet felt stiff and square as blocks of wood, almost clattering over the ridges frozen into the laneway. Downhill felt better than up. Down along the road. Where was her mother? Off to her left moonlight polished the mill windows to perfect ebony rectangles. Something was wrong with the mill door. The wind had blown it open. It rocked closed on its hinges with a creak and bump each time the wind stopped to take a breath, then flew open again with each new gust. Rachel's feet found the path. Stones skittered out of her way as she bumbled, rush and stop and skid, down the steep slope. Rachel stepped up and crossed the threshold of the mill, slipped in out of the wind and felt the physical relief of shelter.

"Mama?"

Moonlight caught the whiteness, nothing but the white bundle swaying from the end of the rope beneath the trap door, swaying ever so gently in the wind, limp and cold and white and swaying.

CHAPTER EIGHTEEN

PENELOPE

I WOKE TO FIND MYSELF ALONE, TO FIND FIRST CHARITY, THEN Rachel, missing. Panic ignited my heart and exploded outward, taking everything. Thought could not survive the blast. I remember only action, only running, only searching, only finding. Rachel, in the first rays of dawn, huddled by the dam where the mill offered her some small protection from the wind, where roaring water swallowed cries. She had curled herself into a ball no bigger than a milk pail. When I touched her skin it was cold as death. But then she lifted her head, turned to me with eyes wide. She opened her mouth to speak but no sound emerged.

And Charity. I cannot speak about this. The doctor signed the death certificate. Scarlet fever. We buried her in the churchyard.

I BUNDLED THE CHILDREN AGAINST THE COLD. Rachel clung to me like a wide-eyed monkey while we lowered her mother into the earth. She had not uttered a word since I found her by the mill. The three boys crowded in beside me. Without them I could not have remained upright. We stood silent while the minister's voice rose and dissipated into the air, watched the dirt hit the lid of her casket.

Now I had seen all four of my children into this world and out of it. Were it not for the young one on my hip and her three growing brothers I would gladly have lain beside Charity and welcomed the earth over me. But here I remained, seventy-five years old with four grandchildren and this monster who had terrorized my daughter into her grave. And a promise. I owned only my miller's trade, my legal right to live in the house, and a jar of egg money. I could not take the children away and I certainly could not leave them. What was there to do but climb into the waiting wagon and be carried, rocking and queasy, back to the mill?

As Charity had instructed, I kept Rachel by my side day and night, always within sight. Like Charity, she would learn her letters at the mill desk and her numbers from the ledgers. Every night when she woke me with her night terrors I cradled her in my arms, rocking her in the dark. She rarely spoke. There were days we wandered aimlessly through a field or along the brook while the mill sat idle. On one such day I came across Laughlin, drunk as a lord, by the brook below the dam. Of course I abhorred the sight of him but more than that it sickened me to find us bound together in secrecy and shame. I scooted Rachel up the hill, directed her to wait for me up on the road. I knew she would not venture that far from me but she pulled back into the woods at least where she could peer at me from behind a tree. There lay her father, sprawled on the rock ledge above the pool from which the boys had pulled countless trout over the years. Merton's Pool. Where Merton died of the drink, of the struggle, subject to the law of all falling bodies. Not a soul around.

Laughlin struggled to his hands and knees, barely sensate. He raised his head and looked at me through his drunken haze. At first revulsion clouded my vision. My beautiful daughter being eaten by worms and my grandchildren at his mercy. I saw only cowardly pleading in his eyes. When I stepped towards him the pleading seeped out of him, turning a steely calm. I advanced and stopped a number of times before I understood. He was not begging me to spare him but to help him through a door he didn't have the courage to pry open on his own. In my grief and dislocation I had not been prepared to see anything beyond his wickedness. But he knew as well as I what a scourge he was. Crawling about here wrapped in dirt and drunkenness and whatever horrors the war had plagued him with. He did not attempt speech; like a dog too old to live, he watched me approach and pause, approach again.

I thought a crime of passion built its own world. I had experience, after all with the crime of love. On that magical blizzard island with Charity's father the world had pulled away, dividing like the double yoke in an egg. The known world was set apart while a new world, without time or consequence, bubbled into existence. But this division of worlds did not happen as I stood over my son-in-law. Should Laughlin die, the mill would pass to his sons and we would all live safely and quietly here until the boys were grown. Industry and thrift had brought us this far and could carry us onward. The children would not have to suffer their father's example, would never know the depth of his cruelty. Perhaps time would dim the memory of this past year and the absent wartime hero would re-emerge as the father they would carry with them. And Laughlin himself would be free of whatever horrors beset him and had turned him from a callow, pampered youth into this beast. If he drowned drunk in a pool I would be freed from seeing his hideous face each day. My daughter's death would be avenged. The world would be well rid of him.

I imagined Laughlin could see, too, where our common interest lay. When he tried to stand he toppled backwards, landing mere feet from the rocky bank. We locked eyes and then, trussed up with drunkenness, his head lolled to the side. He tried to speak but most of his words were aborted before they reached his tongue. One garbled syllable rolled sideways onto the rock. Please? Perhaps he said please. Perhaps. In any case I understood with utter clarity that he was not pleading for his wretched life but for his death. A single crow cawed from a branch somewhere overhead. For a long while I remained motionless staring down at him. Finally I turned my back on him, picked up my granddaughter from where she hid huddled behind a tree, and set off back up to the house.

If I was set a moral test that day I do not know whether I passed or failed. The fates did not claim him and he did not hand himself over. He did not tip himself into the brook. He did not drown. He did not freeze. I know that sometime during the night he returned to the house, because as I stood at the stove making the porridge the next morning, his snores from the room off the kitchen polluted the dawn.

From that day forward I lived with a singular focus. I must prepare the boys to leave. I could not be distracted by grief. My three score and ten had been granted and more besides. Every day I worked to build the boys' wherewithal to pull themselves into adulthood and take themselves away from here. I thought if I could bind the three slender branches together tightly enough, perhaps they would find the collective strength to survive. There was no room, no time, for anything that did not contribute to their departure. I lashed them to their tasks, built strength and endurance, brooked no indolence, certainly no rivalries. I treated them as a unit. When I rewarded Yoo-hoo's pluck or Samuel's acumen or Alec's pure scientific intelligence, I rewarded all three boys together. When one was punished for some misdemeanour or oversight, all three suffered. No one rested until everyone's chores were done. Each was responsible for the others. We lived around Laughlin. Some days he was stock to be tended, some days a bout of nasty weather to be contended with. I had no time to waste on rage or recrimination; the time for that had come and gone. Each morning that I opened my eyes, each morning that I set my aching feet on the floor, each morning that I watched the dawn brighten the millpond, was a victory that brought the boys twenty-four hours more to prepare for their independence. With every season that passed I grew more confident that with their labour and their combined strengths they could save themselves.

But the girl? A woman can work her life away for nothing but dependence and scorn. For Rachel there was only thin Christian pity. Our story, at least, I could give her—truth, for its own paltry sake. I held Rachel close and poured our story into her. I told her all about where she came from, about her mother, and me, and about that wretched mill that ground us all to dust. I held nothing back. I began with the evening in Reverend MacLaughlin's parlour when I first set eyes on Ewan MacLaughlin's plans for his mill. I told her all about my life, my children, her mother, herself and all that happened. Soon the story flowed so easily I could leave off the telling when my attention was drawn elsewhere and pick it up again without losing a sentence.

I told her all, and then I began again. And again. What more could I do? I loved her. I poured all we were and all we had been into her until the story filled every crook and corner of her heart and limbs and mind. "This is the story of how you were loved." Rachel said nothing but I saw her listening, even when she looked away. At least this is what I chose to believe.

THE LORD ALLOWED ME THREE MORE YEARS. And with this gift He turned me grateful, left me humbled. In the fall of 1922 we had been at the late summer oats for a while but this bright September day brought the first early wheat of the season. This I remember—the wheat. The novelty of its fresh aroma transcended the hardier scent of oats. It was mid-morning and the two younger boys had just begun their school year. Yoo-hoo was downstairs on the meal floor checking a belt. Rachel hovered by my side as always. As I lifted a small sack of wheat into the hopper a dreadful tightness gripped my chest. The weight grew suddenly oppressive and I staggered backwards against the wall, the pain squeezing my heart and lungs. Grain spilled out across the floor, and I cried out in surprise. Yoo-hoo came running but I banished his questions and sent him out to lower the sluice gate. Overcome by a great weariness I sank back, flat on the floor where the boards carried the mill's growling vibrations directly to my flesh. An odd sense of knowing tingled along my limbs, numbing my fingers and toes. When the waterwheel creaked and heaved to a halt I knew the boy had reached the sluice. Beneath me, through the floorboards, I felt the giant spur wheel slow. I felt the space between its rotations stretch, felt the power ebb. Even as my mind grew sleepy, I checked off the parts of the power train: the main shaft, the drive pulley, the spur wheel, the stone nuts, the grinding stone. Slow, slow, stop. Rachel patted my cheek. As the mill slipped into silence the roar of the waterfall rose up in a mist of white noise.

* * *

SHE LAY STILL, THE FAMILIAR SCENT OF HER LINENS, THE PUCKERED stitching of the quilt beneath her fingers. Thoughts came to her and perched, then flew off again in their own time like crows resting on a signpost. Odd, she thought. And calming. Free. So much of life can be spent in fear of death only to arrive at life's back door to be greeted by the relief of inevitability. Control relinquished. She slept and woke. The boys stood by the bed. Were all three there? It crossed her mind that she could count them and name them. Over the past three years she had prepared these boys with precise instructions. They knew where to find her casket in the barn, her gravesite beside her children's in the churchyard, her accumulated wealth, such as it was, in the small wooden box with the mother-of-pearl inlay at the bottom of the flour bin in the pantry. In her account at MacKinnon's. One of the boys was telling her about the harvest train. Yes. This was one of the many scenarios she had practised with them. If the time was right—the harvest train, the great open West. Go with the other Maritime men and boys. Work hard. After the harvest move towards a town where there will be work. With all that grain there must be mills. Or other work—it doesn't matter at first. Be watchful. Be careful what you trust to others. Move away from greedy people and towards the compassionate. Find work together, find a room to rent. It will need to be adequately heated and have a strong lock. Above all, stay together. All this the boys knew as well as they knew their names.

Time folded over before her like the turn of a great stone, as though the stone were inside her, or she inside the stone—as though she had turned upside down, then inside out. But she was not afraid. She felt the boys grown to men. For an instant there they were, strong and complete with their Western wives and children. And she beside them. Yoo-hoo smiling and alert, prosperous from business, his burly frame beginning to run to fat, his family large and boisterous. Samuel the teacher with a pretty wife and two kind, quiet daughters. Alec the engineer, practical and intense. Good men, all. So powerful was the feeling of recognition that Penelope could no longer focus her eyes on the boys by her bedside. She felt suffused with pure happiness and must have smiled because she could hear the boys speaking to her. They had taken her smile as a sign. Good. This was the truth she had to share with them. Go. Keep your promises. All will be well.

When she woke the next time Rachel was nestled in like a cat beside her under the quilt. Perhaps she had been there all along. Yes, the warmth, the occasional squirm, the fragile weight.

Maggie Heighton would take Rachel. This had been arranged. But such sadness surrounded the little girl. She worked her leaden arms around the child as best she could and Rachel burrowed deeper. Again the tilting of the stone—but this time she could not see so well. The boys had appeared so clearly but the girl's future lurked, murky and stringy and so intertwined with her own she could not pull them apart. Perhaps it was the proximity of the child or her tender age. There was a lost daughter and a terrible pain. Then a flash of clarity with Rachel—elderly now—with a granddaughter of her own. Both curled around a sadness as great as her own. Fortunes turned and turned back again, season after season, along the generations. Elderly Rachel and her granddaughter huddled in a crocheted blanket made of hundreds of little orange and brown and yellow stars. The child wiggled her fingers through the crocheted loops, pressed her head into her grandmother's bosom. Rachel held her granddaughter and stroked her silky little-girl hair. *This is the story of how you were loved.*

"Nana." A whisper absorbed through her skin and into her blood. A tide of warmth rose through her weary flesh. Could she manage a few words?

"Rachel."

She drew what breath she could. The child raised her head and set a soft cheek on hers, ear to lips and lips to ear. She whispered into the ear. "This is the story of how you were loved," she managed.

A thin voice came back to her, barely audible at first, then clearer. Rachel's voice in the flat rote of a reciting child. "This is the story of how you were loved. I first met Ewan MacLaughlin on a winter evening. I had begun the evening in my room as usual, arranging my students' lessons…"

She smiled.

Maggie Heighton stood guard over the bedroom. She did not give way to the older women who pursed their lips when she declared the child could remain curled up in bed beside her dying grandmother. She did not give way to their scandalized faces when she let the child rest a while embracing her grandmother's lifeless body. Rachel knew her grandmother was gone. She had felt her leave, felt her hand let go, felt the body alter. An aroma of flowers kissed the air as though her grandmother had left her a bouquet she could breathe in and carry with her. When finally Maggie Heighton picked her up and carried her out to the waiting buggy that would take her to her new home at the Crossing, she gave no more resistance than a sack of flour. This is the story of how you were loved.

ACKNOWLEDGEMENTS

I WOULD LIKE TO MENTION A FEW OF THE SOURCES THAT WERE PARticularly helpful to me in writing this book. First is the archival material left by Pictou County miller James Barry, which includes account books, day books and, most importantly, a daily diary covering the second half of the nineteenth century. The character of Ewan MacLaughlin is entirely fictional and in no way representative of Barry. Next is *The Young Mill-Wright and Miller's Guide* by Oliver Evans, which was the standard millers' reference throughout the nineteenth century. The passages Ewan quotes are lifted from the text. Although I originally accessed this book from the Provincial Archives of Nova Scotia, conveniently for me the book was reissued by Algrove Publishing for Lee Valley in 2004. Another work I found both fascinating and useful was *Sojourning Sisters: The Lives and Letters of Jessie and Annie McQueen* (University of Toronto Press, 2003) by Jean Barman. It offers glimpses into the lives and perceptions of two young Nova Scotian women in the late nineteenth century.

Many thanks to the Public Archives of Nova Scotia for access to sources, to the Balmoral Grist Mill (Nova Scotia Museum) for real-life experience, and to Nova Scotia Tourism and Culture Arts Partnership for financial support.

Thanks to Dean Cooke for his efforts. Thanks to Joel for patience. A special thanks to editor Kate Kennedy for stellar work and to Bev Rach at Roseway Publishing.